Backstrap

A NOVEL

Johnnie Dun

PEARLY BAKER PRESS

Editors:
Lisa Borders, Boston, MA
Alexis Orgera, Savannah, Ga

Design:
Cover: Jeroen ten Berge, Wellington, New Zealand
Interior: 52 Novels
Imprint Logo: Stephanie F. Jones

Published in the United States
by Pearly Baker Crimes,
an imprint of Pearly Baker Press.
ISBN 978-0- 9979683-0-9

For Joan & Bob

backstrap, n. –

1. *A simple horizontal loom, used esp. in Central and South America, on which one of two beams holding the warp yarn is attached to a strap that passes across the weaver's back.*

2. *That part of the revolver or pistol frame that is exposed at the rear of the grip.*

1

Earthy bubbles settled glacially down, not up, counter wise from sense, in the black peat-colored pint of Guinness. If she were stoned, it would have been mesmerizing. But Callie Byrne was trying to shake an inner dread and the urge for a fix while waiting impatiently for the Irish brew to settle at the pace of evolution. Tending bar was not distracting enough tonight.

Franklin's Grave Tavern was an oasis of close comfort and upscale clientele in the brick-lined streets of the Society Hill section of Philly, a posh section of town near the Delaware River waterfront. A mirrored-glass back bar combined with black molding stood out in the wood-paneled room to make an eclectic décor—trendy retro, postmodern, colonial club lounge. Her thin, white-girl dreads pulled snug, Callie moved smoothly in command in her black uniform. At one point in her life, she'd done army fatigues in Iraq as an MP. Then it was ripped jeans at punk festivals and indie rock clubs with Peter Jagg, an intense, bang-away guitarist. The old Callie Byrne lived for adrenalized street adventures with boys. She'd been drinking since fourteen. Nearly failed out of high school. Signed up for Iraq. Ran with Peter. Then met Tony Maul, Punk Promoter, a slit-eyed, black-leathered boy-man sitting next to her and Peter in a punk club up in New York. Another kick at life to kill the genetic Irish ache.

She had been arguing with Symington Wandreth III, a trust-funded, Philadelphian blue blood who lived in Society Hill and owned Cruickshank's Rare Books off Rittenhouse Square. He opened for business periodically—the rest of his time, he drank at the Grave.

"True?" she said. "Truth is dead. There's only self-deception and selling."

"That's true," Sym said. "I've almost died from both."

Callie was blunt and could talk with anyone, but tonight Sym's witty banter was just barroom white noise. Her mind was preoccupied with worry. Both she and her oldest friend, Rachel Martelli, were getting harassed by her ex-dealer, Tony Maul. She leaned on the bar looking at her phone. Yesterday, Tony sent a text message. *Once a junkie always junk. Stay out of it.* Stay out of what? She knew he was shady but had no idea what he was talking about. All she knew was that a few weeks ago, Rachel threatened to call the cops on him and refused to tell Callie the details. Which led to Tony scuttling around up in Lower Manhattan psychologically abusing both her and Rachel with his cell phone.

While Callie was in rehab from painkillers and this invisible thing assigned the letters PTSD, her counselor had suggested changing her "circle of friends," as if Tony Maul or Peter Jagg were friends. More like a noose than a circle. Their presence haunted a dead zone within her, and she was having trouble escaping it. She had deleted Tony's info six months ago. But he was addicted to his own menace, like a house fly you couldn't kill. This afternoon a package was waiting for her at the Grave addressed in Rachel's scratchy handwriting. A return address from a ranch in Guatemala of all places. The manila envelope sat unopened below the bar on the ice machine. She was waiting for a quiet moment to open it. Mail in the twenty-first century was rarely good.

Now Callie was in black tight jeans and black tee sized for clientele cleavage viewing, attempting a sober life. The tee showed off still-compelling biceps. The glass windows, back-bar mirror, and the web of steel lights hanging from the ceiling made it look as if there were three of her.

She plunked the Guinness down in front of Father Tim, "The brew of Christ," she said, giving him her ritual quick peck on his old pale cheek. "You're lucky I know how to pour one. I'm lousy at making Virgin Marys."

"Only the Virgin Mary could save a Virgin Mary," he said, toasting her. "*Ad novam vitam.*"

She knew his usual toast. *To new life.* She thought *Death to old life* was better. What was the Latin for that? Back when she'd met Peter after coming home from Iraq, nobody had seen a woman like her working security with the usual football tackle bouncers. She was unafraid to use her body, a Taser, or MP training with a handgun. Came in damned handy at the sometimes bloody shows of raw punk bands. But those tickets were now torn up stubs. Peter and she had split while she was pregnant. Middle East sectarian war? Roadside IEDs? None of that seemed to twist up new life versus old life as much as a man, a son, and trying to live in a country addicted to money, Starbucks, and sugar.

It was a busy Labor Day weekend evening. The flat screen TV in the bar's corner showed a reporter in Kabul riding in a Humvee. Another male drug war gone mad, Callie thought, picturing fields of poppies and radical Taliban. To Callie, governments and media conglomerates were like dirty old men with satellites and video surveillance trading in the porn of fear.

She glanced at Father Tim. He looked worn, his pasty cheeks older than his years. He'd have his one Guinness and then head back to his parish's rectory. He had been caught in the unlikely role of assisting the archdiocese for the last six years in "managing" the sexual abuse scandal. One night, after he had three more than he should have, he'd confessed to her (he to her, the irony of that): he'd been an anonymous informant to a reporter at *The Philadelphia Inquirer*. She had put a whiskey up for him on the house, and said, "Recite five Hail Marys and have a whiskey on Jesus." Then kissed him on the cheek. That started the little ritual. Without words, she was thanking him for his help after her rehab stint and for standing up for innocents. But it seemed the price of his secretive acts of justice was a permanent crease in his brow and a tremor in his drinking hand. It fluttered now, as if caught in a spider web in a Vatican cata-comb. Thank god she had met him *after* her Troubles. You couldn't argue with somebody who accepted you when you had nothing left. She never acknowledged what he had confided. It was the sort of se-cret that held the life of another soul in it. Callie knew how to hold a thing like that.

"You don't ever fully forget an old life," rambled Sym, sitting next to Father Tim in his usual stool. "You just wrap new ones around it until it's buried enough. Believe me, I've done it." He toasted Father Tim and Callie with his Grey Goose.

"Thanks, Professor Wandreth. I think you'd know, considering you've shed more skins than a snake," Callie said. She saw in Sym's sad eyes something like, *Here's to me and my distilled generations. Look at how terrible it is to be born lucky.* She understood failed families, and images flashed at her despite herself. Sym's father spe-cialized in psychological abuse. Hers was a hard drinker who liked to verbally abuse and berate the world, and use his fists to remind his children how much he did for them. . Her mind would flash with images, like film cuts, epiphanies, and splices of other people's suffering. She saw Sym's childhood next to her own: *Symington the Elder berating the boy for clumsiness near a sideboard full of Limo-ges. Her own mother shoving her out the front door of their brick façade rowhome with her drunk father cursing from the front door. Father Tim is there too, on the phone to a reporter.*

Sym was Main Line trust fund. She was the hard-ass tomboy who learned to box in the Great Northeast, where blocks of row houses were proudly adorned with Irish, Italian, and Eagles flags, green plastic awnings, and Virgin Mary statues on plots of crabgrass. Her wiry, stubborn mother finally took the kids and left. Tommy Byrne was good justification for teen self-abuse. She thought she'd escaped that ghost with punk rage and signing up for Iraq.

"Are you sure you don't want to do the south of France with me? I could buy you Bordeaux all day long in exchange for love and af-fection. That should help bury things satisfactorily. You could bring Dillon. We could read Beckett and bake magnificent baguettes."

Callie waved off Sym's harmless daydreams about marrying her and raising her son, Dillon. "I might have skipped college, but I've read *Godot*, asshole. Bread is better." Although, given the package from Rachel and the text in her pocket, who wouldn't wish to disappear to Provence.

Callie and Rachel had met in high school. Rachel had guts and brains with a nose for underground music, punk art, and radical stubbornness. They'd joined the army together. When they got back from Iraq, Rachel moved to Hell's Kitchen in New York to start a new band, then started working for Tony at the Latin Leather Group, a supplier of leather goods and jackets. She had visited Rachel, and they had lain tangled together in bed in a drug haze, looking out the window at a golden-topped pyramid office tower. It had been a surprise to them both and had faded back into friendship with Callie's Troubles. What kind of help did Rachel need? Money? Rachel didn't care much about money.

She moved down the back bar, slid Rachel's package aside, filled an ice bin, flipped three stemmed glasses on the bar for cosmos, finished shaking a martini, and scooped the head of a draft. She felt safe back here, slinging her comfortable act, pacing off the constant dull ache in her heart. She smoothly tended to a group of out-of-town professionals from a pharma company. She imagined they liked lost souls in pain. What's a better market than the masses, full of a deadness they can't shake, in need of opiates?

Callie served a couple a cosmo and martini at a table by the window. She saw them pretend not to look at the tattoos on her lower arms: two boxing gloves hung over a cracked heart on one arm. A guitar hanging from a dripping cross on the other. Callie was still figuring out how ordinary people got through their dull days. Father Tim had his Guinness. Sym was wrapped comfortably in his daily history of upper class self-loathing and midlife bachelorhood, like the same stained blue Oxford dress shirt he wore daily. It drove her crazy that he had no idea who the Ramones were.

She knocked the touch screen quickly in five places with the corner of a credit card for a woman in a teal suit from the pharma company meeting. The woman wore a badge that read, JEAN

COCKER, VP, GLOBAL MARKETING, GLAXOPINE, with no embarrassment whatsoever. Callie could tell by her demeanor she was a woman addicted to manipulating others. Callie had made them feel welcome, mixed a variety of cocktails, and let them feel superior. She was good at playing roles. She had played cop, club security, and now bartender—drug rehab wasn't the best career builder. But she gave the pharma suits graceful service anyway from the underbelly of the American dream: hourly working stiffs doting on corporate professionals wrapped so tightly in their thick security blanket of salaries and health care coverage and Xanax that they no longer felt its presence.

While she closed them out, staring back at her next to the system monitor was a picture of her and Dillon on the beach. He was wearing his Phillies baseball cap backwards, laughing, and clinging to Callie's neck, as a three-year-old does. They had been down the shore. In the background, the Atlantic glimmered. Her sister, Beth, had taken the picture. Now Beth had temporary custody of Dillon, too. Not a moment went by she didn't wonder how Dillon was doing and repeat to herself, *You lost your son.* What was he doing now? Begging her brother-in-law to take him out to play catch in the manicured McMansion's lawn? Trying to get another cookie from Callie's flaky mother, Paula? She was going to see him tomorrow. Another bout of reckoning from Beth and Paula. The nausea of shame wasn't subsiding into the past.

She didn't regret having Dillon, despite the fact that Peter turned out to be a confused neurotic who could record tracks with Bloody Wrist Productions, Tony's indie music label, but couldn't hold a job. The men she had spent her late twenties with were a mental dive bar full of selfish intensity, amazing piercings, and beautifully warped, leather-clad bodies. After the Mosul patrols and military life, a wild freedom had kept the deadness at bay. She'd been drinking and doing bouts of drugs since high school, tough enough to beat her brothers, hard enough to swallow Iraq. But the Home-from-Iraq-Years in New York with Peter were just domestic nightmares of dead-ends and oxy. The Bloody Wrist Band of A-Holes Era: Peter, Tony—Self-Promoter (born Anthony Pavlik)—and a dozen others she was trying to forget. They all had created a surreal haze of posed reality, anxiety, and blood loyalty based on degrading each other in fabulous ways—until she had finally broken into pieces on a two-day binge during which she tried to kill the deadness by kickboxing the crap out of Peter for screwing a female drummer.

Driving back to Philly on the Jersey Turnpike, she had stopped her car on the Benjamin Franklin Bridge and tried to climb the pedestrian fence over the Delaware River. She stopped herself for some still-unexplainable reason and got back into her car. She proceeded that night to do heroin with Angus Kistler, a gentle giant she and Rachel had served with in Mosul. Angus carried Narcan like most people carry breath mints, but she had already left his apartment when she went one fix too far and OD'd. She collapsed on the floor of a 7-Eleven in the candy aisle. A pair of paramedics revived her and brought her to Jefferson Hospital. She was arrested the next day and started an agonizingly slow legal process that had ended in a plea bargain. Callie submitted to rehab, counseling, and six months in a halfway house while her sister had custody of Dillon. She had lived in a shared room with an anorexic from Allentown and a tough West Philly black woman who had stabbed her boyfriend with a barbeque fork. If Peter ever showed up again, she liked the barbeque fork idea.

But she was not going back.

Finally, as the night slowed, in a lull of drink orders, she pulled out her phone again.

Once a junkie always junk. Stay out of it.

She picked up the packing envelope from Rachel and opened the envelope with single rip. Inside was a note and a flash drive. The stationery was pre-printed: GUADELOUPE RANCH, SAN OLVI-DADO, PETÉN, GUATEMALA. The note was in the same scrawl as the envelope:

Byrne,

Okay, sorry to do this, but I need help with Tony. You still boxing? Can you kick his ass please? Latin Leather is dirty. He's working with some real low lifes. I was in charge of inventory, right? Keeping track of orders coming and going, keeping the system updated, right? Shit work to pay the bills. How many pants, bags, jackets, that kind of shit. Mostly from Guatemala. Some from Argentina. Well, I saw some funny crap, like more payments going out than product coming in. Especially to the plant in Guatemala. Last weekend Tony comped a few of us tickets to a Vicious Delicious show. I was back stage. I told him the books were messed up. This guy named Hector who works for Tony in Atlantic City was there too. (Angus knows him, I think.) Runs an escort service in A.C. Next thing you know, Tony decided I should take a little 'vacation' to Central America. "Get to know the business down here." He promised me a bunch of cash if I went. I'm supposed to meet a guy named Slinger who runs the operation, but I'm pretty sure it's way more than leather, Byrne. I'm supposed to get him to accept a wire from Tony he's been turning down. I think I'm into something I shouldn't be. This flash drive has copies of Latin Leather shipments, payments, accounts, and invoices. If something happens to me, at least you know what I know.

R

She held up the flash drive with a black logo of an LL stamped on it.

As the end of the night came on, Callie grew more worried about Rachel and was in no mood for Sym's blather. He asked her what was wrong. She wanted to say, *I fucked up my life.* But she said a version of the truth: "I'm just missing Dillon." Sym was trying to help, but he didn't live in the same world she did. Or even *this* world. He lived inside the twisted flourishes of a family crest and a beaten-down trust fund from somewhere in the stone ages of the twentieth century.

She went through the kitchen, hoping to get to her car with no other surprises from Tony. *Stay out of it.* Like he could dictate what she would do or not do for Rachel. She wanted to get to her car, get in, and hide her fragile new life from her reckless history. And there was what she would do for Dillon. There was only one way back to Dillon. Keep your job, keep out of the Troubles.

The kitchen smelled like scallops, burnt butter, and mushrooms. She nodded goodnight to Mike and the other chefs, who were sitting around having a beer. The stainless steel kitchen was clean and looked as if chaos had never reigned there earlier that night. She stopped to razz them. "You know, it's really fucking annoying how content your fat asses look."

They laughed, and nodded their beer bottle necks goodbye at her.

For most of her life, she had loved being around guys. But she felt a million miles from any man now, as if she saw the male species through a telescope—small, faint, and insignificant to her. That was a thing with addiction; you don't really care about anybody else except those just as busy being addicted. The men she knew were just as busy being addicted to themselves or some sad replacement for a self as her. Now, she was learning to carry her sadness around, to live with boring routine as a matter of existing within so-called normalcy. But she had lost the ability to interact with men from any position of comfort in her own skin.

She swung open the back door, glanced down the alley past the green dumpster.

Her Honda waited down the block. Her beat-to-shit haven. When Sym said he called his old Mercedes Rocinante, she had dubbed her old Honda Ramona, after the little troublemaker in the children's book. As she walked to the car, the composed facade she'd been behind bar crumbled. She felt grim and exhausted. Inside the Honda, under one of her mother's coverlets, were all of her clothes, her books, her music, her hair wraps. Everything she owned. Toiletries, razors, tampons, a vibrator (dead battery), her box of beaded jewelry. Nobody but Father Tim knew it had briefly been her beat-to-shit "apartment." Everything she had saved from the Peter Jagg and the A-Holes Era had gone to pay lawyers, probation fees, and support for Dillon. After rehab, she'd moved into her mother's house—and she'd nearly as quickly moved out—lying that she had rented an apartment, that Peter had put away something for her and Dillon.

In reality, she just couldn't stand sleeping in her old childhood bedroom after all the places she had survived. That, and in the dead greed of getting her hits before she was sober, she'd stolen money from her mother. One of her really low moments. Paula's purse had dark pockets of black-lined shame that Callie couldn't handle if she let herself remember too much.

So, even though she'd found a temporary place to live, what she had to her name she mostly carried with her: Ramona the Honda and a threadbare filament of a new life in the alley behind Franklin Grave's Tavern.

Now she sat in the front seat holding Rachel's envelope and flash drive. She texted Tony, *Don't know what you're up to. And don't care. But leave Rachel alone. Or I will fuck over your shows with the cops right behind me.*

She turned the key and held it. Ramona's weak battery chugged reluctantly and finally turned over.

Stay out of it?

She'd been in it since she was born.

2

In a little room on the second floor of the Mercy of St. Helena's Women's House on Twelfth Street, Callie was staring at a cheap print of the Trevi Fountain and thinking about whether the Pope who had commissioned it cared more for sculpture or the poor? She couldn't sleep. But Father Tim had found her the room in the Mercy House—after the first few nights in Ramona's passenger seat, she wasn't going to turn it down.

Tony had sent another text while she was sleeping. *Rachel is sunning in the tropics. She contacts you—piss off. Get yourself some yoga pants and take your precious little boy to the playground with the other mommies.* Staring at the Trevi print, she saw an existential corruption hovering behind the water-stained fountain that angered her. Behind everything beautiful was something sinister. It was as though Sym, Father Tim, Tony, and Rachel were hidden somewhere in the twisted creatures. That's how her mind worked. But what the hell was really going on that had Rachel going to Central America?

Over the doorway, the nuns had hung a cross. They were the only two objects on the cracked walls. The woman in the next room snored like a bulldozer repaving the Turnpike. She could hear some of the Sisters downstairs in the kitchen. She tried to talk to them as little as possible. It seemed the most respectful way for a dread-locked, recovering addict and army vet on probation to behave in a

Catholic shelter. She was grateful for the bed, but that didn't mean she had to share it with Jesus.

She had put Rachel's flash drive in her knapsack and kept it with her just to be safe. She'd have to forget it momentarily because today was a visit with Dillon. There was no time for letting the past overcome her. She put on a smile, even if it meant enduring Beth playing the role of Dillon's mother with overdone responsible propriety as her unspoken judgment on Callie's life.

Callie went down the hall and put herself into a shower stall in the common bathroom. Two Latina women were using the sinks. They didn't look at her. She ignored the soap on a rope—props to the nuns for that—and let the hot water flow over her, as she glanced at mold in the corners of the tile. She ignored that too. Army life grew you thick skin. She started the long process of washing her dreads. This would be the second time seeing Dillon since she'd been clean.

Callie had found out she was pregnant about two months after a once-in-a-life time lark. Tony had a friend who offered her backstage security work on an Amy Winehouse tour. She invited Peter to come along. There had been crazed benders in London, a resort stay in Georgetown, Grand Cayman, and Winehouse's terrible last concert in Belgrade, Serbia. Two months later, Winehouse was dead and Callie was in the bathroom of a club in Brooklyn peeing on a test stick. The white circle was blank, and then from the nothingness emerged the + sign. That was a nice touch by the test makers: "+" —one more addition to the planet. Like the streets in Iraq, life changed both quickly and never at all.

When she told Peter she was pregnant, he said, "We'll just have to cancel that show, won't we?" He didn't want it.

Prior to that conversation, she had been sure she would abort it. She want home to visit her mother, and twice over the next week, she stood outside the Planned Parenthood Clinic at Twelfth and Locust Street.. She had morning sickness and withdrawal and everything she had done to herself pulsing through her. She was strung out from holing herself up in her apartment trying to dry out while her hormones popped. There was no way she could think straight.

Her body was a rack of bone, smack, and pain. She left with no decision. The second time, a few nights later, standing like a lost tourist on the street of her own city, looking at the black wrought-iron gates at the entrance, she saw two homeless men watching her from a pile of blankets set up against the corner of the building. She imagined them taking bets on what she'd do. She said out loud, *I'm going to have it.* And that was it. She would start again. Get clean. It was a terrible, inspired decision, but it was hers, the first real decision she'd made since signing up for the military. She had stayed clean for the next ten months but just couldn't keep off after he was born. That was the beginning of the really bad time—ending up on the bridge and in court.

Since then, she'd been continually surprised how many times you have to start again to start again.

After the shower, she flung her thin dreads around to the side and squeezed the water out. She enjoyed squeezing the bundle so tightly her hands hurt. She put on a pair of jeans and clean white shirt, then wrapped her hair with a bright red band she had gotten in LA with Tony. She'd have to find her bikini somewhere in the back of Ramona. She felt good, like she was ready to see Beth, ready to attempt the part-time role of Dillon's Messed Up Mom. She spoke to herself. *You're here. You're alive, taking care of yourself. Just do today. Just do today.*

3

She put ten dollars of gas in Ramona. After the forty-minute drive into the suburbs, she arrived at her sister's house. Beth, the Successful Suburban Sister. The four-thousand-square-foot white brick façade monstrosity looked like it might have housed four families. There were twenty or so similar houses in a closed circle, each a reproduction of Beth's, with three or four mass-produced "unique" variations. This was Glen Lea. American Self-Made Status architected into the form of great rooms and three-acre plots with new maple saplings. Her mother's old blue Buick was in the driveway—she'd moved in with Beth to help care for Dillon. Just in case her mother came out, Callie took her blanket and used it to cover over her belongings in the back seat. She didn't want her mother having any inkling of her living situation.

She headed up the walk, then ran back to the car, grabbed the Phillies Jimmie Rollins t-shirt she had bought Dillon. He was traded now, but that didn't matter. She rang the bell and stood at the doorway, braced to engage with a wall of unspoken resentment and judgment. She sensed the impending onslaught of domestic achievement and the intense effort it took to breath beneath the dense atmosphere of Restoration Hardware décor. She felt so out of place she might as well have been entering a resort spa. But she also felt something untouchable about her own failure. It held within it a certain kind of freedom, achieved through individual disaster. There'd been a time that Beth's life, house, IT executive husband, and golf club would have made Callie feel like a loser, but today she only felt something close to an adamant contentment. Once you have lost everything, the little things matter just a little less. She knew meth heads and heroin addicts who had far worse to deal with. She had been to Iraq. She had tried running with Tony and had been all over the world until that fast life crashed and burned. Now it was all slow, ordinary going. She met Father Tim, and he had found her a room. She had a job at the Grave, knew city people like Sym. It was *almost* a life. It made Callie less afraid of Beth's Department of Homeland Security.

Beth opened the door, and a scrawny creature practically tackled Callie's leg. "*Mommy! Mommy! Mommy! Mommy! Mommy!*" Dillon screeched. Beth forced a welcome. It was like meeting your own family in a hotel in a foreign country. Callie knew that they told Dillon his mother had to work in another state and was going to be gone for a little while. Callie reached down, picked up Dillon and flipped him upside down, hugging him as he laughed. She pulled him out to the large front lawn and rolled him around, saying, "We're just going to roll you in this grass right here until you're a steam-roller." His giggles were like salve.

They spent Labor Day at Beth's country club. Callie parked Ramona at the end of the lot, right next to a silver Mercedes that had parked deliberately set off to avoid any possibility of contact—and it surely was a *his* parking job. She inched Ramona just close enough to disconcert the owner, but with enough room to make complaint unjustified, and headed for the pool. After that, she felt as if she were in the first day of summer, rather than the end of it. She dunked Dillon and helped him learn freestyle. Beth sat the whole time in her chair, like a lifeguard, though it was Callie she clearly worried about, not the water. Callie helped Paula down the ladder and they both passed Dillon back and forth in his floaters, chatting about Dillon's life.

The day skipped by as a quickly as a kid running to the snack bar. Around four o'clock, as the autumn day's sunlight softened,

Callie's mind lazed in confused images of hope and regret. Country clubs, overstuffed fabric sofas, marble kitchen islands, and bright stainless appliances floated by in Beth's aquamarine life, but Dillon resting under his towel into her chest, she felt little hands that needed her, and that was all she needed. In her brown, rundown life of Ramona, she saw the black clumps of clothing in her secret room. Beth Byrne-Varry and Callie Byrne, two poles of light and dark, sitting so near and far away at the same time. Callie had to admit that Beth had refrained from any negative comments so far. She had let Callie have a good day. She'd say thank you for that, something they didn't say very much to each other.

She picked up her phone and held it over Dillon's head in the blue sky above, checking for messages. She had two.

One was an email from Rachel.

Byrne, two men showed up to the ranch. I'm supposed to go to the warehouse to meet Slinger today. I'm worried. Loved you. Jesus. That wasn't good. Callie caught the strange past tense, but quickly answered, *You too.* She didn't know if Rachel saw it.

The other a text was from Tony.

How's Dillon? Your sister pop him with pills too? Leave Rachel alone, and don't fuck with me.

Jesus, once a sick asshole is in your life it's like black mold in your walls you can never get rid of. She had her Troubles, and they were supposed to be over. She could feel her heart tighten and Dillon's warm little body breathing easy on her chest under the swim towel. She let him stay where he was.

She looked at Beth reading *People.* She could tell her. Beth despised Tony. One time at a club in Philly, Tony had thought it was a funny joke to splash sangria on Beth's white pants, like he was Jackson Pollock. But it would just sound like she was still hanging with the sordid people she was supposed to have left behind. The sunlight hurt her eyes even through her sunglasses. Tell the cops? He hadn't done anything yet. And it would take months for cops to infiltrate whatever Tony Maul was into.

She lay in the glare, listening to kids yelp and splash. Little shouts echoed around the pool, disappearing into the atmosphere as easily as Tony Maul and his Band of A-holes flew in and out of people's lives. She watched two men strolling to the clubhouse in lime green shorts, striped polos, and preppy whale belts. Successful hedge-fund managers probably. Bred by headmasters. The FCC of the USA: Fucking Chums of Capitalism. She felt them glance at her tattoos and label her: Cheap Dreadlock Druggie. Bred in Public High School Parking Lots. Working Class Slut. Christ, she hated selfish men. She wondered if she'd ever meet another good one.

She grabbed her phone, thinking, No, don't fuck with *me*, Tony. I could blow your world apart before you even know I'm there. She replied to Rachel: *R, Getting weird messages from Tony. He thinks I'm helping you. Let me know you're okay. Like give me an email once a day?*

Maybe she could calm Tony's paranoia. What Latin Leather details were on this flash drive anyway? Was it better to play it or hold it back? She typed and retyped ten times, debating how to walk the line between calm and kickass. Tony might be self-involved, but he was always intense and thinking. Finally, she had: *Nobody's after you. Just leave Rachel alone. Or I will flush whatever business you're into down the shithole.* Like mixing a cocktail, just the right blend: an offer to walk away with the obvious hint of a bullet in the chamber if he opted for stupid. She hit send.

She sat up from the pool lounge, "You need to be careful with Dillon."

"What do you mean? *You're* telling *me* to be careful?" Beth asked, dropping her magazine.

Callie realized it had come out wrong. She extracted herself slowly from beneath Dillon.

"Cover him. He'll burn," Beth said with patronizing care before Callie had a chance to fix the towel.

Callie wanted to say something else but said, "Thank you for the advice, Mom, I know," putting the towel back over him. "Just keep a close eye, okay. I can't be here all the time."

"You can't even be here *some* of the time."

"Back off, okay."

"He doesn't understand, Cal, you just disappear."

"I'm not *disappearing*." The word snapped at her. Beth had no idea what it meant for life to disappear. Like patrols that came back short a soldier. Like the girl you once were, lost somewhere in a chest full of ache so tight it could burst your aorta or make you want to burst it yourself. She restrained herself, "I don't understand either, really." She tried to soften Beth, "Thanks for today. Best day I've had in a long time."

Beth ignored Callie's gratitude. "You better stay clean, Cal."

Callie Byrne, danger to society. She sat breathing for a minute, controlling herself. Everything around her was making the deadness come. As if she were on a never-ending trial, her sister had granted a reprieve, in the style of a chaperone, "allowing" certain behaviors with ground rules. The court had set no rules on visitation, but Beth did. Dillon and Callie could "go to the pool, as long Mom and I come with you."

Between Tony's harassment and Beth's superior advice, she was getting worn as thin as an old dime. "That's such helpful advice. I am, but a friend's in some trouble. And don't start with your ultimatums."

"All of your friends are in trouble, Callie. I'll make a note for the court records."

"I can't argue with that," Callie said, pausing for a second. "Just be careful with Dillon, okay? Tony may come around."

Callie saw disdain under Beth's golf visor. As if Tony's existence were Callie's fault. But she knew her past had made it her fault.

Beth sat sideways on her lounge, "Don't worry about him. Get your life straight. Dillon needs stability."

Callie leaned over, calmly, "Do you know what a second chance means? People with perfect lives don't need them, right?"

The thin mouth under the visor and beneath the fashion shades spurted out, "The court reviews your case in six months. What are you going to do about it?"

"What am I going to *do*? I'm doing my job. I'm clean. What do you mean what am I going to *do*? What else is it I'm supposed to *do*? Turn the fucking clock back for you?"

"We'll see what happens, I guess." Back up went the false front of *People*, as if Lindsay Lohan's rehab troubles made for happier poolside distraction. She wanted to rip that fairy-tale rag out of Beth's hands. Pharmaceutical reps. *People*. Fuckers in whale belts. How could they not see that America was like a two-hundred-year-old delusional addict?

Callie leaned down and kissed Dillon.

"We can't all marry an IT exec. You love judging my fucked up life don't you?" she said to Beth. She walked across the lawn to get a water and calm down. She weaved between people who lived normal lives relaxing in the chairs, wiping her eyes beneath her sunglasses, her heart palpitating with manic tension. She would never be one of the normal people in a lounge chair. At least Callie knew that Beth would go to any length to make sure Dillon was taken care of—the happier she made Dillon, the more she could hold it over Callie.

After dinner, she helped put Dillon to bed. There had been no answer from Rachel. She was torn between seeing Dillon and trying to figure out what to do.

"When are you staying here?" Dillon asked, as she read to him about a balloon farmer. "He likes blue balloons, doesn't he?"

She looked at him, "Soon, honey. I don't know when. But soon." She wanted to promise him but wasn't able to say it. "I like blue balloons too." Just little pills of Dillon, she thought, that's what her soul craved while she struggled to ease the pain in her chest.

Downstairs, she nodded goodbye to Beth and her mom across the great room. Beth waved back. She didn't get up. Her mother blew a kiss. Callie left through the garage. Another day of winning in suburban America. She knew Beth really couldn't understand what fighting a drug "war" meant. Or any war. She wasn't sure it she was right keeping the worry about Rachel and Tony from her. But that was Callie Byrne, all stubborn independence. She drove Ramona back into the city and pulled over in a park by the Schuylkill

River. She needed to think. She got out to walk as a metallic city light reflected off the low clouds and made the river look like mercury. She felt trapped—unable to help Dillon or Rachel. She passed a bronze sculpture of a general riding on horseback. *Look at my sword!* The General Forgottentot, or whatever his name was, posed for posterity.

"Fuck you," she said to the statue, "you probably boned a slave mistress." She looked at her phone. No email from Rachel. If she could have, she would have emailed by now.

Was Tony set Rachel up? Using her for money laundering? She could see him sending Rachel down there to get her out of his business for a while, scare her off. But threatening Callie and Dillon if Rachel came to her for help? Something ugly was veering toward her. The river seemed static. A lone bicyclist's head lamp slid along the opposite bank. A rotting limb swirled in an eddy in front of her, circling slowly over and over again, spinning like a vinyl of raw punk guitar in her head: Tony Maul and His Band of A-Holes.

She finally stopped watching the rotting limb and walked quickly back to Ramona. She needed a laptop.

It was time to go see a few old friends.

Starting with Angus Kistler.

4

Callie parked on Third Street north of Market where the shopping and lights ended and a few dive bars and rundown apartment buildings began. Being on the street at night reminded her of being on patrol. She felt the sweet little surge of adrenaline that killed the ache. She was ready to take somebody down. She thought about bringing her Mike Schmidt Louisville Slugger, the bat she had stolen from her father after one of his nights.

When she was in Iraq, the Phillies went to the playoffs. Then won the World Series. Then had a parade she couldn't go to. She never really like baseball but had listened to the games from Mosul online in the early morning. Everybody in Philly had known Harry Kalas for decades, but thousands of miles away from home in a temporary cement barrack, she had fallen in love with his voice and had watched old videos online of his home run calls. *That ball is outtta here! Home run, Michael Jack Schmidt!* He sounded like what she imagined a good father would have. When she got home from Iraq, she retrieved the bat from Tommy Byrne's basement. He never missed it, and she felt no remorse. That man didn't deserve it.

But Michael was a blunt instrument, more for minor altercations over parking spots or car accidents. She kept Betty, her Beretta M9 pistol—the sidearm MPs carry—strapped to her back beneath her loose t-shirt. She entered the building and went through a shabby lobby. She could hear the floor and cracked walls being pummeled by heavy-metal sound track.

Upstairs, she walked to the end of the hall, where an apartment was crowded and hot.

Toward the back, she saw Lukas "Angus" Kistler lazing his thick, tattooed arm across the back of a chair, balancing his large frame on its back legs. As she approached, she watched him quietly listening to two steam-punkers argue about the best method of suicide. Angus, so dubbed by their army unit for his bulk and his German-American farm upbringing in rural Pennsylvania, was stroking his thick beard, always looking as if he knew the answer to a confusing mystery but was too preoccupied to bother with it. As she made her way to the kitchen, Angus saw her and gave the smallest twitch of a smile. He grabbed a Yuengling beer and bent through a back door onto a fire escape. Callie pushed through the tightly packed kitchen and stepped out to the rusted iron with him. She sat down on the steps facing him. He leaned against the railing.

"Callie Byrne-Out," he mumbled, eyes glinting from kitchen light.

She could tell he was using. "Tony never was funny, Angus."

"I know, sorry, you're right. Tony's a dick. Just first thing came out." Angus gargled a laugh. "How you been?"

"You heard that I got clean after the mess?"

"Yeah. I heard. That's great," he said, nodding in approval with his level-one buzz cut pale head bowed.

"You didn't call me."

Angus shrugged. "Nothing anybody can say when it's between you and yourself."

She thought about that. "Don't be so right, asshole."

"What brings you to Fishtown?"

"Tony's fucking around with me and Rachel."

"It's night time. Cockroach time."

Callie almost laughed. "Probably sitting at the bar right now with sunglasses stuck to his head."

"Like a bug." He flicked obsessively at the military compass watch on his wrist. Angus kept himself tightly organized. "I hear you're at the Grave?"

"Regular think tank," she said. "We talk sexual ethics and the concept of truth in documentaries. You should drop by."

"Nah, I don't do thinking."

"Don't pretend you're not fucking smart."

"If you stop thinking you're smarter than everybody."

"Angus, something's fucked."

He looked up. "You piss him off? Or Rachel owes him shit?" Before they went their different ways, Callie, Rachel, and Angus had all been hired to beat a few heads now and again for Tony at Bloody Wrist shows.

"Hell no. If anything he owes us."

"For what?"

"Mental pain and suffering."

Angus shrugged. He didn't bother with suffering. It made Callie jealous, who felt every isolation, injustice, and heartless act. The perks had helped ease the ache, like rubbing salve on a body of burns and sending her into nightmarish visions.

"You know Rachel's in Guatemala?"

Angus had liked Rachel, but she had always turned him down, except one drunken night, and then promptly returned to the same dismissals. But Angus kept a protective ring around women he cared for, no matter what. It made him a strange combination of rural Pennsylvania beef farmer, twenty-first century army body armor, and old world chivalry. "I still have that picture of her you took. That was a nice shot." He seemed to be admiring Rachel's imaginary vision. "And no, I didn't."

"Tony sent her down there to work something out around some deal for Latin Leather, and all of sudden I get—." She almost said a package. She wasn't ready to tell that. "—I'm getting emails that she's worried. I asked her to keep emailing so I knew she was okay. But then she stopped. Last day or two, nothing."

He flicked his wrist and watch, thinking.

"Angus, c'mon, give me something."

He pouted his lips and beard, thinking. He slid the watch around his wrist. "I still work for Tony sometimes when his bands come through. What do you want me to do? Shake him upside down and see if some change falls out? I'm sure she's fine. You know Rachel."

She leaned forward and pulled Betty from behind her. Leaving the safety on, she poked the gun barrel gently into the crotch of Angus's tent-sized camo cargo shorts. He didn't seem fazed, but his groin involuntarily flinched. "What's worse? An asshole boss up the Jersey Turnpike or a friend with an unstable history with cock-n-barrel? And if I'm not mistaken, you poked this thing in Rachel, so at least you can repay the favor."

She lowered it before Angus's adrenaline had time to rise. She had made her joke and her point.

He chuckled. "Still the same, eh."

She thought about that for a second—Dillon, the Grave, getting out of the halfway house. Was she? "No, actually, I'm still different."

He tugged his shorts with his thick hands, as if he had spilled crumbs. He threw his cigarette butt, which bounced between the iron grates, tumbling down into the alley. He pulled another out as soon as it was gone.

"They've been at each other for months," he said.

"Yeah, I know. She came down here couple of times—she was getting worried even then."

"She wasn't here to see you," he said with a smirk of self-satisfaction.

"Yeah, right," she said, skeptical of his suggestion.

"I am right. I asked her to move back too."

"You asked her to move in with you?"

"What? I can't be thoughtful man?"

"It's a stretch."

"Well, I did, Byrne. She didn't tell you everything. She was trying to let you move on with your boy."

Callie realized that was likely true. She thought of the note, the flash drive, and Dillon. Rachel wouldn't involve her if it wasn't serious. But maybe she wasn't the only person Rachel trusted.

"Why didn't she stay with you then?"

"She didn't say." He shrugged his big shoulders. "Just told me she'd see me when she wanted to. And I think something's up too. They had me work some shows down in Atlantic City. Tony's got this new guy down there. Hector Perez. He's still doing the same strategy. But it's getting fucked up, I think. We were supposed to have shit for all the fall shows."

Tony had grown Bloody Wrist Productions with a fine recipe: hard music with stiff drugs. People knew up and down the East Coast that a Bloody Wrist show was going to produce a long, crazy night for everybody. Bloody Wrist bands had no trouble selling out. Callie, Rachel, and Angus knew they hired local dealers to walk the floors like vendors at a ball game. "I heard they were supposed to get supplied through the Halloween shows by now. But nothing so far. Tony said he was done with his old guys. I've heard this Hector's set him up with a new source."

"Where? In Guatemala?"

"Maybe. Seems to be the case from what you're telling me. I guess he sent her down there to shake shit loose?"

"Could be. Or he wanted to shake her loose." She stood up and leaned over to head through the door to the kitchen.

Angus held her shoulder for just a moment. His hand was like a heavy blanket on her shoulder. Then he let go just as quickly. It was the first time she had been touched since Peter.

"Where you going?" he asked.

"Nowhere." She stepped back down into the kitchen full of twenty-something girls with cartilage piercings who seemed to be waiting for something dramatic to happen. Try Mosul, she wanted to say to them.

She heard him following behind her. "Nowhere's a funny place to go." He squeezed his heft through the fire escape doorway like a limber parade float.

"What's that supposed to mean?"

"Let's go down the shore," he mumbled.

She knew Angus was trying to help. "I like the ocean better when nobody's there."

"You want to meet Hector Perez or not?"

Christ, she thought, he had a point.

5

Callie watched the silhouetted buildings of Camden in the night glare as she and Angus drove in Ramona over the Ben Franklin Bridge into New Jersey. The same bridge where she had climbed the fence during her OD night. She felt herself driving the wrong direction, away from Dillon and her fragile new start at the Grave. But this time was different—she wasn't indulging for herself. Tony's reckless business was wrecking people around him. Angus was already leaning his head against the passenger window. She drove down through the pine barrens of New Jersey, through pit-bull-breeder country and sandy scrubs of dilapidated farm stands. They crossed over a long causeway across the bay. The casino buildings dazzled in the night, neon reds and golds dotting the coast like lighthouses of vice, TRUMP'S, HARRAH'S, WYNN'S.

"Look at that neon mess. It looks like a psychotic scrawled all over the night with a glow stick," she said.

"Beautiful," Angus muttered. "Too bad half the city is bankrupt."

She pushed Ramona up and over the Intracoastal Waterway bridge and down into Atlantic City, with its dismal city blocks of traffic lights, tour buses, and waitresses in bowties riding on employee shuttles back to park-n-ride lots just off the island. Beneath the golden Trump lights, Callie felt like what she was: a homeless woman dwarfed by the Real Estate Media Mogul's world of immense, inscrutable capitalism. Who made the world like this, she thought? The boardwalk was empty except for a few stragglers trying to walk off whatever conditions haunted them. She saw the cloudy dark of the Atlantic, a string of lights along the coast lining a sea of black water, white surf visible every few moments that melted back into the night. It made her think of Dillon. And soldiers killed in Iraq. In rehab, Callie had counted the lost people she had known: live human beings gone to black. While greedy people like Tony seemed to persist unscathed.

With Angus's directions, she drove north into the city's blighted neighborhoods, whole blocks of abandominiums. They stopped in front of a rotting, boarded-up storefront, a few check-cashing joints, a few thrift shops.

"Hector keeps an apartment up there." Angus pointed over a former hair salon with a faded pink sign that had lost all the hope of some stylist's dream. The nearby expressway sounded like a river of tires and wind that never stopped.

"Somebody once made other women feel pretty there," she said, nodding at the salon.

Angus stared as the salon. "Damn shame."

"You're a bundle of sympathy."

"Hey, I'm serious. As a professional slob, I respect people who want to look put together."

"I'm sure today's t-shirt qualifies me."

Angus identified himself on the intercom to Hector. "Hector, Angus." They were buzzed in. Upstairs, a Puerto Rican man in drab, oversized gray sweats opened his door and disappeared back inside. In contrast to the gloomy hallway, the apartment was a surreal Eden of red leather, gold lamps, red walls, beads hanging everywhere. On the wall were photos of tropical beaches, some photos of A-Rod in his Yankees uniform, and a prominent print of the San Juan Capistrano Mission in California. In the corner was an old desktop computer and monitor sitting on a desk.

Angus introduced her. "This is Callie Byrne. We're having some problems with Tony Maul." His tone made it obvious they wanted Hector's help.

Hector nodded. "Yeah, so we have something in common. I got a problem with him too." He looked like a man who had not left the apartment in a decade—unshaven, overweight, full of soda, burritos, and creamed corn. Hector's round, pockmarked face was drawn and reflective, his eyes purple and baggy. He seemed tormented by some restless anxiety.

"Thought that might be the case," Angus said.

"What's Tony so worried about?" she asked.

"Isn't everybody worried?" Hector said, staring at her dreads.

"Tony sent a friend of mine down to Guatemala earlier this week. Rachel Martelli? Do you know why he'd send her down there?"

"Tony Maul doesn't think. He's going to fuck up a lot of people with his crap. But I suggest you forget it."

"I don't forget things very well."

"The Evers Corporation doesn't either," said Hector.

"The Evers Corporation?" she asked.

Hector looked at Angus like, *who is this woman?*

Angus explained, "Manuel Evers. They call him El Mares. The Seas. Has an entire merchant marine network of cargo ships, crews, customs agents. West and East coast ports."

Hector added, "Controls two shipping companies. Manzanillo, Mexico and Colon, Panama. Has private wharves in LA, Newark, Baltimore."

"And Tony is working for the Evers Corporation?"

Hector didn't respond. Callie pulled the picture of the Capistrano Mission off the wall. Hector looked at it, then said, "I'm doing you a favor, perra. Better to stay stupid. But you know, girls don't listen."

She hung her head to the side and ran her hand through her thin dreads. "I'm listening," she said. "And I'm a girl."

Hector's eyes glared. "Look, go see Tony. All I did was introduce Tony to a distributor down there."

"Rachel said she was supposed to go see a guy named Slinger. What's the problem between them?"

"Why don't you head down there and go fuck yourself."

"That's just what I'm thinking actually. Except the fuck myself part. Maybe I'll love it down there, hang out with my friend and sun bathe." She put the picture back on the wall.

Hector started to get up. Angus was behind him and shoved him back down into his seat. "Just relax. I'm wondering how come Tony doesn't have his shit for the fall shows?" asked Angus. "I thought Tony always had a plan for that?"

"A plan?" Hector said to Angus, picking up a plate full of pinto beans in front of him. "Who's plan? This is the plan: you can live for a long while or be dead in a few months. Just depends."

"On what?" he said.

"If you're stupid."

"I'm not fucking stupid," Angus said.

"Nobody thinks they're stupid. That's the thing with being stupid. Stupid people don't know they're stupid, 'cause they're stupid." Hector tapped his temple with his index finger.

"What's in Guatemala?" Callie asked.

"Just go till everything looks like it's melting," Hector pointed down the coast.

Callie changed tacks. "I bet it must be a problem, Tony sending some woman down there in the middle of your shit. You can't like that."

Hector peered at Callie. "What do you want to know this shit for? Once you fucking know, you can't fucking unknow."

She had hit on something. "Tony is fucking around here with something he shouldn't, isn't he?"

Hector considered Callie, then surprising little nod. "Evers is a brilliant businessman. Gets himself into all kinds of community help and legit businesses—bananas, coffee, leather. But you fuck with his real business, he disappears people onto garbage barges."

"And people are fucking with his business." The whole thing was beginning to take a shape. Tony was trying to play in the big leagues.

Angus said with near-admiration, "It's true. I heard what he does if you screw him over. He stuffs money in your mouth, straps exercise weights around your arms and ankles, then puts you on a garbage barge headed out to sea. Bloop. Bye bye. Into the fucking fathoms."

"El Mares will dump Tony. Dump me. Angus. Your friend."

"I got the point," she said, trying to ignore El Mares's preferred dumping method. So Tony was disturbing business as usual somehow and Rachel was disturbing whatever Tony was trying to get in on. She thought about Tony's text, knowing Rachel would be talking with Callie. *Stay out of it.*

"I gotta piss," said Hector, and got up. He went down a thin dark hall, and closed a door.

Callie undid Betty's holster behind her in case Hector decided to come back with an attitude. He wouldn't shoot anybody in his own apartment, but she didn't want him escorting them to some Atlantic City wharf for a one-way cruise on a trash barge. Callie scanned the room. Pictures of a younger Hector in casinos with various girls. She quickly opened the desk drawers. They were full of junk. She saw a small spiral notebook. She flipped through it. First names of men and phone numbers in front. Then another set of pages with girls' names and numbers. All the fixings of an escort service. Scribbles, meandering prayers, and notes of appointments. In the margins, Hector had maniacally doodled lots of crosses and swirls and had written *Vámonos Vámonos Vámonos* up and down the sides of the pages.

When she heard him come out of the toilet, she put the notebook back. Angus positioned himself against the far wall near the hall.

Hector came in fixing his sweat pants. "I got kidney problems." She held up one of his notebooks. "How's business for you, Hector? Can't be good with all the casinos just a pile of bankruptcies."

He leaned into his red sofa, laughing. "I make ends meet."

"My friend Rachel. You met her with Tony a few weeks ago. At a show."

"Don't remember."

"Angus, Hector's getting older. His memory sucks."

Angus picked up an iron lamp on an end table, and unplugged it so the sofa and Hector were now half in the dark.

Hector reached between the sofa cushions.

Callie pulled Betty. "I wouldn't clean out your sofa out right now, or you'll be another stain on it."

Hector lounged back again, palms up. "Easy, bitch. I remember, okay. Nice ass, purple hair." But his voice sounded deadpan, as if he hadn't remembered anybody in years.

"You like your little life here?"

"Love it," Hector said, but his tone seemed indifferent, his face a mask of frowning.

"Why would Rachel be in Guatemala?" Callie said.

"Maybe you should go home," said Hector.

Callie lowered her voice. "Listen, you probably been holed up here so long you've forgotten what self-respect looks like. But I'm trying to get my life straightened out. Tony Maul is becoming a problem. I'm not leaving until I get somewhere."

Hector seemed to register the fact.

Callie reassured him. "I don't want to fuck up any business or bring in cops. A friend of ours is in some trouble. That's it. So I want some fucking help before we leave."

"Fuck off, I'm not—" said Hector, but before he could finish, Angus wrapped the lamp cord around Hector's neck and pulled so hard the sofa was leaning back along with Hector's head. His bloated body flailed and gagged under its own weight.

Callie stared Hector down, letting oxygen deprivation have its effect.

Finally, Angus let the cord slack, and he plunked back down. He wheezed, and his heavy body heaved as he caught his breath. "Okay, okay. This guy, Slinger. He runs the Latin Leather distribution plant for the Evers Corporation in the northern part of Guatemala. Tony made me introduce him to Slinger. That's what I do, make network connections. Slinger's built up his own inventory, and he's getting ready to ship thousands of kilos of heroin to New York. Tony's pushing him to sell to him. But Slinger doesn't know him so he's ignoring Tony. Then Tony started threatening to go to Evers if Slinger didn't sell to him. So nothing's moving. If Evers's security guys find out about the whole deal, we'll be dead in a few days."

She remembered Rachel's note. *I'm supposed to talk to Slinger.* "Where in Guatemala?"

"I don't know exactly. But Latin Leather operates near Flores. That's all I know." He leaned over, elbows on knees, trying to gather himself. "Now get the fuck out. And be my guest. Go and see your friend."

Callie thought about Hector's story while she gazed at the San Juan Capistrano Mission on the wall behind Hector and his fat, scatological head. Father Tim's undercover operation. The Trevi Fountain. The Mission. She was haunted by Catholicism, and she wasn't even Catholic any more. The sacred and the profane, saints and fuckers, she thought.

Hector saw her looking at the image of the Mission. "That's where the motherfuckers lost me." He spoke more to himself, as if remembering some unspoken shame in his boyhood that seemed innocent by comparison to his life.

Her mind was turning schemes into cubes and shapes. Tony inserts himself into Latin Leather to have a front business. He throws parties for Bloody Wrist acts around the Northeast. He's got big win-win going on both sides. Tony Know-It-All sees no reason not to go for more. He makes Hector introduce him to Slinger. So maybe Rachel sees the deal? Rachel asks a few questions—bargaining herself? Innocently, or looking for an edge? Then gets used as courier?

"I have a proposal for you, Hector."

He rubbed his neck, waiting to hear what she would offer.

"You tell this Slinger that you met a woman who will cut out Tony Maul—"

"I'm in too," Angus nodded to Callie.

Callie didn't need to look at him. She knew exactly what he meant. "I'll help get Tony's mess sorted out. I don't give a fuck about any of your business. I just want Rachel Martelli back safe and my family left alone. That's it. If Tony's MO looks anything like the way he's been messing with Rachel and me, it means he's inserting a bunch of drama, threats, and problems into your business, right? That can't be good."

Hector ate some of beans off a paper plate. She had him thinking about it.

She continued, "Look, Angus and I know how Tony. You tell Slinger I'll help him out. Slinger gets to sell his shit to whoever he fucking pleases. Tony goes back to his small shite life. You run your little life booking escorts in Atlantic City. Life goes back to one big fucking bowl of normal cherries."

"How you going to do that?" Hector asked.

"That's my problem. What do you have to lose? Right now, you got a shipment going nowhere."

She saw Hector try to weigh the odds of getting Tony out of Slinger's shipment. She added one more angle. "Tony asks, I never came here. That work for you?"

He chewed the side of cheek and smiled at her, "Yeah, what the fuck, that works. I'll call Slinger."

She nodded at the Mission photo. "What'd you mean, 'where the motherfuckers lost you'?"

Hector's old face became proud and worn. "I was born near there in California. It reminds me God ruins everybody."

"Uh huh. Maybe that's why God has so many enemies."

She and Angus headed for the door.

Hector mumbled something that sounded like both warning and threat. "Don't be another lost girl."

As they got back onto the street, trajectories of Tony, Slinger, and Hector shot in multiple directions across the long avenues and cross streets of Atlantic City. Angus walked next to her, telling her she was crazy. But she wasn't listening. She headed back to Ramona through a dead block of foreclosed failures and crack houses, a neighborhood of lost gambling addicts, loners, crazies, and self-destructive souls of all kinds. Selfish, rotten men seemed to roll in and out with the tides, like salt air, seaweed, and the trash-laden marshes.

Were she and Angus really jumping in the middle of all this? Could she just let Rachel fend for herself? *Don't be another lost girl.*

They got in Ramona. Her mind was whirring. She sat staring out the front windshield. Seemed like any of them could turn on each other, but they had ankle weights and probably millions of reasons to play things out. She thought again of Dillon and her time with Rachel. She needed to change the game. The tenuous line between her past and the Grave seemed simultaneously connected and divided in two, like standing on the edge of a canyon. She stood on the edge of an old life with no place to go. Far off on the other side, she wanted Dillon and an ineffable future. For a moment, Callie had a nauseating premonition that she could never cross it, that she might not see Dillon again. There would only be the memory of the pool a few days ago. She felt a normal life had been assigned to everybody but her.

"We going to drive or just sit here?" Angus asked, his hands on his large knees like an overgrown school boy.

"You say one more thing, you'll be sitting on that curb on your ass."

He reclined the seat back and looked out his window like a boy. "You really going down there?"

She sighed. "That's one more thing."

They both knew that if Tony discovered she went down to Guatemala, he would retaliate. Callie felt as if a continental spider web vibrated between New York and Philadelphia and Central America, between Tony and Rachel. Now it had spun underneath her life at the Grave to this abandoned street in Atlantic City. She sensed something significant, one of the places in her life where a decision would move time and not be undone, like a sculpture or a structure that stands for centuries. Across the street in the doorway of a grocery store, a neon sign flashed ceaselessly with CHECKS CASHED, CHECKS CASHED, CHECKS CASHED.

Then for the first time in a five years, she realized it wasn't her that was lost. She knew exactly where she was, and she was just confirming what she and Angus already knew in their guts. "Yeah, I'm going down there."

"You mean *we* are."

"No, I mean *I*."

"I have money." You had to give Angus credit. When in doubt, he believed money was the root of all good.

"Where'd you get money?"

He shrugged. "I don't buy nothin'."

"I don't want your money, Angus. I have a Patron Saint of Old Philadelphia Money who likes me. You can pay your own way, though."

She thought of Sym sitting on his stool, obsessively playing Clash of Clans on his iPad and talking about an F. Scott Fitzgerald first edition.

"Actually, I'll see if Sym can cover you too, if you can help me with some security?" "Okay, for what?

"I need some guys who want to keep an eye on a McMansion for me."

"No problem," he nodded.

She put Ramona in drive and floored the accelerator. The car waited a few moments to listen, then the poor engine rattled toward the AC Expressway. "The Grave is closed. I need a computer."

"What for?"

"Research," she said.

He didn't push her. He knew any good operation needed intel. "Paul Paul at Dahlia's."

"Will he still be in his office?"

"He's always in his office."

6

Callie and Angus rehashed most of the way back.

She drove Ramona up North Front Street alongside the empty Interstate 95 up to Dahlia's Den Gentlemen's Club on Spring Garden. Dahlia's sat under the elevated highway, as if the crumbling Eisenhower-era cement and steel had been poured right over it. When she got inside, the dancers were all done for the night. The center runway was empty but for that special purple shade of klieg light, probably called "Foxy Fuchsia." The bar was closed, and a few regulars were avoiding speech, too drunk to do anything but wallow in their own self-induced anesthesia.

They went straight to the back and saw Paul Paul DeLone.

Paul Paul was night manager of Dahlia's. He was a large, wheelchair bound man who sat every night, seven days a week, 364 days a year (he took off on his July birthday and visited his mother in Delaware) at the rear of the club in a motorized scooter holding a Livestrong water bottle filled with Smirnoff and clamato. He had been put on a ventilator since the last time she saw him.

He was arguing with one of the girls about whether fake tits brought in more cash.

"You should do some market research on that," Callie interrupted. "You'd think you'd know the answer, Paul Paul. You're getting slow."

"Finally here to apply for a job, Byrnsey?" He nodded at Angus and winked.

"No thanks, I've given up the pole, Paul Paul. Listen, I need a favor. Can I borrow your computer for a half hour or so? I need to do some quick research."

"Fuck no, I have all my WikiLeaks documents on that."

She snatched his water bottle from his cup holder before he could grab it.

"Refill?"

Paul Paul waved her back to the office while Angus grabbed a table. Paul Paul's gurgled voice sounded like he could barely pluck out the words from a vat of lard in his neck, "Hey, Dread. Help yourself. Youse ain't still popping killers, right?" She could tell he was goading her as an entrance fee.

"Fuck off," she said.

"Duly noted. I like a cold woman. Reminds me of my mother."

Paul Paul's office was surprisingly creative for a strip club manager's. A large double knee-hole, leather-topped desk held a green-shaded brass cock lamp with two balls for pull chain switches. Oak paneling affixed with more breast-motif sconces. A black-framed degree in Latin to Paul Paul Delone from the *University of Pussylvania*. Vintage portraits of naked dancers in impressive poses from old burlesque clubs in European and Asian cities. She said, "Your office looks like it should be a 1920s bank president's. With a sex addiction." On the desk were two framed photos, one of Paul Paul and his mother in front a South Philly row home, and the other of Jeanette, an older woman that Callie knew had been Paul Paul's house mom at Dahlia's for twenty years before dying of lung cancer.

He spun his scooter around into the doorway after her. She sat on the door side of the desk, turned the monitor around toward her, and put the flash drive into one of the slots.

"Hacking into the NSA?"

Callie ignored him. There was a list of spreadsheet files and PDF documents. But one document was just a plain text file called *Contacts for Callie*. She opened that first. It had only a few names.

John Slinger. Guadeloupe Ranch. Petén Guatemala.
Hector Perez, Atlantic City.
Ixchel Cante

She opened several spreadsheet files with different dates. Shipment orders with columns of details, products, and dates. Another file was a list of Latin Leather Group employees. She scanned down the list of names, dates of birth, and addresses. She found Rachel's and saw her Ninth Avenue New York address listed. She stopped again on the odd name. *Ixchel Cante.* She had no home address listed. Instead it just listed Flores, Petén. Ixchel. She saw Hector Perez and his address in Atlantic City.

One of the sheets listed product codes in alpha-numeric combinations (10a/4g/95), colors, measurements, serial codes, and various repetitions of letter codes (XAL, SOB, KJF, LHP, IAM). They seemed like ordinary inventory data of leather goods, sizes, and products. Another file was an alpha-ordered list of customers. There were hundreds: clothing retailers (*Coach, Kate Spade*) and strange Chinese furniture companies (*Guangzhou Sofa & Home*). She scanned to the Bs. Ball & Stoners and then Boa Imports. No Bloody Wrist Productions. She re-sorted the list to be sure. It was definitely missing. So Tony kept the two businesses unconnected.

Callie paused, then did a Google search for *Guadeloupe Ranch Guatemala.* The ranch was in a small village called San Olvidado, not far from Flores, and appeared to be a working horse-and-cattle as well as some kind of Catholic Charities volunteer station. There were photos of generous white volunteers with big smiles and cute local children. She took down the address, phone, and an email address for Vera Granger, Ranch Manager. Callie felt a twinge in her gut—the same quiver of necessity, curiosity, and pull that had her walk into the US Army Recruiting Station up on North Broad next to a sneaker store in a strip mall. If life were a map, you could pick out the route you were supposed to take by following the lines. So far, Callie just had her gut.

She went back to Google, ignoring the moneymaking schemes popping up as Internet ads based on Paul Paul's digital behavior for

Vegas NFL betting, erectile dysfunction drugs, and the Detroit auto show—microscopic pixels of too late American boyhood dreams. She searched Petén, Guatemala, and saw a large dollop of blue in the northern section of Guatemala. Lake Petén Itzá, in the Petén Department. Francis Ford Coppola owned a resort in Petén not far from Tikal, the Mayan ruin, in the northern jungle region.

Around the monitor, almost on both sides he was so wide, she saw Paul Paul smiling at her. "Where's my refill? Time's up."

She thought of everything that spun inside the heads of selfish men and how they made life spin inside out for everyone around them. She couldn't let Dillon turn out like that. She stood up. "Back up your training wheels, Paul Paul." She poured him his refill and put it in his cupholder. "Thanks for the IT support. I'll stop back another time for the pole dancing." She waved at Angus. She watched for some joke about staying, but that wasn't Angus's style. He got up with the same indifference to the naked dancers as he might have had to a mass with a droning priest—just another in the long, simulated fantasies of civilian life that interspersed episodes of intense meaning that rarely came. As they left Dahlia's, the swiveling kliegs, the balconies, and curtains of the club were surreal and disorienting.

"I'll put it on your tab," Paul Paul wheezed.

She drove Ramona over the Vine Street Expressway, which ran through the heart of Center City as a sunken highway beneath the office towers. They were both quiet now. Tony's behavior and Rachel's involvement worried them. Layers of male ego towered over the night, repeating themselves in concentric circles: the ship decks of past Chinese opiate traders; the delusions of Christopher Columbus looking for his "Indians"; Capone and his jazz liquor and cocaine; the boards of Corporate America; the desert bunkers of Bush-Cheney-Rumsfeld; the air of so-called civilization so dense most people never saw it. As far as Callie could see, the earth was just layers of mad male dirt and desire that killed women and children like birds smashed by eighteen-wheelers rolling up and down Interstate 95 with consumption in bulk.

She parked on Angus's street for him to pack his duffel.

Angus got out and leaned into the window, "I'm thinking."

"Well that's a first," she said, starting to move.

"Why don't I go. You need to stay here for Dillon."

There was that farm boy chivalry she counted on.

Her conscience kicked. The way Beth had looked at her at the pool. Sleeping with Rachel in a foggy haze. The messages from Tony that were meant to put her in a box of inaction. The message from Rachel that had an absolute trust in her to act, just as Rachel would do for her or Angus. Life had almost been easier in rehab, where you just took care of yourself. In her experience, any domestic thing involving more than one human being led to the three circus rings of disputes, debts, or death. But war for some greater good led to living.

"No, *I* need to go for Dillon. *We* need to go for Rachel. Just talk to your boys and tell them about the excitement they could havepatrolling Glen Lea McMansions."

Angus hesitated. "Yeah, okay. Fuck."

He paused, as if he were thinking about something. He sounded almost remorseful. "Rachel's one of my girls." He was staring down the street now, talking to himself.

She noted his proprietary *my,* and yet there something undeniably innocent and generous about it.

"Go pack. I will let you know the flight. Meet you at the airport."

She drove off slowly. There was a cop car sitting in the bright street lights of Market Street. In the past, she would have had vials of killers. Out of habit, she signaled carefully and hoped she didn't have a blown tail light. She remembered Tony telling her, "The key to a good dealer isn't black-tinted windows or chrome wheels. It's the fucking driving habits of an old lady." Then he laughed that nervous, cocky laugh—as if everybody loved him and he had been figuring out how to scam the world since elementary school playgrounds.

She headed for her room.

She called Sym and woke him up. After an abbreviated version, he agreed to help her with airfare and some spending cash on loan.

"Thanks, Sym," she said. "When I get back, we'll go to Paris." She almost meant it too. It was a relief to have somebody besides the US Army—an actual human being—believe in her.

"I know we will," he said. "Will get your plane ticket to you in a few minutes."

She hung up.

As she packed her own duffel, including an unloaded Betty and ammo, she pictured Hector pimping from his depressing apartment. Her mind was busy calculating variables, looking at the information she had, wishing she were in a swimming pool holding Dillon, with no help required from Angus or Sym or Beth. No Peter Jagg to fuck when they were out of their minds in that crammed studio apartment. No Tony Maul. What had she actually done with her life? The dead ache felt stuck in her heart. The endless sadness of failure hung in her like the night sky over that fire escape, over Philadelphia, over all humanity. Angus understood it somehow. Some people could see it, some never do. People who've seen bodies blown apart by other human beings can't stop seeing it. In that dark sky, an internal cloud of despair occupied her, despite any good she had done, despite all effort at responsibility. Now she felt in Dillon's small body, in Angus's and Sym's help, a new chance.

Callie lay down and stared at the Trevi Fountain again. Still the same stupid print flat frozen on the wall. Water draped. Horse heads twisted in mid-stride. Gods whipped their minions. Her mouth was dry as stone.

She forced herself up and picked up her phone again.

She looked for a message from Rachel.

Nothing.

She turned on her side to try to sleep. But it was just prostrate anxiety.

Her dreads hung over the side of the bed, as if she were some anti-Rapunzelian rebel. As she closed her eyes, she imagined Dillon climbing toward her.

7

Callie and Angus walked across the tarmac of the small Belize City airport in the hot midday. It was closer to Flores to fly to Belize and drive west than fly to Guatemala City. A tourist group of older couples who apparently had just completed a cruise passed in the opposite direction looking tired beneath oversized visors. She envied them, heading home to comfortable routines. As soon as they'd landing, she was looking for Rachel's purple hair and black Chuck Taylors. She wanted to see them walking through strangers toward her and be done with this whole mess. She could buy their return tickets to Philly and be back before her next probation hearing. Back to the Grave. Back to a day down the shore. Back to reading about balloon farmers. She passed the cruise couples toddling along. She saw the women eye her and Angus, who must have looked like two private-contract soldiers heading out.

At baggage claim, they quickly eyed their army duffels. Callie had loaded hers with a mix of hand-drawn jeans, t-shirts, her copy and a backup she made of Rachel's Latin Leather files, and Betty in her case. She slung it easily over her shoulders. Mrs. Granger's email had said to look for a man named Anthony with a sign. Outside the terminal, taxi drivers and luggage handlers yammered at each other. Angus said no thank you to several, who spoke to Angus first out of habit, one with bad teeth, one with fat cheeks, one with an aged Nike *Just Do It* t-shirt. Finally, a potbellied, tall man in a black cowboy hat, boots, jeans, and a checked shirt came up with BYRNE scribbled on cardboard. He reached to grab her pack.

"No, that's fine, I got it," she said, holding the pack firmly. "Anthony, right?"

He ignored her hand and sucked on a toothpick, staring at her. "I'm Jorge," he said in a slow, indifferent voice. His head was large and his dark brown eyes sagged beneath a cowboy hat tilted back on his round forehead. His face looked like a clay mask that peered emptily at everything in the world.

She was aware of him examining her: a sensuous body, a hardened face that made her look older than her age but not old, her army-issue pack. She thought she saw him scowl at her dreads. "Mrs. Granger said an Anthony was picking me up?"

"We have long drive," is all he said and nodded at an old black Chevy Suburban.

"I just want to change my shirt first. I sweat when I fly. Nice humidity you have down here. Worse than Philly in August." She put her pack in the back while she was talking, took out a pile of bandanas and panties, and shoved them into Angus's chest, "Here can you hold these for a second. And no smelling." She held up a new shirt, looking at the two men. "Mind?" Angus and Jorge walked around to the side of the SUV. She took off her black t-shirt, and put on another identical shirt. She retied a red bandana around her dreads. She reached into the pack, flipped open Betty's case, and took it and a clip out with several other shirts. She slipped the pistol into her rear holster, pulled down her shirt, and covered the case back up.

"All set," she called to them.

Angus awkwardly handed back her things, and she stuffed them back into the duffel. "Ready to go, sunshine," she said, slammed the back door, and let Angus ride shotgun.

They drove out of the airport and into the country. Inside, the rear-bench vinyl seat was faded and ripped, and she tried to settle during bounces into a spot between yellow crumbling foam. Angus said little, so she tried some small talk. All she could extract from

Jorge was that he was originally from Colombia, so she stopped attempting conversation. She fought the urge to fall asleep after the long night before with Angus.

At the border into Guatemala, they drove up to a set of gates and waited in line at a customs building with bulletproof windows. They crossed without hassle and the "highway" turned into a dirt road that wound through empty valleys of marshes and fields crosshatched with paths and irrigation. Villages looked more like camps on a dust floor. She had little to do but brood on what was happening. All that mattered really was she was getting closer to Rachel and to getting Tony out of their lives. She missed Dillon when she saw some boys kicking a soccer ball on a dirt yard. Twinges of doubt and the dead ache came back and weighed on her. Maybe Dillon was better off in Beth's McMansion and country club world? What kind of mother drops everything and goes to the middle of Central America with nothing but a backpack and a US Army-issue pistol?

Finally, the road hair pinned over a mountain pass and down into the valley of Lake Petén Itzá. The Lake sprawled the tropical heat seemed about as deflated as she felt. She hoped there would still be a chance to salvage whatever situation Rachel had stumbled into. She knew first hand that salvage operations were for scrap metal; for human beings they rarely worked.

The town of San Olvidado was on the north side of Flores, the department capital. A set of tin-roofed houses jutted up a hill near the Lake, like a jigsaw puzzle made of colors and porticos and rust. Along the side of the road, she saw women and men of all ages walking. They appeared to have no particular destination. Wearing old Nikes or leather sandals, they carried sacks and plastic bags. Blouses were as multicolored as pebbles at the bottom of a streambed. They hit a pothole, and she held onto the door. Jorge swerved around a mule and a small child holding a toy bat, who swung it with a big smile, waving hello. A mutt skittered sideways onto the road, saw the SUV, and barked at the vehicle for violating its territory. Jorge hit the brakes hard, but seemed preoccupied by some other matter in his head. He eased the truck forward and let the dog bark at him as if he were not there.

"Things jump around here, don't they," she said.

The radio blared dance music. Jorge didn't respond.

"You pathologically introverted or just rude?" she asked.

Jorge didn't respond.

Angus looked back. "Pathologically rude."

Driving out of town, they passed plots of ragtag gardens, rickety metal windmills, and more irrigation ditches crisscrossing the valley. A few men in straw hats worked the fields by hand. She was surprised that it all looked somehow familiar. Fertile but dry, everything seemed where it was supposed to be. Yet it was as disorienting as a façade on a film set.

The Suburban pulled into a dirt lane with a small chain-link gate. Mounted on top of the gate, a makeshift wooden sign read, *Guadeloupe Mission of Jesus Christ—GMJC, Loving the Lowly.*

Angus mumbled, looking at the sign. "Nice touch. Some balls to front as a Catholic mission."

The lane crossed a bridge over a shallow river, and they stopped in a dirt parking area.

She started to get out, "Is Slinger here?"

Jorge glared at her beneath his hat, chewing a toothpick, looking in the rear view mirror. "Hector said you're here to fuck this new guy with us?"

Hector seemed to have done what she asked. But it was tenuous. They could still disappear them any time they wanted. "Yeah. You can call me Ms. Fixer."

She got out and Angus had hauled their duffels out of the back. She noticed on the side door of the truck a faded stencil that read *GMJC*, with a faded cross underneath it.

"How will you fix?" Jorge seemed overly interested for a driver.

"I'm only supposed to talk with Slinger," Callie said.

Jorge didn't move from the driver's seat. "Fine. But you're in my Department now. You fuck with me, you may never go home. Understand?"

"Understood. Thanks for the warm welcome. Didn't you ever hear the expression, 'Don't kill the messenger.'? You want your problem cleared up or not?"

"Slinger said meet him at the airstrip tomorrow morning," Jorge said. He pointed at the house and headed for the driver's side. "Go find the old lady."

The Suburban threw up dust behind it.

She took a breath. They were here.

She saw a few ranch hands up the hill working in jeans and cowboy hats. She felt the strange shape of her body, as if the ride from Belize had taken her farther away from herself and into a foreignness that could not be hidden. There was the wonderful, thick sense of being alive and lost at the same time. She remembered arriving at Camp Bravo in Basra. It was the first time she'd felt that grand sense of civilizations tidally shifting, just an insignificant soul witnessing the past and the living, the survivors and the erased. How many others felt their own ghosts of Cortez and Lady of Guadalupe as they arrived in a new place filled with a passionate, guilty desire to mold a piece of time and earth that is not theirs? Yet, she loved the shedding of home, the sense that no matter what failures, traps, or roles you manage to set upon yourself at home, when you hit the road, you meet a redemptive life despite yourself. Because the creatures you see when you get there are undeniably alive at the same time as you. As she hiked up toward the main ranch house, she bore her whole being and these thoughts on her back like the duffel: Mosul, punk-band tours, Dillon, dreads, her beige shorts, the Doc Maarten boots heavy on her feet, her Irish skin ready to burn in the sun, her fresh Pearl Jam t-shirt.

She followed Angus's bulky waddle up the scraggly path from the riverbed toward a set of buildings. Angus could hike twenty miles with a fifty-pound pack, but watching his rear and his gear gave her a laugh.

Angus turned, "What's so funny?"

New arrivals surrounded by a world that had not asked them to come. What was funnier and more deadly than that in the entire history of human beings?

"Your ass, Conquistador Kistler. Your ass," she said.

8

The ranch house was a mud-colored, single-story home beneath a canopy of palms, surrounded by several paddocks, barns, and out-buildings. A second beige stucco building with a large blue cross over the doorway sat across the way. Callie could hear a few children's voices inside chattering.

A woman appeared on the front porch. Paisley skirt, yellow blouse, and wispy gray hair.

"You must be Mrs. Granger," Callie said.

"That's me! Come around to the office," the older woman said.

She watched Mrs. Granger wave at a mosquito and flutter her hand over her unkempt, frayed hair as they walked past a large cage of cockatoos and parrots. "Jesus knows we're here."

Angus didn't miss a beat, whispering to Callie, "It's about time."

They entered a pink stucco addition to the main house, and came into a paper-strewn office. Inside, Mrs. Granger pointed at a star chart. "The birds and the stars talk to me. Perhaps they will talk to you?" Mrs. Granger seemed to speak to herself more than Callie and Angus. Her tanned face seemed more cracked earth than skin.

Callie didn't know what to say to that. "Maybe they will."

"You're here for how long?"

"I don't really know. Is the other American girl here? She's a friend of mine," Callie asked.

Mrs. Granger took their passports and said, "She was here for a couple of days, but she left yesterday. She hasn't been back. Ixchel is back though. Strange, you all here within a week. And I've been living for the last year with nothing but Slinger's twenty men. That's something, eh? You ever live with twenty men?" Mrs. Granger spoke somehow with both straightforwardness and a haunted regret, as if living in a time twenty years ago but fully prepared to go to the barn and birth a foal. And that name again. Ixchel.

Cement block buildings. Platoons of men. Calls to prayer over loudspeakers over the roofs. Callie gave a nod at Angus. "Yeah, I did. In Iraq."

"Then you know," Mrs. Granger smiled at her. "So you both work for Latin Leather?"

"Sort of," she said.

"You can't *sort of* work for Latin Leather."

Angus helped. "Yeah, we are here to meet with Slinger about some business."

"So you met Rachel Martelli?" Callie asked.

"I met her. She was here for two nights. Jorge and one of his men came and got her yesterday. She said they had some kind of meeting. She hasn't been back since then."

"That's why we're here."

Mrs. Granger seemed to think about that. "Good. Go see Slinger. He'll know. Watch everything you do and say here, do you understand me? They let me stay here on my own ranch that they took right out from under me. I'm just their goddamned cook and maid since they forced me to sell. You can stay in one of the old volunteer cottages."

"Can I pay you something?"

"Go wash up, and we'll have dinner at seven o'clock."

It didn't feel right, but the woman's generosity also meant Sym's cash would be good for a few weeks.

It was getting toward sundown after a long day of flights and driving.

As they stepped outside the office, the dented black Suburban with the bad muffler pulled up at ranch gates on the other side of the small river that flowed between the valley road and the ranch's main house.

"Jorge's crew is back," Mrs. Granger said. Her face tightened. "We used to be a mission and these cabanas where you are staying were for our volunteers. Americans. Canadians, mostly. But some Europeans would come here. We were helping teach English, do projects like build schools. All kinds of things. Then we started protesting the trafficking. That's when they came. Slinger said we had to sell…"

She didn't need to finish the thought.

Angus and Callie stopped next to Mrs. Granger, army duffels still over their shoulders. They watched the Suburban bounce across the shallow river and come up the hill toward them. For some reason, Callie felt like she was waiting for Dillon to get back from school. A group of local men got out of the truck. The crew looked disheveled and exhausted from a day's work, boots and jeans covered in dust, shreds of trees, and mud. They might have climbed out of a half-dug grave. Then behind the group of men she saw a young woman carrying a machete, just as muddy and dusty as the rest but dressed in a colorful orange and blue top that flowed over a small, swollen belly. She carried a baby in a body wrap. She had gauze on her left cheek. The girl had large eyes, and her black hair was tied up in a bun. Beneath the grime and the bandage, Callie could see she had a pretty face. She walked up the lane, staring with disdain at Mrs. Granger and Callie, as if Callie were trespassing. Her left hand seemed glued to the machete handle.

"Who's the girl?"

"Ixchel," Mrs. Granger said. "Ixchel Cante."

Ixchel Cante.

"She worked all day with her baby like that?"

"She won't let her out of her sight."

Callie thought of Dillon. "She won't even let you watch her?"

Mrs. Granger seemed pained by the question. "She won't let me. She's worried they'll take her."

"Why?"

"You can ask her tonight." Then Mrs. Granger stared at Callie, as if Callie could change things. "Jesus has a plan."

"I'm sure he does, but I doubt I'm in it." Callie said. She was more worried about Tony's plans in Flores, Guatemala.

"I raised Ixchel as a foster child. She just had Sylvia about a month ago. So does that make me a grandmother? Now she's back and has her own girl." Mrs. Granger waved a hand at the mountains and jungle. "People here have visions. They see Jesus in the coffee fields. They see him along the side of the road. He comes here. The desperate have deep souls. That's the reason I stay with these men. I believe in sinners. And if I weren't here, I would have missed Ixchel and Sylvia. Jesus has a plan for us."

Callie pulled her hair off her neck. The Catholic talk made her nervous, as if she could have been a better woman if she had invoked a faith. But there was something authentically sacrificial about Mrs. Granger, some kind of forcible will for good hung around her regretful face like the wisps of her hair.

Callie watched Ixchel go into the screen porch and into the back of the main house. Then for some inexplicable reason, perhaps because this expatriate had made a life in a new country, Callie shared with Mrs. Granger the only tenet of her life she could articulate: "I guess I believe in women who roam."

Mrs. Granger picked up one of her dreads off her back, curious, as a little girl might have been. "Well, we're all converts to something, right?" she said, looking at Angus now.

"I like women who roam too," he said.

Mrs. Granger smiled. Then she reached up to pat his big shoulder, and said with ominous warning. "You'll be happy here then, because so many want to leave."

She went toward the kitchen to make dinner.

Angus shuffled off toward his cabana on the far side of the yard. Callie started toward her assigned number three.

Above the cabana in a tree, she saw her first howler monkey. Dillon would have loved it. Memories and images came. Dillon curled up on her lap at the pool. Rachel sitting on a fire escape in the night. Beth reading *People* by the pool. Tony standing off stage at a punk club in New York. The monkey watched her intently as she crossed the yard, then chattered into the air. He slouched back into the crook of the tree, moving his lips and shaking his head at her, mouthing something like, *no, no, no, no.*

She watched his cocksureness, his languid indifference and ignorance of global trade routes, of diseased men like Tony Maul or Manual Evers.

"Fuck off, Mister George-in-the-Bush," she said aloud, exhausted from hours of traveling, her brain, the resentment for Tony's mess, the worry over Rachel. Tomorrow she'd be at Slinger's warehouse and would hopefully meet up with Rachel. She flung open the screen door enough to get by it with the bulging pack. She continued talking to the howler, "Callie Byrne has arrived and has a very limited set of social graces."

The screen door bounced against the pack. She stumbled inside, wanting a fresh shower and a private respite from a dense jungle canopy of drug runners and Jesus hunters.

9

At dinner hour, Callie walked across the ranch to the main house. A large screened-in porch jutted off the back of the house. There were two rows of picnic tables set with simple wax candles on top of faded, handmade tablecloths. Twilight was turning. The sky pulled a thick purple over their heads. Angus wasn't there yet. She didn't like that, like a missing bulldog out looking for garbage or a leg to hump.

Through a doorway to the kitchen, she saw Ixchel cutting mango on a steel table. She wore a colorful pink-and-azure baby wrap holding a little baby with deep black hair tucked against her front. Mrs. Granger was pulling parts of roasted Cornish hens apart, her hands full of grease and meat, wiping her forehead with her upper arm. There was an unspoken tension in the air.

"Callie Byrne, this is Ixchel and Sylvia. Mi Hermosa. My Beautiful."

The young girl ignored her, continuing to slice fruit. The large knife snapped into the butcher block table. She did not look at Callie. She had a sullen, almost angry hunch to her. She gripped the knife so tightly bones bulged through her thin but swollen, red hands. The entire left side of her face was bandaged.

"Anything I can do?" Callie offered.

"You can put out this jug of water, please. Slinger's men will come in soon."

"We sit on the left. The men on the right. You can put that at the end of their tables."

When Ixchel, Mrs. Granger, and Callie sat down, they remained by themselves. No Angus. That probably meant he was in a state. A yellow bulb above was the only electric light. Mrs. Granger lit their table's candle. Mrs. Granger said a prayer to Jesus their Savior who died on the cross. Soon about a dozen men wandered into the porch. They seemed to be in their twenties or thirties. They served themselves and sat talking on the other side of the porch. They spoke Spanish in crude, abrupt tones. Callie had seen young Iraqi men who had the same look: ready to maim or kill but not really knowing why, other than they hating the world and themselves.

Mrs. Granger saw her watching them. "'They know not what they do.' They are still God's boys."

Ixchel spoke for the first time, under her breath. "They're devil shit."

Callie raised her eyebrows. Impressive.

One younger man seemed to be making a joke. They all turned around and looked at Callie. He was imitating brushing long hair and picking at it. "What are they saying?" Callie asked.

"They say your hair has bugs in it," Ixchel explained, with a tone that implied she should have known what they were saying.

Mrs. Granger ate slowly, glaring at the man who had started the joke. She spat out some Spanish at him. The men turned around, but the joker pointed at Mrs. Granger and Callie, as if threatening them.

Ixchel kept eating and rubbing Sylvia's back beneath the bright wrap around her front and shoulders.

"You work for the Evers Corporation?" Ixchel asked.

She had to make a quick decision on this girl. She opted for an approximate version. "Not really. I'm here to find a friend of mine who came down here a few days ago."

Ixchel nodded, "I think you're too late."

Callie probed, "You met her?"

Ixchel hesitated, as if there were more to tell. "Yes. Purple hair. We spoke two nights ago right here. She wanted to know about

Slinger. Jorge and another man left with her yesterday to go to the air strip."

"Do you know where they went after that?"

"No."

"What air strip?"

"Slinger's."

Mrs. Granger explained for her. "Jorge is leading a team clearing it."

Callie focused on Mrs. Granger. "You run this ranch by yourself?"

"I do now. Like I said, we used to have this place full of volunteer missonaries. But not since Slinger bought the ranch last winter. It's just me and Ixchel and Jorge's crew."

"Are they local?"

Mrs. Granger frowned. "Some. Most of them are from Guatemala City or Mexico. Some work the fields, some at Slinger's air strip. I don't ask a lot of questions, as long as they keep business peaceful. They know I treat them all the same. That's the fragile deal I have with Slinger."

"What deal? We have no choice," Ixchel suddenly said. She was picking at the bandage on her determined face.

Mrs. Granger interrupted her. "Of course we do. I've been here for twenty years."

"There aren't any fucking do-gooders here anymore, Vera."

Mrs. Granger brushed it off and gazed at nothing. "We would all pick a project back then. There's an old list on the wall right there." She pointed at a faded blue paper that appeared to have been taped to the wall for years. "Look at what we did." Mrs. Granger started reading it aloud:

!!VOLUNTEERS FOR CHRIST NEEDED!!

Location/Project

Camanchaj: Security wall for medical clinic

Chucam: Classrooms for Catholic school

Chuisamayac: Adoption support with local families

Lemoa: Kitchen/dining room at Catholic Retreat Center

"Fuck all that history," Ixchel snapped. "It's over."

After that, the three of them ate in awkward silence.

Finally, Mrs. Granger broke it, as if she'd been thinking about Ixchel's blunt remark. "Jesus led us here for God's work," she said, looking at Callie. "I came here to love human souls and teach them."

Ixchel whispered, staring down into Sylvia's face. "God's work is a fucking mudslide."

"You left Jorge, didn't you?" Mrs. Granger said.

"Yeah, because I'm keeping my daughter." Sylvia was squirming and started crying.

The two seemed to have no boundaries around Callie. It was as if she were not there, and they were arguing an unresolvable history.

"Something brought you both here," said Mrs. Granger. She looked at Callie. "Ixchel just came back here last week. Don't you think it's strange? Your friend, then the two of you coming one right after the other like that?"

As she got up and left the table, Ixchel mocked the older woman's 60s idealism, "Oh, it's cosssmic."

"You have to pursue reckonings. They don't just drop from the sky," Mrs. Granger said.

Ixchel came back pulling a baby bottle from a shoulder bag painted of Mayan design that seemed to hold a closet full of beauty products. It reminded Callie of Ramona's back seat. "It doesn't matter anyway. I don't plan on being here very long," Ixchel said. The girl had a plan in mind.

"Ixchel wants to go to New York City," said Mrs. Granger, as if going to New York were similar to going to the International Space Station.

"And you know why." Ixchel was fiddling with her bandage. "I almost had enough saved up."

"Everybody needs more money in New York," Mrs. Granger said.

"I can make it. I don't care what I do there. I will find my father."

"Do you know how she was planning on going north?"

Callie guessed. "Something with Slinger?"

"Close. She sold Sylvia for adoption. Her job wasn't paying her enough, apparently."

Callie was surprised at this, but she finished the plan's logic. "And then use the money for one of Slinger's coyotes?" She knew there were smugglers who ran people north to the States. Callie felt a tundra of brush blow through her mind, stray sleeping bags and blankets left behind in gullies and streams in southern Arizona.

Ixchel corrected, as if Callie should have known. "But I changed my mind. I should get some credit for that. I'm still right here where I was fucking born."

"Do you know anybody in New York?" she asked Callie.

Callie hesitated, thinking of Tony. "Not anyone who can help," she said. The men were all talking loudly with each other. She spoke in a calm, casual voice to avoid attention. "The guy I know in New York is trying to do business with Slinger. He sent my friend down here as a courier. But I don't really know why."

They fell quiet. It was obvious they both believed Rachel was in a serious danger but were not saying more.

"I wondered why she was here," Mrs. Granger said. "I can call Inspector Piñada."

"Vera's 'boyfriend'," said Ixchel with a sneer. "Like he's any help. You need to understand what goes on here."

"He's a good man. He can't help what he has to do."

"I think my friend Rachel found out something she shouldn't have."

"You think so?" said Ixchel with the condescension of a teen with no patience for stupidity.

"Ixchel, this Rachel and Callie need our help. And could help you."

Ixchel seemed doubtful. "I don't believe anybody can help another person."

Callie let that go. Philosophical dead ends were not productive. She needed more history from Mrs. Granger and Slinger. She had no time for normal social boundaries. Rachel was missing. She'd been at the ranch. Rachel's life had somehow become intertwined with theirs.

"You said you've been here for twenty years?" Callie asked Mrs. Granger.

"Three lives' worth. I came from Kansas City. We had a ranch back there too. Raised cattle. We were down here on a mission with others from my church for a few weeks. And then Jesus told me to stay here. He came to me one night while I was crossing under that ceiba tree. He stood right in front of me and told me this is where he wants me. He didn't say why. Just looked at me and told me I had to live here to do what I was born to do. No visions since then. But one is enough, don't you think?"

Callie paused, then said, "I wouldn't know." But she did know. She saw visions of things all the time. *Walking on patrol in Mosul. Standing on Twelfth Street and Locust. Dillon floating on the sliding waters of the Atlantic. Climbing the chain link fence on the bridge.*

Mrs. Granger was still talking. "Richard never had one. He died about three years ago."

"I'm sorry."

"He hadn't had a drink for eighteen years. Then he started drinking again. One night he went down to Jamón's and decided to drink mescal with Slinger. We've known Slinger a long time. He started as our ranch manager years ago."

Mrs. Granger faded into her own head. Callie didn't press it. She watched Mrs. Granger's hands and eyes. They seemed disconnected, as if her hands were fluttering over a blanket she was making with scraps of hand-woven cotton fabric.

"It's been a Catholic mission ranch for twenty years. But after my husband passed, I couldn't keep it up on my own. Slinger came to me six months ago. Some of these men started coming here trying to recruit and intimidate people around Petén for the traffickers. He said if I sold him the ranch, he would protect me, if not they would probably drown me in the Lake. He put up good money. What was I supposed to do? Latin Leather's warehouse is a few miles down the road. He's knows bad people, I know, but we have a kind of understanding. He left me and my ranch hands alone for a few months.

But then Jorge said these men needed a place to stay. I didn't expect that."

Ixchel had lifted the baby Sylvia from the sack and started feeding her. "So, you came here to find your friend, eh?" There was a softening tone now for some reason, but she still held a skeptical glance. "What can you fucking do though?"

Mrs. Granger could not help mothering. "Ixchel, please. Her friend is in trouble."

Callie took a sip of water, glancing at Ixchel and Mrs. Granger. "It's okay. I get it. I have trouble helping myself let alone anybody else."

"Welcome to Guatemala," said Ixchel. "You help me and Sylvia get to New York, I'll help you."

Callie recalled the cold drive from Belize City with Jorge. She looked at this hard, young girl staring at her. "Okay. I will do what I can. Can I ask, what happened to you?" She nodded at the bandage.

Ixchel shifted Sylvia to her other arm. "Do you know what I fucking realized last week?" Ixchel said. "Something your friend should have."

Callie waited, realizing Ixchel was coming around to her question but was contemplating something.

"I realized a woman needs to plan every fucking detail better than they do." Ixchel nodded at the men across the porch. She searched Callie's face.

Callie nodded. She understood exactly. She had seen it in female recruits.

Ixchel continued, "And that's the only reason I didn't kill Jorge last week in the middle of the night."

Callie could tell Ixchel was not joking. She was pointing her finger at the sky, waving it back and forth. There was an element of TV drama in the gesture, but Callie sensed she was conveying a real willingness to kill him and a desire to show it off. Callie waited a moment, letting this proud, scarred girl go at her own pace. "What happened?"

Ixchel held up her free hand. "I had swollen fingers, that's what happened."

Callie saw in Ixchel a passionate, Latin flare for the dramatic, an expectation that whatever she said should be understood because she had expressed it.

Mrs. Granger stopped her, nodding at Slinger's men. "Better wait until later."

"I don't care about them. But okay. The front parlor after dinner. You want to help your friend, you have to help me. Simple as that, American Dread Woman."

"I said I will do what I can," Callie said bluntly.

Ixchel cooed to Sylvia. "Baby, watch out for Americans who talk dreamy."

Callie was going to defend herself but let it go. Mrs. Granger was watching the baby, brows furrowed as if she had forgotten something important. "I have a daughter too. One day she called us and said she wasn't coming back. She wanted to stay in Seattle. She wasn't coming home. I went into a depressed fog for three years. I didn't even realize it. She's a very important businesswoman there. For Microsoft. Have you been to Seattle? We know what it's like to live in the rain."

"No, I've never been there."

"One day I'm going to Seattle for Christmas," Mrs. Granger announced. She was like a hopeful prisoner awaiting early release.

Ixchel stroked Sylvia's soft head and said to Callie, "And I'm going to Long Island on the Day of the Dead. I'm going to hunt down a rich white man in white pants. I've seen *The Great Gatsby* with Leonardo." Ixchel laughed at her own imagination. There was something so dense and experienced about Ixchel that Callie couldn't help being compelled by her. It was like meeting a girl whose soul had been sacrificed on a Mayan temple a thousand years ago.

"She has a mind of her own," said Mrs. Granger.

Slinger's men had risen to leave the porch. A few of them started their imitation of picking bugs from her hair. "Bugs! Bugs!" they teased.

The one joking about Callie's dreads was glaring at her. Then he lifted his shirt, and unsheathed a knife from his hip. He poked at his hair, as if killing bugs. Then he put the handle on his crotch, waving it back and forth as if marking territory at the three women.

Callie stood up slowly and walked straight at him.

"Callie," pleaded Mrs. Granger, "don't bother with Rodrigo."

Callie stood right in front of Rodrigo and his knife and raised her fork straight at his left eye. "You like to use that little shaft down there, eh, Mr. Rodrigo? Didn't your mother tell you you'd go blind? I'd be happy to enlighten you."

Ixchel was laughing behind her. "See Rodrigo, women can have bigger balls than you."

Rodrigo glared at her. The other men stood outside, watching them now. Then he spat on the floor near Callie's Doc Maartens. He turned and walked into the twilight.

"Night, Rodrigo Little Shafty," Callie called behind him.

He cursed something in Spanish as he joined the rest of the work gang.

10

Just as they finished dinner, Angus arrived to eat. He followed them into the house, like a dog trailing the scent, and grabbed a plate of food on his way. The main house smelled of molded teak and damp fabric from the humid, tropical air. Mrs. Granger led them through the kitchen into a hall covered in photos. The original ranch house from the 1950s. Aerial views of the jungle. Tikal rising out of the canopy of trees. The photos were arranged on a wall where steps ascended to the second floor. An odd closet door shaped in notches was cut beneath the steps.

Ixchel opened the small door, and pointed in for Callie and Angus. "My cell."

Callie looked into the one-bunk room. The ceiling was the underside of the stairs above her head. It had the appearance of a third-class berth on a ship or old train. The wallpaper, decorated with steamer trunk stickers of cities of the world (*Paris! Amsterdam! London! Tokyo!*), curled and faded. A single bulb hung from the underside of the stairs. A small shelf with old magazines hung over the head of the bead. The room had a certain child-like adventure coupled with minimalistic dollhouse.

"Still has the photo of Pam Rodriguez I took when she came here." Callie saw an image of a beautifully airbrushed model taped to the wall from a fashion magazine. "She's part Guatemalan."

"She's part sexy," joked Angus quietly.

Callie swatted the back of his head. Despite herself, she thought, Jesus, it was good to have him here.

Ixchel nodded, though, "Si, some tight little body, eh? You know why I have that picture? I wrote her. I wanted to become a model in LA. You know what she did? She came here and stayed. She said, 'Why can't you be the first Mayan supermodel?'"

Angus grunted through his beard, which seemed to take up half of the small hallway now. "I say why not too."

Callie was more interested in why this little compartment had become Ixchel's bedroom. It seemed a surreal version of an American teenager's room. Callie felt like she was now really in a new country—she did not understand anything at all about Mayan culture or Guatemala. But one thing the army trained you in was military courtesy. Thank you, sir. You're welcome, ma'am. And Callie had walked down a hundred streets abroad with that attitude of universal courtesy and come to this conclusion: everybody wanted to live out their lives with their families without being killed—and everybody wanted sweets after a meal. People knew immediately, like any animal in the wild, who wanted to kill them and who was offering chocolate. So even though she had no idea where she stood in this place, somehow she knew that she and Ixchel did not need to understand ancient Mayan or Irish Philly history to understand each other. They both savored chocolate.

They proceeded up the hall and entered a parlor at the front of the house. The room seemed frozen in the last century. Drooping shelves were crammed with pottery, and woven baskets were stuffed with rolled fabrics faded on the top by sunlight; oranges, purples, and blues hung in mazes of blankets over the sunken furniture; ten-year-old issues of travel magazines for theoretically bored volunteers in the rainy season were splayed in a perfect fan on the coffee table. Nobody had picked them up in ages. On a table in the corner, a half-emptied chessboard where two ghost players seemed to be battling; a stone fireplace with dried wood waiting for future lighting by yellowed newspaper; a plain wooden, dusty crucifix over the mantle, which was apparently decorated year-round with a Nativity. There were three different seating areas, including the rattan sofa, where Callie and Angus sat, covered in a washed-out red, green, and white cockatoo pattern and pillows zigged with zags. A dusty throw blanket lay behind them on the back of the sofa.

Ixchel sat crossed legged in a dark, rattan chair with a fan back that seemed to wrap the thin beauty of the girl in a halo. Mrs. Granger sat in a flowered arm chair.

Ixchel held Sylvia in her lap and waved her head at the room around them. "This is the same room where my father left me."

"Don't do this, Ixchel," the older woman said.

"Why not? It's all related. On that sofa. I was seven. It was late afternoon. Sunlight and shadows striped from those blinds. Vera gave me lemonade."

Mrs. Granger said, speaking to Callie, as if a trial of some kind were in progress, "I wanted her to know I loved her."

"I'm sure," Callie said.

"No, she wanted to get rid of the guilt."

Mrs. Granger remained silent to the charge.

Ixchel continued, "I remember the smell of the mint leaves and the tall glazed glasses etched with GRANGER. The lemonade had bits of raw brown sugar. It's funny what you remember, no? I swirled them while my father and Mrs. Granger talked about what to do with me."

"Your father was making sure you were cared for," said Mrs. Granger.

"My father was getting a strange justice where he could. He was talking short and fast, like he always did. He had removed his cowboy hat, and it looked big sitting on his little legs. My mother's accident was like BG and AG. Before Guadeloupe and After Guadeloupe. My father goes to New York. I stay here. I haven't seen him since." Ixchel's eyes welled, but her face refused to crack. "Sylvia and I will find him."

Callie saw the determination in Ixchel's eyes. It was the same determination that Callie had to stay clean for Dillon.

Vera Granger didn't look at either of them. She sat playing with her hands. "We all leave our mothers somehow, but they are not supposed to leave us."

There was a silence in the living room, as if all their mothers' souls wanted to pass through the room but were cast out now into exile. Callie felt her blood carrying the name *Dillon*. Her own AWOL motherhood was an existential ache that emanated head to foot, like a splayed network of muscles hung on skeletal bone. It was screaming inside her for a fix to ease it.

Ixchel said, "That's what happens when people die unexpectedly. The little things in life turn into monster snakes."

Callie thought of her own mother, who had fought hard for Beth and her. She'd gotten the will and discipline of a soldier from Paula. She wondered if she would ever feel that kind of strength in herself again.

She felt for this young, strong-willed girl, who reminded her a bit of herself. She leaned forward on her knees, looking at swirls in the faded Oriental rug, processing the history, the world, into which she and Rachel were enveloped.

"So my talk with Slinger should be fun," Callie said.

Neither woman responded, but she sensed they agreed.

"I can't wait," Angus murmured. He sat like an oversized boy in a church pew, empty dinner plate on his fat knees.

Ixchel picked up one of the magazines and was flipping slowly through a thick *Vogue Latina* magazine. For some odd but appealing reason, Ixchel held them up to show Callie. Glossy pages of photoshopped, simulated female bodies flipped by. "Mr. Angus, do you know we get grabbed on the street any time by a man here? Do you think these women get grabbed in New York like that? We have to stay quiet or we'll get beat up, or worse."

Angus looked for help from Callie, not knowing what to say. The golden floor lamp shone in the corner, and mosquitoes had come through rips in the window screens.

Callie changed the subject. "So what happened with Jorge?" Callie asked.

"What's the point? What will that change if I tell you?" Ixchel asked. For some reason, she pointed at a magazine model as she said it.

This time Mrs. Granger put Ixchel on the spot. "Tell her, Ixchel. Or I will."

Ixchel looked directly at Callie, reading her intentions. Then, having made a judgement, she recounted the story to her like a sister.

11

Ixchel's hands had always been thin and small-boned. After Sylvia, they were swollen and hurt. She couldn't sleep. The moonlight made her night a restless one. Sylvia was sleeping. The room in the Hotel Palm where Jorge stayed smelled of rotten cantaloupe and his stink. She had been furiously listening to Jorge snore like a pig. She thought, who could stop me from taking a kitchen knife and just stabbing a man like Jorge? She got up and went to the studio drawer and pulled out a large knife. It was perfect. She could stab him so many times before he stopped her that he'd bleed to death. She crossed the room to the window and looked out at the night and the alley below. Lita Ruez would sit every day in that alley weaving blankets by hand.

Lita had sat for years against the crappy egg-yolk yellow of her son's house. But in the moonlight the yellow was just the right for killing—sick yellow. Ixchel held the knife so hard her hand throbbed.

She looked at her swollen fingers, and they felt like someone else's. That was the thing that struck her, that her hands were not her own. She'd sold them. Then she thought about how you couldn't kill somebody with a kitchen knife without gloves. Even more if he is a man with lots of corrupt police friends in Petén. If you actually wanted to get away with it, you needed a plan. You needed to *think*.

You needed to have every detail organized into the right time, place, and order.

She got back in bed next to the snoring pig, and waited.

The next morning, she sat looking out the slats of the shuttered window.

Four boys kicked a soccer ball behind the rooms where the Ruez family lived. Lita Ruez sat against the wall, smiling, weaving a blanket. She looked contented with her life in a way Ixchel could not grasp. The alleyway was narrow, but the old woman seemed miles from her. The boys, too, ignored her, living the kind of childhood she could not remember. Had she played with other girls? Before her father went to New York and her mother was killed in the Granger accident, she remembered playing with a boy named Roberto until she had to beat him up for grabbing her ass. He never came back.

She liked to look at the Ruez's house in the daylight. Now the yellow was the color of deep gold and contentment. Above it, someone had painted a skein of clear blue sky. It was beautiful and light. Sometimes Lita Ruez would look up at Ixchel sitting in the window. Ixchel could see a world of thoughts in her lined, tan face—but Lita Ruez never revealed anything. Her simple smile was maddening to Ixchel.

Behind her in the darkened room, Jorge was on his bed. He looked like a long sack of mud with two rodent eyes peering out from a hole. She had been coming to his room for a few months now, since right before she had Sylvia. An old transistor radio sat on the table playing lounge music, a twisted soundtrack for a sordid place. When she had started seeing Jorge, she thought she had been tough and smart about it, had known what she wanted. But the longer she stayed with him, the more Jorge withered her, the more foolish she realized she had been.

But last night, with her deliberateness, she separated from her mistake from herself somehow, as if her own body were as elusive and distant as New York City.

"I'm not staying here anymore," she said.

He lay on the bed throwing a bead sack into the air and catching it. It was the most activity Ixchel ever saw from him beyond satisfying his stubby member. His round head looked like a heavy medicine ball that nobody would want to carry around, followed by a pot belly that appeared to be over-stuffed with the beef and chicken he gorged on, and then his spindly legs.

He didn't answer her. Just kept tossing the sack toward the ceiling and trying to catch it. It was at least a small consolation that when he missed, it would glance off his head.

"Did you hear me?" she said, looking back outside at the boys. She despised those boys, shouldering each other happily, feet scuffling and flailing, and kicking the ball through their makeshift goals of old sneakers set up in the alleyway. When they got bored, they would kick the ball over Lita Ruez's head, who would curse them off, her hands busy weaving.

"I hear you," he finally mumbled.

"And?"

"You can go any time you please," he lied.

He was reminding her she could not go anywhere she pleased.

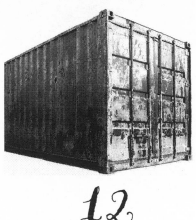

12

How did she get into this situation to begin with?

When she had started work at Slinger's plant packing leather, it didn't pay enough real money to make her dream possible.

Ixchel didn't care about leather or whatever else they did with the Evers cartel. Everyone in Flores knew Jorge was involved with Slinger's operations, but what she cared about was Jorge's *other* business as a *buscadoro,* a baby broker, who had informants nose around the clinics and streets keeping their ratty little eyes out for pregnancies, despite the state ban issued halting adoption. Jorge had a brother who was a "lawyer" in Guatemala City, an expert at fake paperwork. They had their little nasty trading system: families were made and unmade, started and ended, born and traded, no different than a banana plucked from a tree and bundled on a ship.

At nineteen, there was no reason you couldn't know what you had to offer and what others could offer you. She had heard what other girls had done. She wanted a baby because she wanted the money. She wanted the money to go the States. She wanted to go to the States because she wanted to live with her father. That's what she told people. Secretly, she believed she was born to be a fashion model.

But she knew how life worked: something does not come from nothing.

So she met up with Jorge at Jamón's cafe one night to do the first major piece of business she had ever conducted in her life. He sat in the back booth, where they said he would be. He was with Slinger, an American with a ponytail, a flapping plaid shirt, and jeans. She wondered why some gringos with lots of money would dress so poorly.

She had little idea how such things were done, so she said straight out, "I want to do some adoption business with you."

Jorge looked at her, cutting into a thick sirloin, eating with his fork upside down. He said nothing. Just kept chewing and looking at her. Slinger was writing in a notebook and was paying no attention.

Ixchel was afraid of what they could do but somehow not intimidated by Jorge's face staring at her. It seemed she had known of him her whole life. She'd seen him many times around the city. Her friends had told her about him, a middle man in the corrupt black market in the region: fresh fruits from farms to the tourist hotels, cuts from tour guides to Tikal, boat engine parts, licenses for fishing. And babies. One of his two brothers wasin prison, the other a crooked lawyer, and he had a reputation for drinking and beating girls who worked for him.

She stared back at him, while she thought, *He's just a part in a movie.* The more she repeated that the more she could taste the reality of New York City. She knew her father worked somewhere in New Jersey tending plots of grass and island gardens in shopping malls and condos. She wanted to be there. There was nothing left for her in Guatemala. In New York, you could dream of anything, and it would be somewhere on the island waiting for you.

"You need a cock, eh?" he asked, pointing a corn on the cob in the air.

"I can find somebody else, if you're going to be rude," she said getting up. "You seem unable to eat and talk at the same time."

He waved the corn at her to sit.

Ixchel worried that people around them noticed her, but a quick glance saw men with their beers talking to each other, paying no attention to her. She sat back down.

"So how does this work? I don't have time to wait."

Jorge introduced Slinger.

"I know who he is," she said. Everyone in the area knew him. Slinger did not appear interested in her.

"Yes, you do. You work in his warehouse after all. Here's how this is going to work. You're going to continue to work for us at the warehouse until we say different. The police don't like girls who steal cash from tourists when they should be making their beds and cleaning the toilets."

She had never stolen when she was a maid at the Flores Hotel and Resort. But she knew they could easily fabricate that and have her arrested if she didn't do what Jorge demanded.

"See, I work a lot of places," he said, chewing quickly, showing his crooked teeth in a grin.

"I heard ten thousand is the rate for a baby," she said.

He scoffed. "You're crazy," eating his grilled corn. He held it like a club.

"How much then?"

"A thousand US."

"For a baby or a dog? You're the crazy fucker."

He pointed at her with the cob, "You know, do you? There's many, many babies. There's many, many people." He waved the cob at the outside world.

"But they're not *me*," she said.

He guzzled his beer and said, "You think you're important? *You* are the least important thing in the world."

It was unheard of for a girl to talk the way she was to a man like Jorge. What did she have to lose at this point? She ignored his attempt to belittle her. She was genuinely engrossed in the possibility of the deal, in her own dream-visions.

"I want a thousand and a trip north," she said.

"You want a trip? Then you come stay at my place for a while too. We'll see what you get. Or I can talk with Piñada about your hotel activities. You'd probably only be in jail a few months."

Ixchel looked at Jorge and saw an ugly man, but one with connections. Wasn't he sitting next to a gringo who flew to Florida and California as he pleased? Wasn't he the man who took van loads of men into Mexico headed to Texas and Arizona? He probably drank with Inspector Piñada.

"No," she said, "I'll see what *you* can do, old fucker."

He waved his corn at her to be off.

"And you eat like an old cow. I'm surprised there are not swarms of flies around your eyeballs," she said.

She heard Slinger laugh to himself, head in his hand, writing in a notebook.

13

Now she turned from the window, picked up her bag over her shoulder, and went into the toilet. After she'd had Sylvia, she had started again dabbing coke between her legs or on her gums. She felt around her bag in a flurry, anxious and frustrated. She wanted to burst. Then she remembered she had flushed her last stash in a fit of concern for Sylvia. She sat on the toilet, breathing hard, getting ready for what was coming. "I'll find another way to get the money," she said through the closed door.

When she came out of the bathroom, Jorge hadn't moved.

The bead sack bounced off his hand and next to his head. He reached up without looking and found it.

"I changed my mind."

He knew what she meant.

"You can't. She's sold. Look at her now, because she'll be flying soon."

The stupid little radio played a Latin guitar ballad. She picked up Sylvia from the baby pen. A quiet bongo and a man singing, *I have watched you all my life / I have died and I watch you from the moonlight.*

"I can do whatever I want," she said.

Jorge got off the bed.

She backed up a few steps.

He was boiling water for his coffee.

Then he threw the bean bag at her head, grabbed the boiling pan off the stove, and rushed at her. He grabbed her by the hair and slammed her head up against the wall. She gripped Sylvia. He smashed the bottom of the pot into her face and held it there. He didn't bother covering her mouth. She was screaming and punching. He was saying coldly, "You work for me, puta! You work for me!"

She kneed him in his balls, pushed him off, and managed to run out the door.

Even carrying Sylvia, Ixchel was quick. She heard his smoker's cough. She ran down the hall and hurried down the back stairs. Her face felt like a hot fire. She climbed over three old bicycles and out the back door into the alleyway. She tried to be careful, knowing she was shaking a baby as she went. The boys ignored her, all kicking at a neon green soccer ball and each other's legs in a cloud of dust. Lita Ruez did not look up from her blanket as Ixchel turned to look back.

Ixchel imagined the old woman thinking, *That girl is trouble because she has bad friends and her little jeans are too tight.*

She felt relieved to be out of Jorge's room and the little prison of his old transistor radio. Then from the window where she had just been looking down on the alley, the shutters crashed open and down came the closet of her life, spilling out onto the ground. Colorful shirts in bright turquoise, hot pink, patterns of orange sun floated down into the dirt. Panties in black, bright white, fuchsia, and red stripes fluttered noiselessly down in the breeze. Her toiletries came down in a sad pile, hitting and spilling out. Sharp-heeled shoes landed on their sides.

She didn't move or run but just watched as Jorge spilled her life onto the street.

She knew she could not live in Flores any more. Or in Guatemala. Until she could leave, though, she would need Slinger's protection. He was the only one who had anything to hold over Jorge Mercado. She wasn't sure why, but she knew he would protect her.

She started picking up her clothes, trying to shove them in her shoulder bag and hold Sylvia at the same time. The boys stood nearby watching her, stunned at the TV drama unfolding in front of them. They pointed at her and laughed, but then her leather boots came crashing down between her and the boys, cluster, and they ran off. She shoved a fistful of panties into her shoulder bag, kneeled down to get her shoes. The pebbles and dirt ground into her knees. She heard shuffling. Lita Ruez held out a cotton sack with a draw-string that she used to keep her thread. She had emptied all her thread next to her loom and was easily bending over and putting Ixchel's assortment of t-shirts and jeans into the sack.

She heard Jorge from the window above in a low voice, "Pick up the shit, old lady and little girl slut. The police are coming."

She watched Lita just continue to put her clothes in the knitting sack, and she got up and put her hand on Lita's arm. The shoulder bag and the sack were both as full as she could manage. Lita handed her the sack, and put the two draw strings over Ixchel's shoulder. Then she took her old hand and wiped something off Ixchel's hot face.

Then she felt her feet running on the cobbles heading down toward the water as if her body were not her own. She smelled grilled chicken and burnt corn husk. Between the narrow buildings on either side of the street, she could see out to the Lake. She had been born here, but she hated Lake Petén. She walked along an open quay on the waterfront now, carrying Sylvia, her shoulder bag, and Lita Ruez's sack.

She waited for the ferry to take her across the Lake.

She had a place she could go, but it was akin to returning to a home that's been sold to strangers.

14

The bright green skiff bobbed as Ixchel sat on a narrow bench beneath a small roof. The water was relatively calm, unlike Ixchel's stirred-up emotions. She was humiliated by her mad departure. On the other side of the boat, four annoying birders wore various American t-shirts, vests, and binoculars hanging around their necks. They were so comfortable in their lives that they could be away from home and seem perfectly at ease in a foreign land. The two men wore canvas bucket hats, while their wives wore matching sweatshirts.

They were trying to talk to her about how beautiful Guatemala was.

She nodded and smiled at them. They asked more questions. She pretended to be shy and gave them cursory but polite answers. She looked down the Lake. She did not want to look back at Flores. She could see fishermen with their boats along the shore. One of them was likely her uncle, her father's brother, who was a little dull in the head from being hit by a motorbike in Guatemala City. The water lapped along the side of the boat as the ferryman sat with the small outboard, and Ixchel let her hand drag in the water. Above the Lake were the mountains, and Ixchel saw the Hollywood Man's resort up on the hill. She could see cabanas with thatch roofs dotting hills of dense green where people with money could play with their lives, drop in to see the ancient Mayan city of Tikal, wander the streets of Flores, and have coffee on the Lakefront in the morning looking at maps. She had tried to get a job at the resort before all this, but there had been no openings.

When she was younger, she had resented the happy eco-tourists and the tour groups of Germans and Canadians. Crossing the Lake now, she felt a renewed indifference toward that world. She was a separate island from the business of displaying Mayan ancestry, the Hollywood Man's resort, and the local machinery of catering perennially to American dollars. She felt the promise of leaving for the first time in her life, and being in the middle of a large Lake on a crossing made all of her past feel equally distant and diminished. The alleyways and cobbled streets of Flores had seemed impossibly large to her, and now they were nothing but a collage of small blue, mango, and coral dabs. Her pregnancy, Jorge, her father in New York, and her own dreams made Flores an island town of worry, looming despair, and the all-encompassing effort of scripting her escape from it.

As she crossed the Lake, as the rush faded, as her legs felt the bags of all her belongings between them, she believed for the first time that she would reach New York. Wasn't this ferry moving away from Flores? Wasn't she out of Jorge's apartment? Wasn't she now capable of working, stealing, or otherwise negotiating her passage with Slinger? Nobody had to tell her that Slinger moved things to the north. Her father and many others had gone north through Mexico—a chain of vans, treks, pickups, and migrant-worker shuttles.

Sitting across from the birders, watching the white beard talk with his wife, the world was an inverted mirror above the Lake. She would be like a bird migrating. Here she was in their sight, then she'd be gone, nothing but a sighting report. Ixchel's mind seemed to see the world from above. Lake Petén was a puddle. Flores was a toy city. This ferry was a pilgrim ship. The resort on the hill was a boy's model of fragile balsa. Beneath the water, where her fingers dragged, minnows were as large as tarpons. Men who had power and money were infants; she was a giant beautiful film being played against the screen of Lake Petén. She looked at the birders in their hats, necks hung with binoculars. The small Yamaha outboard buzzed steadily behind them.

At San Olvidado Ixchel disembarked. Then, in a moment very unlike her normal reticent state, she volunteered to the birders one of the best trails to take and how to find it. She did not ordinarily give local information to tourists. In fact, she had been known, if asked, to provide deliberately misleading information or steer them toward depressing locations. This time she had helped them.

They thanked her with open smiles, as if she had personally shown them a yellow-bellied bananaquit. The man with the gray mustache offered her a ten-quetzal bill, worth about a dollar thirty. He had apparently pre-folded a set of them neatly into thin rectangles for just such interchanges. She took it and asked, "Do you know anybody from the Queens or the Brooklyn?"

He looked surprised, but answered politely, "No, we're born and bred Oklahoma Sooners" and pointed to a confusing red logo on a bright white t-shirt. She thanked him anyway and headed off, leaving the group puzzled about the girl carrying her clothes and questions about New York. She headed out the valley road, winding through soy and corn fields toward the ranch, the shoulder bag strap digging into her bony shoulder.

She wondered what the room under the stairs looked like now.

15

There was a long pause. Nobody said a thing, each of them thinking about Ixchel's decision.

"You know Guatemala is one of the baby-factory countries, right? It's just a fact," said Ixchel. She said it matter-of-factly, the way an American would have said, You know the best deals on toilet paper are at Costco, right?

"Despite an international ban on adoptions," Mrs. Granger added.

Ixchel interrupted her. "Don't speak for me. Just because I'm nineteen, there is no reason I don't know shit. One of Slinger's men told me there was a Latin Leather man in New York who could get me a fashion agency. That I could work for him."

"Tony Maul," said Callie.

"Tell him I will help him get his shipment."

"How?" asked Mrs. Granger. "Aren't you into enough trouble?"

"That's how life works," Ixchel nodded.

"And how does life work?" Mrs. Granger asked.

"Criminal supply and demand. That's what life is, right Vera?"

Mrs. Granger was shaking her head, disagreeing with Ixchel or God or both.

Ixchel answered her own question. "Yes it is. People's secret desires are just fucking business. People who want a baby who can't have one—in Germany, in Texas, in California—and people like me provide them. When each of us does the dark thing we want, the universe fucking wobbles along." She looked at Callie as if she were stating a law of gravity.

"So I said fine, a thousand and a trip north. But I couldn't do it after I had Sylvia. Slinger said I could come work for him until I figured something out. He said Jorge wouldn't touch me." So that was it. It's an evil thing I put in motion. But I'm not good at being good anyway."

"Don't say that," said Mrs. Granger.

Tear streaks were running down her left cheek, overcoming Ixchel's efforts to deny them. The bandage obscured the right side.

"She came home, at least," nodded Mrs. Granger.

The huff from Ixchel made it clear she disagreed. "Home? People born in the wrong place don't have one."

Mrs. Granger grimaced.

Ixchel got up and stood in the doorway. She looked at the older woman and then said to Callie and Angus, "I don't trust Too Good People. Did they come here to help us? Sure. To provide medical care? To build schools? Sure. But they come from another world. And some try to convert you to believe. They give you hugs like sermons. They smile at you. But they smile that way to everybody. So while they talk to you as if you are special, you feel like a nobody at the same time. A special nobody.

"I'm sorry your friend came here—it's a lost place. Tomorrow, you can talk with Slinger and see what you can do with all this." Ixchel turned and walked away. Callie heard the door to her room under the stairs open and then shut out everything in Guatemala.

Callie and Angus got up and said goodnight to Mrs. Granger, who seemed to be having a private war between faith and despair. After she had been so dismissed by the girl she had raised, it was the latter that seemed to be winning.

16

A mosh pit that has turned into a crushing crowd. Vicious Delicious are playing all out, the noise against normality at a fever pitch of ecstatic rage and escape. Dillon is on top of the ride of hands and waving arms, and then he is flaying at those around him with chains. He waves at Rachel and Callie to join him atop the crowd. He's laughing as if it's all good fun. Then the mood of the crowd changes. Tony starts yelling, "Fuck the System! Fuck the System!" The crowd wraps belt loop chains around Dillon's legs and arms while twirling him in the air over their heads. Then the band on stage cranks the volume louder yet. The room is exploding in energy and pounding decibels. The crowd throws Dillon down under their feet, and the whole room starts jumping up and down.

Callie awoke panicked, disoriented, and sweating. The strange, quiet room made her throbbing heart rate more intense. Her mind was both continuing and dispelling the nightmare at the same time. *Dillon is stomped to death.* Where was she? She heard alarmed bird screeches. Where was Dillon? She peered at the window. Sunrise was coming around.

Then she remembered. She had flown to Guatemala. Rachel. Tony Maul. Jorge Mercado and Ixchel Cante. They all came to her in one flush of anxiety.

She forced herself up and doused her face with cold water in the bathroom. She pulled on her jeans and a plain white t-shirt. She was going to meet Slinger. She started running through the plays she could make with him. She hoped he had as many objections to Tony as she did. She walked down the dirt driveway of ruts and bumps along an old fence by one of the fields. She crossed a foot bridge across the stream. When she got out to the main road, it was a barren, dusky view.

The dusty road curved through some fields and hills and she could see occasional shacks, lean-tos, and sheds scattered here and there. The fields looked like tufts of thinning hair on a sunburnt scalp, with irrigation wrinkles spreading across the land. A single small power line crisscrossed the road. They said electricity had only been in the area for twenty years or so. Near the few houses, clothes-lines carried dress shirts, t-shirts, blouses, and baseball jerseys in the breeze with the arms outstretched, like ghosts flagging a rescue plane. Coming the other way, a farmer with a hat and a bright blue shirt rode his bicycle. The man ignored her and made his slow way down the valley hunched like a question mark.

She recalled the facts she heard last night. Ixchel's mother had been killed in a ranch accident. Her father left Ixchel here at the ranch. Vera Granger raised her. She started working at Latin Leather but wasn't making enough money. She cut a bad adoption deal with Jorge Mercado to get money for a trip north. She had a baby girl. Then a week ago, she decided to keep her baby, blew up the deal, and returned to the ranch at the same time Rachel arrived to find Slinger.

She returned to the house. Mrs. Granger was in the kitchen, and Callie quietly ate some toast, an orange and drank a strong coffee. Neither Angus nor Ixchel appeared for breakfast.

Jorge's Suburban came down the road and splashed through the river, bounced over the rocks and ruts, and came to a stop. Red clay dust blew in Callie's eyes and mouth. Angus and Ixchel both walked down the road toward the house. Callie watched them. Could they have slept together just like that?

Sylvia's wrap bounced side to side. Ixchel carried the same machete. She did not look at Callie but opened the side door and climbed in with the men. Jorge stared at her but waved her on.

Angus walked past her to get in the Suburban. "Stop staring, Dreads, it's impolite."

She climbed in after him, and the Suburban pulled off to Slinger's.

17

They arrived at the Latin Leather warehouse, a long gray building with a few lame swaths of yellow graffiti striped across it. Faded letters spelled out ROBERTO BANANAS. The air smelled of preservatives and chemicals, cowhide and humidity. Callie was surprised at how large the building was, stretching out like the cavernous warehouses in the distribution hubs back in North Jersey. She joined the group of workers getting out of the truck.

Angus was directed into the warehouse. Callie was handed a machete similar to Ixchel's. Jorge pointed them toward the brush. It was only a few minutes in the humid air that the machete grip was sweaty in her palm, as she swung it at the thick brush. She just wanted to go find Slinger and Rachel, but she wasn't sure how. She figured she'd just play along; she'd have to bide her time. Slinger knew she was here, and hopefully why.

The men seemed quieter in the morning with the anticipation of a full day in the heat. They had their own lives to think about, and the sound of bulldozers grading the airstrip drowned out any talk. While they worked side by side, Ixchel gave Callie a rundown of what she had gathered on the men working for Latin Leather. Some were originally from Guatemala City. Some had been road crew. Some were sons of farmers who had spent years working coffee fields. Despite Mrs. Granger's impression, there were local men who had surreptitiously worked for Latin Leather before Slinger had become the regional director. Rodrigo, the young thug with his waving knife, was a nephew of Jorge's, always assuming the protection of nepotism. He had groped Ixchel just about every day she had been there.

At a break, one man came over to Ixchel and Callie. He had a thick neck, wide lips, a bloated torso, and his arms were covered in several gang tattoos. He stood too close in front of Ixchel. He smelled like cigarette ash in a public toilet. He reached out and put the back of his hand against Sylvia. Ixchel flinched.

"Jorge said you backed out," he said, while speaking English and eyeing Callie purposefully.

"She's my daughter. I can to what I want," Ixchel said.

"You think so. But you have no place to hide. She has no place here. You work for the Evers Corporation, just like the rest of us."

Ixchel smacked his arm off her.

"Nothing to say? Too good for us? Rodrigo, look at this, Ixchel Cunte, the talky bitch is quiet. And look at this, she brought another American this morning." He looked at Callie now. "We must be lucky. Two American girls in the same week."

Callie gripped the machete. It would be a pleasure to take a swing at his thick neck to make his mouth stop talking about Rachel. She stared back at the puffed face. The muscles in her arm wanted to hack the blade into his left thigh. She restrained herself, and turned back to hacking at the brush, thinking of women who for thousands of years worked in fields, worked fires to cook for men, worked their backs into the earth. Callie remembered her own belly pregnant with Dillon. She felt the hips and bellies of ancient women above her in the mountains, beneath the dense jungle in the old earth.

At lunch, she sat with Ixchel and Sylvia. The three of them were at a picnic table by themselves, while two other tables were crowded with the men. Men with AK-47s guarded the perimeter. They were inside a work camp—nobody was coming and going of their own free will.

18

Across the compound, emerging from the warehouse, she saw Angus with a pale, long-haired man wearing an untucked cotton shirt and cargo shorts. He seemed to be squinting at the day for the first time. Angus waved directly at her. The man slouched his way toward their table ahead of Angus. She knew this must be John Slinger. He sat down across from her, offering an odd grin, carrying a black notebook. He reached out and took her hand. "Welcome to Latin Leather, Guatemala—the home of magical mystery tours."

His breath and skin smelled of alcohol, sweat, and coffee beans, which he chewed, crunching them like hard candy.

"It doesn't have to be tarmac," he said, nodding at the runway. "Dirt's all we need. I'll be gone, and they can fly in and out of here till the cows come home. Let's go talk for a bit." Ixchel started to get up with Callie and Slinger. "Not you, Ixchel," he said. Ixchel shrugged at Callie. *Fine, go.* Angus stayed with her.

"Cigarette?"

"No thanks," she said, feeling him peer out from beneath his greasy hat, his face a dirty set of whiskers.

He nodded sideways at the airstrip. "I learned to fly at a small strip in the Jersey pine barrens and made my first money flying advertising banners over the South Jersey beaches. That's where I met Hector. *Scanties! Tonight! Live Music!* I've made and abandoned a dozen of these. You fly in, unload, torch the latest Cessna, and drive off. That's my kind of goddamned freedom."

"You're an inspiration," she said.

"I am. Over the last seventeen years of my private war, I've flown for whoever pays me. I know airstrips all over Colombia and Mexico. This is my last shipment. I'm going to retire to an ocean-front villa in an undisclosed location, where I'll watch movies and drink mescal till I'm dead."

"An inspiration *and* a go-getter."

"Historically speaking, I've been too lazy to get involved with ambition. A life of invoices, transfers, and runs in and out of Mexico have been fine by me." He flicked his head toward the warehouse. "Come with me."

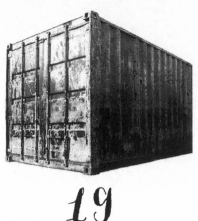

19

As they walked toward the old sheet metal warehouse, Slinger's eroded mouth rambled onward like confusing jazz: he knew trade routes, agents in Mexico, producers in Hollywood, and dock workers in Elizabeth, New Jersey, who transferred shipments of crap like baby strollers from China to trucks going to Cleveland. His hair looked like straggles of brown and gray vines. His paunchy middle and flapping shirttails could blow any direction, like a flag in the wind. The smell of burnt palm and ash came floating down and mixed with his cigarette smoke. He had the demeanor of an intense professor bouncing around tropical ports in search of his next discovery. He seemed nervous, as though he had the interior life of a desperate squirrel, scurrying busily to make his horde before winter.

Inside, monstrous lathes, hand trolleys, multiple rooms were puzzled together into the Latin Leather finishing and shipping process. Long alleyways of hanging leather looked like clotheslines of skin. Men strolled from one station to another wearing headphones, some carrying blue folders, others red ones. Callie saw women wearing rubber boots standing in shimmering pools of a silver chemical that flowed into collecting pools outside, spilled into hellish versions of drainage channels, then emptied into a stream that fed down into Lake Petén Itzá and sank into sludgy silt.

"C'mon," Slinger said to Callie. "Come into my office."

Callie felt her antenna go up.

Slinger flopped down into the crooked chair.

"You tell Tony you're here?"

"Not yet."

"Okay. You ready to tan your innocent illusions of *Thou* out of your flesh with chromium sulfate?" He raised his eyebrows, expecting a response.

"I don't really know what that means, but I forget when I was innocent," Callie said.

"We're innocent when we die. Before that, we're alive."

Callie thought she sensed a veiled threat. She watched groups of men in orange company t-shirts moving piles of skins that looked like they had dripped there for hundreds of years, stacked up like layers of bluish rocks in a cave. Callie thought of the animal rights smartasses back home who protested at pharmaceutical companies and forwarded videos of PETA fanatics chasing Japanese whaling boats. Here in Guatemala, making leather from cow skin seemed part of some ancient ritual to clothe the gangly human frame. It was something significant and raw she hadn't seen before.

Slinger explained, "Guatemala is divided into departments, like states. And I have Petén Department connections. That's why all this beautiful hide is here."

"Inspector Piñada, right?" Callie asked, recalling Ixchel's story of Jorge and his brother, and how Piñada turned a blind eye.

"So you've done some homework, eh? He's made a career out of creative bureaucracy."

"I try."

"So Ixchel's your little mission."

"No, she's not my mission."

Callie saw Ixchel's wiry arms moving quickly, her round face and large brown eyes blankly looking at nothing, somehow separated from her body.

For some reason, maybe stalling, Slinger showed Callie various work stations: the tanning area, the loading docks, the packing girls, who stood beside piles of finished hides and placed them into crates by color—light browns with light browns, chocolate with chocolate, black with black.

The finished skins were moved off the floor into an adjacent warehouse and shipping area where a second team packed. Slinger had arranged an entire operation in this room, his second shipping operation within the leather operation. From the shipping port in Belize to docks in New York City and Hector in Newark, the Slinger & Co. branch of Latin Leather was an ecosystem of symbiotic organisms exchanging supply-chain logistics, shipping, customs payoffs, small planes, radar, Border Patrol, and Coast Guard interdiction avoidance methods.

Slinger grinned. "You want the life you have or you want a new one?"

She said nothing.

"I don't force anybody to go where they don't want. You understand?" He pointed at her. "I didn't ask you or your friend here. You invited yourselves. You can invite yourself out now or be in for the long haul. But come on. You help me, I'll help you."

He led her back outside and leaned against an old blue Toyota pickup.

"This is my final operation, you understand what I'm saying? I don't need trouble. What I need is product loaded in Belize City, and the ship at port in New York. Hector said you want to provide some assistance with this Mister Tony Maul?"

Slinger's scrubby airstrip had a burning dream surrounding it, like heat coming off a cast-iron skillet. In the pit of her stomach, Callie understood why Rachel had been scared. She was deep into illegal territory.

She offered up the information she had. "He's pushing to go bigger. He's been supplying clubs to support his bands in clubs in the Northeast. I think he wants to expand, go national. Get acts up and down the East Coast. Break into the West Coast maybe."

"You came down here to tell me that?"

"No. I came down here to find Rachel." She had been thinking about the stalemate between Tony and Slinger. It was the opportunity to exploit to reverse the cards on Tony, to get some kind of chip to have Rachel's and her life cut loose from his. From what she knew, Tony was itching to be "the man" in New York who knew players in Central America. "I'd like to get him down here to help find her. And maybe that helps you both out?"

There was a pause. She saw him nod, and there was an un-spoken understanding between them that anything could happen if Tony showed up here.

"You think like a cop."

"Well, I used to be an MP."

He turned to her. "I know." Slinger saw her conflicting reactions. "Yeah, we do our research too."

But she'd already gathered herself again. No reaction or sign of intimidation. "Okay, so if you can hold up for a bit, I'll get him down here. You can work out your deal. I can discuss his treatment of women. If this is your finale, what do you care? As you said, you'll be gone."

"I'll reflect on it."

"How about reflecting on where Rachel Martelli is?"

"I met her."

"So where is she?"

Slinger lifted his long, scraggly hair off his neck. "You probably won't believe me, but I don't know."

"You're right, I don't believe you."

"We just met. You don't know my Boy Scout history."

"She has no intention of getting in the way," she said, still hoping to persuade him to give her some information.

He lowered his voice and wiped his mouth casually to cover his words. "Maybe not, but Jorge doesn't think that," he said.

Given the atmosphere, she could tell he wasn't just playing dramatic.

"Look. I'm a shipping agent," he said under this breath. "But Jorge Mercado's dangerous, and he's got side gigs. He thinks he's going to be as powerful as Evers. They love him around these parts—the man who pays them decent money. The man who brought them all together. Takes care of them."

He spoke of himself as separate from Jorge, but he was also a man who seemed to be playing three roles in his head at once. "I've heard," she said, letting the implication of insider knowledge linger in the air. "That's why I came to you. I need some help."

"What exactly do you have in mind?"

Callie watched Rodrigo sit down next to Ixchel and Sylvia. He was oddly rubbing Sylvia's head. Ixchel snatched her away from his hand. "You want Tony Maul out of your deal?"

"To put it mildly, yes. He's apparently a fucking idiot?"

"To put it mildly, yes. Delusion topped with greed, and a side of self-aggrandizement."

"If he tries to play the Evers Corporation, anything could happen."

"I've heard. Garbage barge refuse."

"I know men who are now at bottom of the Atlantic. And I don't plan on joining them."

"So, like I said, what if I get Tony down here?"

"I'd say that would be helpful."

"If I do, I want Rachel on a plane back to Philly with me." She nodded across the yard. "And have Rodrigo sent out on a barge, please."

"I don't make promises I can't keep. I can't do either of those."

"Why not?"

He looked at her with an expression that said he didn't control as much as she'd thought. "Because, first, I don't know where your friend is. And second, Ixchel and Jorge are a domestic dispute. I don't do social services. And I would advise you to stay out of that. If you consider an old, depressed drug runner's advice worth taking."

Rodrigo was smiling over at Callie. Then he suddenly turned and grabbed Ixchel's arms from behind and dragged her off the picnic bench and onto the ground. It was such an abrupt, grotesque thing that Callie watched frozen in disbelief.

Ixchel flopped to the ground, legs and feet up, but held Sylvia tightly.

Angus jumped up and was atop Rodrigo choke holding him before he could pull Sylvia out of Ixchel's arms

Callie jumped toward Ixchel, but several men with semi-automatics waved them casually at her to stay put.

Nobody intervened, and the three of them struggled on the burnt out dirt, Ixchel jumping up and kicking Rodrigo in the head while Angus choked him. A few men eyed Slinger, but several others watched the fight. A cowboy on a bulldozer was driving along the edge of the jungle like a drunk driver with a pack of men behind laughing and whipping their hats around, as if they were penning calves. They drove the dozer toward the melee.

As they did, Rodrigo had started to weaken with the head blows, Angus's weight, and lack of air. His face was bleeding, desperate and gasping with an eerie lack of sound.

Callie thought Ixchel might kill him. But she finally stopped her kicking and ran toward Callie with Sylvia.

Angus maintained the hold, and soon Rodrigo was clawing at his arm for air.

Slinger said, "I told you. Unfinished domestic business. Jorge and his ill-tempered animals are what happens when you get involved." He had an odd, defeated tone to this voice.

The bulldozer was nearly to the two men on the ground.

Jorge stood across the parking lot, hands in his pockets. He was smiling. Callie was sick to her stomach. She didn't understand why Slinger couldn't do anything, but she heard herself respond with a helpless, "Bullshit."

Slinger was drawing on his cigarette contemplating something, then yelled, "Stop it! Fire the weeds! I have planes coming in here!"

Jorge nodded at man driving the bulldozer. He stopped the machine a few feet short of the two men, jumped down, walked toward Angus pulling a handgun. He lowered it directly at Angus's left knee and pulled the trigger.

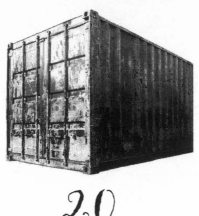

20

Angus lay curled on the ground, holding his leg, grunting in pain through his teeth.

Rodrigo scrambled away on his hands and knees.

Callie ignored Jorge's men and the bulldozer and ran toward Angus. She already had her t-shirt off and wound into a tourniquet. At the same time, she saw a sedan had pulled quickly into the field near them. An older woman wearing a scarf over her head emerged. The woman was watching Ixchel and Sylvia. The whole thing had been arranged, and Sylvia wasn't supposed to be in Ixchel's arms anymore.

She saw as she got to Angus the heavy blade of the rusted yellow bulldozer sitting a few feet from them.

Ixchel was looking in all directions at once, checking to see who might try to approach her. Her face clenched, her eyes screaming at the world, but her mouth stubbornly silent.

"Way to get yourself shot on the first day," she said to Angus.

He tried to speak but was in too much pain.

Slinger took Ixchel by the arm and walked over to them. "Turn that dozer back around! I said smoke it!" yelled Slinger. "Jesus-fuckingchrist, enough of this," he mumbled and waved his fingers through his long hair. He too seemed distraught.

"What are they doing?" Callie asked.

"Well, I'd say Jorge was trying to take Sylvia to Guatemala City," Slinger said.

"You bastard. Do something."

"I told you, I can't just *do something* and make this all go away. At least not at the moment," Slinger said under his breath.

Laughing, Jorge ordered the men around with nothing more than pointing. Then he waved off the woman driving the sedan, who got in and drove off as mysteriously as she had arrived. Jorge took off his brown cowboy hat and waved it around like he was rounding up loose ideas, commanding, "Enciende el fuego! Enciéndalo!"

The men started lighting fires around the perimeter with gasoline cans. Others followed lighting matches, and the edge of the jungle went up into flames and smoke. Smoke billowed up over the hills like somebody had blown another careless puff into the hazy mountains.

Jorge sauntered to his Suburban next to Slinger's truck, leaning against the hood. Callie hated Jorge's face, his round unchanging face and indifferent eyes. He popped a handful of sunflower seeds. His cheeks bulged as he mashed the seeds in his mouth. In the tropical green, his stare had the metallic edge of a machete.

Callie yelled to Jorge, without thinking, "Why don't you take me instead?"

Jorge nodded, "Not instead. *Too.* You want to know your boy someday, no?"

She wasn't surprised, but she felt nauseous.

Ixchel's face looked torn between resigned survival and despair, but she tenderly wiped Sylvia's face with water from a plastic water bottle. Slinger scribbled in a notebook to himself, like a demented child immersed in a fantasy world.

Jorge laughed. "This is how business works. Your purple-haired bitch shows up. You think I'm going to let some New York fuck send this woman into my business? No, no." He wagged his finger. "Your friend should have stayed in New York," Jorge said.

As Callie tried to ease Angus and keep him from bleeding out, Slinger was talking as if to everybody and nobody. "We have a fifty million dollar shipment sitting in a dock warehouse and a fucking beater cargo ship. And our little necks on the line. Out of nowhere a Mr. Tony Maul from New York wants in? Some asshole music producer who has no connection whatsoever to my supply chain—or to Jorge? Then one of his girls—your friend—shows up here. In case you don't read the news, cartel security teams do not fuck around. Most are ex-military and special ops. If Evers intel agents sniff us out, we're all dead, you know."

"We have to get you to the hospital," she said to Angus. He nodded back, trying to sit up so he could get to a vehicle.

She looked at Slinger. "I just told you I was here to get Tony out of your hair. And you're telling me Rachel and Jorge aren't your problem? Fuck off."

"They aren't. Believe whatever you want. I'm a game theory expert with a focus on international trade, flight routes, and a pilot's license. Not a thug."

Angus got up to his feet, dangling his left leg. She braced his left side.

She smelled the cutting and slashing and the burning back of the jungle. She felt like an agent whose cover was broken. Somebody had told Tony that she had come here. How else would Jorge know about Dillon. Hector? Angus? Angus wouldn't do that. Ixchel and Callie looked at each other in shock. Sylvia had almost been kidnapped; they knew where her sister and Dillon lived and would try to use them as leverage; and they were no closer to finding Rachel.

Slinger walked Callie and Angus to his truck, talking to Callie under his breath. "Do you see Moses in the burning bush? Believe me, I know more shit in my head than any man in Central America. But I don't control everything."

He spoke with quick and quiet ferocity. "I don't know why she came down here. All I know is she met with Ixchel out here the day before yesterday. I don't think she realized what the fuck she was doing." He looked at Ixchel as if she had made a grave error. Why hadn't Ixchel told Callie about this meeting? Ixchel evaded Callie's look, pulling neurotically at Sylvia's baby wrap. "I've been working more than a year on this shipment. And turns out my local fucking

so-called 'partner' is a paranoid perve with a history in fake passports, illegal babies, and working girls. Fucking great. But I do this
shipment and I'm fucking gone. Retired to Laguna Beach. Become
a sand castle artist to the gods of the Pacific tides and surf stoners.
But right now you've landed in a nest of squirming snakes that don't
like anything getting out alive. Do you understand what I'm telling
you?"

She didn't answer. She felt Ixchel standing behind her. She felt
the wound in Angus's leg. It was as if each of them had just met each
other on the street after a fire ripped their illusion of separate lives
into charred frames.

She said, "No, I don't. Not one fucking bit. Doesn't Jorge work
for you?"

"Goes both ways. Jorge is the only middle man in this whole
region. And he knows it. And he knows he needs me too. You can
use my pickup. Take Angus to the hospital. You and Ixchel go back
to the ranch. They don't mess with the ranch."

Finally, as helped Angus into the bed of Slinger's pick up, Callie
was skeptical. "Why should I fucking trust you?"

He snapped at her. "You realize what I'm doing right now? I
told you, I'm a logistics expert. Not a kidnapper or a killer. It's not
my fault you're in this mess. It's not my fault that Evers assigned me
a local sociopath who loves migrant girls who will pay for a lifetime
trip to Jersey." Callie felt a new wave of anger—had Rachel gotten
herself mixed up in a human trafficking operation too?

Slinger handed Callie the truck keys.

"You're really letting us take a truck?" Ixchel asked.

"You better go to the ranch. And pack."

"Where we going?" Callie asked.

Slinger swung his hair off his neck. "A cargo container. Same
ship as my shipment. We gotta get you out of here quietly."

Callie looked at Ixchel. "You know about this?"

Ixchel's face fell for a second, then adopted a mask of defiance
again. She got into the passenger side. Her silence said it all.

Slinger peered across to Ixchel, "You should have picked better friends. You wanted to get to New York, there you fucking go.

Be careful what you wish for. Go back to the ranch. They will be watching you."

Callie got in the driver side. Angus sat up against the cab in the corner, his leg with her bloodied t-shirt propped up on the sidewall.

They watched Slinger head to the door of the warehouse.

Callie started the truck and gunned it down the lane. If they hurried, the doctors could get operating on Angus. But as they drove down the dirt road, it became clear that driving the bouncing truck too fast was just the illusion of doing something. There was nothing for miles but gentle palms swaying in the breeze.

They approached the main valley road that would take them back to the ranch. She brought the truck to a stop, looking in both directions for any sign of danger.

"Ixchel—"

"I know."

She looked at Ixchel. They both understood: Sylvia was a target now.

Ixchel's chest was convulsing beneath her patterned blouse. Callie thought she might break down right there. But while her eyes teared, generations of suffering seemed to hold the girl together, as if souls of a thousand women were bracing her tough little arms and body. She glanced at Callie angry, undeterred. Whatever might come, she was now forever on a path of unrelenting purpose.

Callie's hands held the wheel and she looked out the front of the truck for some direction on where to go from this crossroads.

Then Callie saw them. Across the road. In a large pasture of turned earth. A fence. She threw the truck into park, jumped out.

"You okay?"

"I'd prefer not to lose the leg, it's all the same to you," Angus said. He looked like he was going into shock.

"Angus, stay with me!" She hurried across the dirt road.

Whoever it was—Tony, Jorge, Evers security, all of them—they had sent their message.

Wrapped around one of the split rails, the laces tied together, were Rachel's black Chuck Taylor sneakers.

21

Ixchel had directed them to the hospital where they admitted Angus. They reacted as if blown out knees were a daily procedure. A nurse told them he would be in prep and surgery for a few hours at least and left them in the waiting room.

Callie couldn't sit still. Rachel's sneakers were in the truck calling out to her, as if Rachel were still in them.

She turned to Ixchel. "We're going to the police."

"That's pointless. And stupid," Ixchel said, feeding Sylvia, who was sucking as if she might never be fed again.

"Then I'm going myself."

She headed out of the one-story building toward the parking lot.

The humid tropical air felt like a blanket suffocating her. She heard Ixchel walking behind her, talking to Sylvia, "She understands about as much as you do. She's just a baby girl inside the whitest skin anybody ever saw."

The Department of El Petén police, the PNC, was stationed in an old colonial gated home in the San Benito section of Flores. Callie pulled the truck down a narrow one-way street. Rachel's sneakers sat on the bench between them. Somewhere in there, Callie was angry, worried, and distraught—the part of her that was the lost, ashamed mother of Dillon. But right now, the reality in front of her required the part she liked best: the MP-trained professional stoic, indifferent to extraneous emotion for the sake of investigating evidence. They had tried to take Sylvia in broad daylight in front of thirty men.

In front of the police building, they sat in Slinger's truck. Neither moved. Sylvia lay asleep in Ixchel's lap. Between the narrow alley of the police station and the building next to it, Callie could see out to the Lake. Two dark blue, yellow-stenciled police trucks were parked on the street.

"We going in?" Callie asked.

"I told you," Ixchel said. "It's pointless. And dangerous."

"What's your suggestion then? Do nothing?"

Ixchel shrugged. "Your friend, your decision."

The risk of asking help from corrupt cops just feet away from them forced a considered silence. Any Evers payroll cop who saw them here would let Jorge or Slinger know they had come. Yet if they could get the Inspector to work quietly for them, there might be a chance for some justice. She had never taken the "good girls keep quiet" option. "Piñada. He's friends with Mrs. Granger?"

"Yes. He comes for dinner sometimes to the ranch. He and Vera sit on the porch. He smokes cigars and drinks tequila. She likes him."

"Does he like her enough to find out about Rachel and keep it quiet?"

Ixchel did not hesitate. "Around here we don't know who the real police are, and girls are just garbage to throw away."

Callie was angry. There was no wound or bleeding to stop—but she felt the two damaged souls in the car. It was like being in a mine boring up toward a surface that never arrived. There was nothing to say.

Callie picked up Rachel's Converses. "I'll go in for Rachel, and we'll see how it goes."

She opened the truck door, and Ixchel got out of the truck behind her.

The cobblestoned street was deserted, as if nobody came to the station much. A brass plaque with official letters in Spanish hung on a stucco wall. They proceeded through the small archway with a gravel path that led into the front door. They approached a turquoise door with the letters PNC stenciled on it. Inside, the atmosphere was like an old school—a combination of old paper stacks slowly molding, musty air conditioners, and stained asbestos tiles on the ceiling.

They asked for Inspector Piñada and were ushered into small conference room with a cheap folding table and some plastic chairs.

Soon a thick-mustached man wearing a simple button down shirt, pressed jeans, and thick black boots entered. Callie noticed he wore a gold cross. He carried a laptop. As soon as he saw the shoes he said, "Come with me." He led them out of the room and up a center staircase of the old colonial home. They proceeded down a dark, carpeted hallway with a set of dim sconces on the wall. He ushered them into a large room with an official looking desk, a bay of windows that overlooked the Lake, and two stuffed armchairs. An afternoon rainstorm was clouding the distant hills and approaching.

Ixchel and the Inspector spoke in Spanish first. He was clearly asking demanding questions, and Ixchel was providing short responses. Callie could tell Ixchel was telling him about the attempted kidnapping of Sylvia because she nodded at the baby periodically. He tapped on his laptop with his one leg crossed casually on his opposite knee. He glanced a few times to Callie, but he seemed to have no more concern for Ixchel's story than he would have filing a report for a traffic accident. The event was already being logged, turned into a statistic that required no action. Finally, Callie's impatience at the fraudulent bureaucracy overcame any hesitancy for being on foreign soil in a foreign government's office.

She put Rachel's sneakers in the middle of the table. "Her baby was almost taken right out of her arms."

He looked at her over his pair of thick framed glasses, then put them on his silvered, balding head. "If they wanted to take her, they would have."

"We know who the men are," Callie said.

He leaned back in his leather chair, a man feigning toughness, but in his eyes she saw a debilitated soul, systemic anxiety, and a fear slowly choking off his own coronary arteries. "And so do I."

"Are you going to arrest them?" Callie asked. "They also have a friend of mine." She nodded at the shoes.

The Inspector's mouth twisted with a frown at this dreadlocked American woman. "It is not so easy as that."

Ixchel was sitting up now in her chair. She had been answering questions with an indifferent skepticism. But something in her altered. "I'm going to leave here and find my father, Inspector. And whether you do anything or not, I will have my report. I am filing this report."

The Inspector looked at Ixchel as if they both knew what this meant. He said quietly, "I know, Ixchel. I know you for many years." Then he crossed himself and made a cross on Sylvia's forehead.

"And?" Callie asked. "What about a visit to Slinger's warehouse?"

"Ms. Byrne, how long did it take you to get here?"

"About an hour around the Lake."

"Exactly. Everything they do in something like that is highly planned. Whoever drove that sedan is already on her way back to Guatemala City or Antigua or some village. Should we stop every vehicle driven by a woman between here and the US border? Then there's the problem of paperwork. Even if we did arrest Rodrigo and Jorge, we would be in a court with no evidence and Jorge's associates—"

"His fucking brother," interrupted Ixchel.

"His brother, whoever, his business partners, will show up with lawyers who know every loophole. They will produce legal documents signed by Ixchel. Or forged. It doesn't matter which, saying that she has officially relinquished her rights to Sylvia. Depending on the judge's mood, he'll either dismiss the case or put the case back into the family services process, where Ixchel's ability to reclaim her is slim to none for the next few years of procedures. Then, should she decide to pursue this fight, we will also have the issue of retaliatory attacks—probably against me, Ixchel, Vera Granger—whoever Jorge Mercado's commanders would target for interfering in their business. So I am sorry for you, Ixchel. But should others suffer or even be killed for your daughter? Or do we quietly build our case against Jorge's network so other young woman are not put into this position?"

"Of course, not, but that's no reason not to investigate."

"Oh, of course we will investigate."

He was lying as easily as if he were commenting on the weather.

"What should she do in the mean time?"

The Inspector hesitated for a moment, reluctant to say any more.

"She knows what she should do. She should leave here, change her name, change Sylvia's name."

There was a long pause.

"Should I no longer call these Rachel Martelli's sneakers?"

The Inspector nodded at the sneakers. "They are whatever you say they are." He seemed unsurprised there was a pair of shoes sitting on the table.

"They belong to a friend of mine, a woman named Rachel Martelli. She was sent down here to Latin Leather as a messenger. She has been missing for three days. Ixchel saw her and Jorge leave Latin Leather, and nobody has heard from her since. We found them on a fence post on the way here."

The Inspector picked them up with plastic-gloved hand. He smelled the side canvas of the shoe.

He held it for Ixchel. "Go ahead, you'll recognize the smell too."

Ixchel smelled the canvas as well, and she nodded recognition as if she were confirming the identity of a body.

"What?" Callie pulled the Inspector's arm abruptly to her and smelled them herself. "What is it?"

Ixchel pointed out the window down the hill. "Water. We smell the Lake water."

They didn't need to explain more, but the Inspector had turned around his laptop. He opened up a slideshow of photos. He slid the laptop over to Callie. It was a gallery of shoes, all women's shoes—Nikes, flats, heels, sandals.

"I have hundreds of these from the last few years, all in this Department, from around this Lake. The Evers cartel, Jorge Mercado's local division."

Callie stood up and went to the window and stared down at the large Lake, the gray-blue waters swimming in her mind. Rachel was drowned. A deep weight of water constricted her chest. Already her mind was saying, I can't leave without her body. Behind her she heard Inspector Piñada describing the situation in an indifferent, neutral voice that was like a body bag wrapped around the remains of a human being.

Finally, she asked, "What happened?"

The Inspector recounted as if he had seen it himself and seen it a hundred times. "They put a weight belt on her. Then they hooked her by the ankles to a rope on the stern. Then they dragged her around the Lake until she drowned. When she was dead, they reeled her in, took off the shoes, cut her loose, and let her drop to the bottom. We'll never find the body. At least not whole. They always leave the shoes for us to find. Usually at the family's door."

She looked at the laptop and then at Ixchel and the Inspector. "Why?" she asked, trying to hold the deadness in its hole.

The Inspector was putting Rachel's self-decorated sneakers into a plastic evidence bag.

It was Ixchel who answered. "Any time the PNC or DEA arrest or kill an Evers soldier in Petén, they drown one woman."

The Inspector added, "Many of them are ex-Kaibiles, our military special forces. So you, see, it's not easy. We show up, there will be a massacre. We just don't know where."

Callie turned her back on them and looked out the window covered by a thin film of dirt. She watched the silvery blanket of an afternoon storm across the valley, a shadow of rains over the densely green mountain that headed across the Lake in a sheet. What had she done? Or seen? Rachel was out there, unclaimed, somewhere beneath fathoms of water and eons of mountains. The sheets of rain were like transparent shrouds, beautiful and terrible in their indifferent shimmer, the earth spinning its meaningless weather over the daily acts of human violations, cruelties, and death. She thought of Dillon in her arms in a pool, holding him gently on the happy surface of a heavy life.

She felt Ixchel standing next to her now. They did not touch, but it was as if they had now become bound in a common disaster of blood and inseparable love for Dillon, Sylvia, and Rachel.

Callie felt the ache that needed a fix, the pain was rising to the point of a suffering that she wanted to obliterate.

She felt Ixchel standing beside her, holding Sylvia, and before she could ask, Ixchel responded.

"I'm getting on the ship." Ixchel whispered so that the Inspector would not hear.

Callie was stunned and in grief. Across the Lake, a small speck of land was being logged and stripped. Flakes of paint chipped off the old window cross-pieces. She smelled the must of old. Ixchel grabbed her upper arm, shaking it for an answer, for another woman to go north on the Atlantic with her.

Callie nodded her head just enough. There wasn't any question what she was going to do; it was just the dazed reality of seeing what had come next that paralyzed her in Piñada's office.

She finished Ixchel's thought. "And take the fuckers down."

"You should go home," the Inspector said.

She turned from the window. She took a photo of Rachel's shoes in the bag. "Just for my records. And Inspector, we don't have a home."

"Well, you should go make one."

"You're going to drag that fucking lake. Or I will myself."

He walked past Callie, carrying Rachel's shoes as casually as if it were a bag of trash on the way to the dump. His response was part condescension at an ill-informed amateur, part institutional hopelessness, and part bribed allegiance to unseen bosses.

"Señorita, the cartel patrols the Lake. Our PNC district no longer has a functional boat."

22

It was nearly midnight. Angus's surgery had gone fine, and he would be out in a few days. Ixchel and Sylvia were in their room at the ranch. Callie had become their de facto body guard, yet Callie felt isolated in her tidy, borrowed Catholic missionary room, with a dread spinning around in the dreadful ceiling fan above her.

She had poured herself half a bottle of straight dark Belizean rum that Mrs. Granger had offered her.

As usual, she couldn't sleep. Emptiness had become full up with sadness for Rachel. She would have shot up if she could, and her thoughts ricocheted. She remembered sleeping beside Rachel. She remembered the loving weight of Dillon on her chest laying by the pool. She felt the regret of self-incrimination, of doubts, and a deep worry about how she was ever going to start a new life. She faced the wall, trying to turn away from a diseased past that was now a full-blown malignancy. She wanted to get high with Ixchel; she wanted to go back to seeing Peter Jagg thrashing his guitar in a dark club and fuck him out of his sheltered life while they were drunk. She wanted to re-do everything that had happened since returning from Iraq. She saw the bridge and the chain-link fence. She was standing with Beth before the judge who agreed to the guardianship. She was fumbling around in the back of Ramona. She was showering in a women's shelter and accepting help from a shrewd priest. She thought of the frozen stone of the Trevi Fountain.

She got up, decided she had no options, and sat outside the door. A sliver of a moon was visible through the jungle trees, and a pin-holed ceiling of starlight and the faintest fog of the Milky Way slid around the viscous sky.

She opened up her phone and wrote to a Dillon somewhere in the future.

> *Dillon, Someday maybe I will read this to you. I'm so sorry I'm not there with you. I am away trying to help a friend. And it didn't work. Be good and listen to Aunt Beth. Do what she says. I saw a monkey here that you would like. Imagine if we lived in the trees? We could grow blue balloons in green trees! Love, your mom.*

Your mom? It sounded like a false ID. She attached a photo of George-in-the-Bush howler. She put in Beth's address. Deleted it. Changed it to her own email address. Then sent it to herself.

She opened another new message, and wrote to Tony.

> *Rachel is dead. Slinger will sell only if he meets you. You need to come down here. Let me know and we will pick you up at the airport. And no crap, or I will come find you myself. I want no part of this except for Dillon and me to be left alone.*

She hit send. She paced the yard in the dark while her email had already wound its way through unknown servers between the jungle and Lower Manhattan.

23

When Angus was released, he insisted on using his crutches and walking out of the hospital to the ranch truck.

"Glad you came for me, I was beginning to think I might need to call a cab," he said.

"We were packing another pallet full of leather jackets," Callie said. "Jorge wouldn't let us out until it was done—and I'm not letting Ixchel out of my sight."

"They ought to call the jacket brand Smack," Ixchel said.

As best they could with his two hundred fifty pounds, they helped Angus arrange his injured leg across the pickup bed. It was like watching an NFL player try to get comfortable on the pad of an injury cart.

"Where we going?" he asked.

Ixchel responded before Callie could. "They killed. Rachel, and now we're going to take down Tony and get on the ship."

Callie gave a small nod to Angus. Tony had written back. *Fuck yeah I will be there.* "She's right. Tony bit. He's coming."

"Are you crazy?"

Callie ignored the editorial comment and filled him in about the Chuck Taylors and their visit to Inspector Piñada and the PNC. "We worked inside packing today away from Jorge. Mrs. Granger has Sylvia for now, and we were at least able to convince the Inspector to send a few men to watch the ranch. I'm not convinced Slinger can keep Jorge away. We're going to meet Slinger at Jamón's."

"Slinger? Isn't he the one who went after Sylvia and had me shot?"

Callie said, "No, I don't think so."

In San Olvidado, Callie parked on a side street. Ixchel directed them to Jamón's. They descended a set of steps between side streets, children in doorways with their mothers.

They walked past a contented woman sitting on the street with blankets of crafts displayed. It looked as if nobody ever came down the street, and yet the woman sat there hopeful, open for business, ready for some luck. They found Calle Trystale, a narrow, long street that ran through San Olvidado like a capillary behind the main artery. The street was made of volcanic cobblestone, with piles of shirts and chickens and racks of clothing and brooms hanging on the narrow sidewalks.

A few pale, fleshy hippies hung in one doorway, somehow remaining impossibly pale in the tropics, huddled like wet dogs amongst sleeping bags, rank clothes, and a patchwork of Mayan serapes. One had a drum that he beat in rhythmic self-absorption. More women sat together behind blankets of trinkets, smiling and chattering with each other. What were they so happy about? A group of men gathered around small bodegas. One waved to Callie as if he had known her his whole life.

Jamón's was a hole-in-the-wall bar and cafe with a bright blue façade and a purple door, like a place from a Dali painting that dripped off the curb and into the gutter. Next to the door were small piles of garbage. She unsnapped her holster, took a breath, and went in. Inside, a few itinerants sat in a corner smoking, the air smelling of cigarettes, manure, and dried brush burning. A man reading a newspaper was behind the bar.

"Is Slinger here?" Callie asked.

He flicked the paper at the back table. Slinger was hunched over, his hair falling around his face, thinking in every twitch of his shaky fingers. He looked like he had just gotten out of bed, hair scruffy, face unwashed. He ate fried plantains and had a mug of black coffee. "So look who's here. The Philly Fuckups." Slinger scribbled notes into a black leather journal, not looking up.

Next to him was a dark, smooth-skinned girl with a permed explosion of frizzed black hair and a gap between her front teeth, one of which bore a gold cap. The girl licked Slinger's cheek, "You taste like blood. What do I taste like, Slinger?"

"Like sucking a lemon. Everybody, this is Lina, Lina, this is the crew that wants to straighten me out." Slinger went back to scribbling in his black book, head down.

"We don't think we can straighten you out," Angus said.

"Good work blending in yesterday. How's the old catcher's knee?"

Angus was nonplussed. "Hard to blend in when you're six foot four, 275."

"Standing out gets you killed. A punk-ass kid came down here last year and ended up shot in the ass because he didn't blend."

"You're Ixchel? The wannabe fashion model with a burnt face?" Lina said, laughing.

Ixchel almost jumped across the table at Lina's throat. Slinger held Lina back.

"You think I'm fucking joking about the kid shot up his intestinal exit?" Slinger said to the whole table.

Callie watched Slinger. "Look, the only reason we're here is because Tony sent Rachel down here, and he wants your shipment. We don't need speeches. We just want him taken down a peg or ten, and we'll head home. He sent me a message last night. He's coming. He'll let me know when."

Slinger raised his head and didn't bother to brush the hanging hair from his face. Lina was chewing a mashed straw. The silence hovered in a tension of distrust. Angus just grinned at the whole plan, almost giddy, and then got up and went to the bar.

Everyone looked at her now. In a split second, her mind was flashing with images and calculating her best move.

She looked straight at Slinger's brown, haggard eyes.

Slinger said, "Well, we can pretend everyone's going home after this."

Callie agreed. "We know Rachel's not."

They all said nothing. Slinger seemed to be calculating something. Callie felt they were deep across an invisible border.

Slinger alternated his looks between Callie and Angus. "You people got yourselves in a deep spot, didn't you? And you've got yourself big plans." Slinger put some hair behind his right ear. "All clear as day, huh? Tony has plans, I have plans, everybody on the planet has goddamned plans."

Slinger slurped his coffee, peering over this cup at Callie. "What do you think, Lina, we may be getting somewhere. The bunghole from New York is on his way." He popped a burnt plantain into his mouth and chewed with his mouth open, then brushed his hand over his forehead, and hair went flying backward. "You know, I just flew back from Bolivia. Had a little business vacation. And when I get back, what do I find? Jorge says that Hector says that a Tony Maul is going to inter-fucking-mediate for my shipment. Then this lady here shows up because her friend is MIA."

"So now we're getting somewhere," Angus said, echoing Slinger.

Slinger scowled at Angus. Callie thought Slinger might just shoot Angus right there.

"Excuse me." Slinger took a soft plantain out of his mouth and crushed it into the floor. Then he sat back and took a drink of coffee. "Bad fruit," he said.

Slinger didn't look up, scribbling again in his journal, his mouth and face twisting around like the letters. "You were not invited here. However, you have connections with the inevitable confluence of circumstantial forces." Slinger sounded haunted; Callie recognized the tone, one she'd employed many times.

She felt the gate into Slinger's world somehow had been lifted, a complex set of unseen conspiratorial connections vibrating around Tony's deal. She felt like the new kid on the job—whole histories of rats' nests hidden around her.

Slinger changed his tone. "So look at us expats getting to know each other. Lina, a little home away from home. Isn't that sweet?"

The woman with the gold tooth smiled at Callie with complete insincerity.

"How's things over at the ranch, eh?" Slinger said to Ixchel, wiping his dried crackled lips, specks of white suntan lotion on his face.

That place seemed humid with history, palpable but unseen. "So you own the Granger ranch, eh?" Callie asked.

Slinger looked up, a wall of privacy and defense. "That's my business. The Grangers and the Christian Rangers. The Lost American Souls of the Mayan Jungle. But Ixchel, feel free to enlighten her."

There was awkward silence, then Ixchel finally recited what all the locals knew. "Teddy Granger was a Kansas rancher. They came down here twenty years ago or so. Something happened to them in the States, but nobody really knows what. What makes a couple up and leave Kansas and come here? They raised horses and cattle, helped with adoptions, and made sure local kids had school and medicine. Mrs. Granger really loves the place. She won't leave it." Ixchel hesitated to finish. "Slinger has helped ease things for her."

Slinger ignored Ixchel's summary, staring oddly at Callie, trying to read her. Then he summed her up. "You've been around, eh? Punk promoter. MP in Iraq. Rehab. Bartender of Note. It's pretty funny the way human beings move around, isn't it? Like they're in a bed and can never get comfortable." He reached across the table and picked up a handful of her dreads, chewing his own cheeks with his teeth and mouth gnawing around at nothing, his grizzled face looking greedy for more bites.

Callie let him explore her, almost like a blind man. She was unfazed.

Lina emptied her cocktail, annoyed at Slinger's attention to Callie. "Order me a drink, baby."

She stared at Ixchel while speaking to Callie. "Ixchel wanted to sell her baby, but a few days ago the little bitch changes her mind and now she wants Slinger to save her ass. Ha! Right, baby?" Lina said. Lina seemed the kind of woman who criticized other women no matter what they did.

Slinger looked at Callie, talking to both Ixchel and Lina at the same time. "Life is the process of surviving the flaws of everybody around you." He took out a small black notebook and scribbled. Then he reached over and pulled Lina to him and made out with her for an uncomfortable minute. He waved to the man behind the bar. "Jamón, a round of mescal."

The pockmarked face under the cowboy hat nodded. Callie saw a split-second grin, as if he'd seen Slinger perform this act before.

Angus smirked at Callie, his eyes glinting, as if to say, *See, didn't I tell you we'd have fun down here?*

Slinger said, "Mrs. Granger wants some American do-good dance from you? Like Ixchel here?"

Callie nodded, "Maybe, I don't know."

"Somebody is always doing something funny." Slinger looked at her, and he laughed in a loud, burnt rasp, then suddenly intense: "I'm financing an operation. Don't fuck with me."

"I won't. I just want Tony out of my life."

They both looked at each other, gauging the other's position.

She had the distinct feeling that no information came from Slinger without some payment due, but that he was going to help her resolve Tony interference and Jorge's thugs.

Slinger got a waiter to bring four shot glasses and poured rounds from a bottle of mescal with a worm at the bottom for the table. "Con gusanos!" Slinger toasted. The others picked up their shots, and Slinger translated. "With the worms. And to the American Nightmare! Ha! People are sick of talking about fucking America down here, aren't they Jamón?" Jamón, sat at the bar chuckling as he flipped through pages of the local newspaper.

They all drank, and Slinger asked, "You know your friend Rachel tried to offer Jorge money from Tony? What was that about?"

Callie hesitated a long time. Then she looked Slinger in the eyes. "I don't know about the money. All I know is she was supposed to meet up with you. Rachel gave me a copy of some Latin Leather files. Tony doesn't know I have them, but I think he figured out Rachel did and sent her down here to find trouble."

Slinger gestured his full shot glass at Callie, "Bring me a copy of the files." He threw back his shot. "Meet me at the airstrip in an hour. Now get the fuck out of here. I'm trying to finish one goddamned meal in peace before I'm dead."

24

They left Jamón's and walked down the main street, among some backpackers and American and German couples on their way to volcanoes and Mayan ruins. Little Hyundais and bicycles hopped past. A man outside his cafe recruited them to try his agouti stew, fresh local jungle rodent.

She thought of Slinger's mental state, and it seemed to be rotating between self-importance, paranoia, and an intense desire for a respite. Everybody was after him, and he was after everybody.

Ixchel walked next to her.

"He knows who killed Rachel," Callie said.

"How do you know?" she asked.

"I listen to what people don't say."

Angus said, "If Tony thinks he can break into big-time dealing, he'll be here in no time."

"He's good at taking credit for nothing," Callie said to Ixchel. Ixchel looked like she wanted to stay out of it, but was also seeing some hope that these people could make something big happen for her.

They headed down to the car. Sun glare off the Lake blinked in her eyes and washed over her face and loose dreads. A hippie sitting on a wooden crate rambled through a thick red beard, "I don't know where she is, I don't know where she is." He shook his head, shaking off flies, his eyes blurred, red, and half-baked, like he'd fried himself out in the heat for a decade. He made her think of Dillon, and she had a flashback of rolling in the grass. She had a son who knew who she was and knew she was gone. This man was somebody's son and was now just nobody on the street.

She couldn't help but feel that human beings had found every possible way to mess up their lives. Stupid boys everywhere. Boys falling apart, and boys growing up to be careless men. She remembered how Dillon threw sand at her at the shore, how pedestrian and vital it seemed to teach him right from wrong.

As they headed to the car, Angus said, "I could stay here."

Ixchel said. "No, let's go where you live." It was the nicest thing she had heard Ixchel say yet.

But Callie also understood what Angus meant. It was dangerous, sad, and alive all at once, something washed out, brown, and lush green around Lake Petén Itzá. She remembered arguing with Sym just a few days ago. Maybe she had been wrong about the idea of truth. With the violence and conspiracy of trafficking surrounding her, the world seemed full of true evil. And that truth was somehow never dead. It was like groundwater—deep underground, clean, contaminated, replenished every rainy season—and always rising to the surface to evaporate and fall again. Somewhere in this valley, Rachel's remains were gradually eroding into the waters.

They agreed to get Ixchel back to the ranch with Sylvia and drove back out the dirt highway in the valley. "I'm scared to fly. That's another a reason I signed on for Jorge's cruise," Ixchel said.

Callie sucked on the rind of a lemon from the mescal, trying to understand how Slinger had become Slinger.

25

An hour later, Callie crossed the dirt landing strip with Angus hobbling along at her side. She knew he'd been on crutches before, when an IED blew up twenty yards in front of him on patrol in Iraq and filled the other leg full of hardware.

She could see Slinger had already strapped himself into the pilot seat and was sitting with the Cessna door open, indifferent, it seemed, to who came or who didn't. The plane was covered in streaks of mud and looked more like clod of earth than pristine bird.

"Been waiting for you. I see you travel with your own personal medic, Angus."

He started going over adjustments to the rudder, flaps, and tail.

"I usually need my daily dose of mescal before I run drugs across borders," Callie said, her head pounding from the mescal.

Angus scanned the plane, as if he could inspect it. "Where'd you get this piece of crap?"

"Came from Honduras with a load. I can shoot your other knee if you'd like."

Angus seemed unaffected behind his aviator sunglasses.

"You gonna get in or you gonna stand there waiting for the sky to fall on you? Callie Dread, up front," Slinger said.

"Where we going?" Angus asked.

"Get some things ready. And get your friend's remains started home."

"What are you talking about?"

Slinger looked up at her. "Your friend. She's in a body bag in the luggage compartment."

Callie and Angus stared at each other.

"How'd you find her?"

Slinger ignored the question and was reviewing his gauges.

Callie climbed into the co-pilot seat, glancing back at Angus. He had a look on his face that somehow a combination of *dead dust* and *Where is all this going?* He raised his eyebrows to question whether they should really get on this plane with Slinger. She nodded her head quickly. After certain decisions are made, everything else is too late for logic. She put on the headset. Slinger started up the engine.

Slinger nodded to them. "For you aviation historians, this is the same model JFK Jr. flew into the Cape Cod bay. I'll try to avoid that."

Callie saw Jorge in the parking lot with a few other men smoking, guns lazily pointed to ground. Slinger buzzed and hummed, like an electrical transformer behind a chain-link fence, a block of energy you secretly wanted to touch to see what it would feel like.

"I could disappear any time," Slinger said. "Another American free from history." Slinger spoke to himself, mumbling about the Cuban missile crisis and Contras in the Eighties. "Castro loved anti-Americans who dropped in for a cigar. I heard Evers met him once. They sat in his box for a baseball game. Said he told him to keep up the good work, anything that sent Americans into rehab or jail or that wasted War-on-Drug money was okay by him. But that's not my deal. We're dealers helping farmers. That's my motto. Every kilo helps. Fill some kind of hole that can't be filled any other way."

Callie looked out the window. Another howler sat in a rubber tree looking at them from his entirely separate existence. It was impossible not to feel the presence and absence of Rachel in the bottom of plane—both there and gone.

"You see these burns on my arms and these pink scars on my neck? I crashed into a soybean field. I climbed out in time and watched the plane burn up. There's a whole junkyard of car and plane parts serving up the AmeriCanDo spirit. One of the cables snapped."

Slinger reached behind him where an old tape player was strapped to the seat.

"I never fly without Jerry." He hit play and a bootleg of the Dead started.

"Still living in '69, eh?" Angus said. "Shoot me now, please."

"I might. If you make it to forty, you'll have the right to comment on time."

Callie felt like she was riding in a '77 Pontiac Le Mans in a high school movie with potheads headed for hazed philosophy and a snack-food binge.

Slinger yelled over the engine. "We have a couple hundred kilos in the back. We're gonna run it over to Belize City. Team up there will load the ship. I have to split up the shipments to keep the flow—some for Evers, some for Slinger, some for Evers, some for Slinger."

"What do the police do if they see us?" Callie asked.

"Depends how they feel. If we're over scrub brush, shit, maybe shoot us down. Maybe track us until we land, hoping we'll lead them to bigger fish like Evers. Maybe wave hello if they're ours." Slinger took a slug of mescal. "Never drink and drive. But a little before you fly adds to the high. I have my routine. One before takeoff and one on the way back from the run."

"Very responsible," Callie said, shaking her head, yet oddly unconcerned about flying with Slinger. She was dealing with a survivor.

"I know! That's how I got where I am! Goddamned, never-ending responsibility!"

The plane bounced and rattled down the airstrip over the washboard dirt, crushing giant red ants into bird pickings.

"Christ, Jorge's team couldn't get this any smoother?" Callie said.

"I have to agree with your construction quality review. And now shut up, Jerry is soloing. New Haven, '77."

"Don't you have any fucking Ramones?" Callie asked.

Slinger pulled it out of the jungle and headed the plane east. They chopped their way through bright sunshine. When they had leveled off, Slinger gave Callie a long-winded instructional—interspersed by Deadhead head-bobbing—and some tries at the controls.

"Not half bad," Slinger said. "You should have been a pilot not an MP."

"So really, how'd you know that?" she asked.

Slinger looked at her as if she were some kind of Fed.

"Sources, missy, sources. I always have three rules," Slinger said. In their headsets, he sounded like an old-time radio show host.

She appeased him. "Okay, I'll take the bait. About what?"

"Everything."

"I'm so curious too," Angus mumbled in the headset.

Slinger looked like the street musicians they'd seen outside Jamón's, his long hair hanging off him, unkempt but with a sheen of care and cleanliness.

"Number one. Know everything about the creatures around you."

The music sounded through the headsets as if it were playing behind a prison cell wall. She'd give anything for pounding loud guitar.

"Number two. Every day is a deal. What deal did you make today?"

He made Callie take control and told her how to hold it steady. The plane jostled a bit but she basically kept calm and held it roughly on course and altitude. Slinger started ruffling through a journal of scrap papers and scrawls and old maps. "I forget the third one. Fucking memory isn't worth shit. I wrote them down somewhere about twenty years ago. Like one of those toy kaleidoscopes you spin around with the crystals? That's what it's like getting old. Pretty, meaningless patterns in my head falling around into flowers and one-eyed illusions. Who the fuck gave us a brain filled with so much come-and-go that we're not sure which pieces go with which other pieces?

"Oh, here it is. Found it. Fucking little piece. Number three." He held up a Club Sandinista napkin with scribbles of black pen on it.

"Oh good," Angus said.

"Rule number three: Nobody gives a shit if you die."

He took back control and peered out of the plane like a mental patient on tranquilizers. She wished she were sitting with Angus in the back. He seemed to have hidden things wherever he went: the tree along the airstrip, the storage room in the leather plant, a secret retirement.

Slinger let go to fold up all of his papers carefully and placed them back in his satchel as the plane wobbled, then started descending randomly. "Ease her back and it'll level. Take it easy, would you? Stop jerkin' off the stick and it'll calm down. We don't want to end up in body bags ourselves yet."

"Slinger, how'd you find Rachel?"

"Don't ask. But let's just say that if Jorge's men find out I know my own fisherman in town, I'll be in one of those dry-cleaning bags too."

From her time in the military, she knew how intelligence and alliances were almost never obvious, that there were alliances and counter-alliances that needed to remain unknown. But the implication for her and Angus was clear: Slinger was working against Jorge, and yet was partners with him at the same time.

"Can I talk with you about something?"

"Now's a good time," he said, waving a hand at the horizon out there. "We're not going anywhere."

"So when Tony gets here—"

He finished her thought. "What are we telling him? You start. You're the one who came down here."

"Tony is a man imploding from his own pyramid scheme. He's got a network of shows and dealers who won't be happy if he stiffs them. All of them expecting a buffet of psychological amenities. He steps up from territory sales to regional distributor. He asks Hector to get an intro to you. He starts trying to sell you on his Bloody Wrist import/export scheme, but all the while he's working with Jorge too. He got Rachel out of the way, but he must think copies of his Latin Leather data are floating around. So he's nervous."

Slinger took a swig from an engraved, inlaid silver flask. "Want some?"

"No thanks."

"I'm listening. The man is a true multi-tasker."

"Make him think you will deal him in if he comes clean on what happened to Rachel? Just long enough to make sure he's gets in some real down time here."

"How you gonna do that?"

"You want him gone?"

"Gone? You have your own ferryman do you?"

She asked him point blank, "Did you have Rachel killed?"

"She wasn't threatening *me*," he said.

"I have a ferry*woman*. Ixchel Cante."

"She's going to knock off Tony Maul?"

"If I wanted to do that, I'd just shoot him myself. I'm a woman, I can think five moves ahead."

"I play chess with old Guatemalans by the Lake every Sunday morning," Slinger muttered. "That helps offset your so-called female advantage."

"I'll give him his files back. They don't make sense to me anyway. Tony's threating my family, but Angus and I have taken care of that. We just need to educate him on his place in the world. I want to prove he had Rachel killed."

"That's five moves? You want me to hold up a fifty million, two-year operation to get a confession out of a stone?"

"Not a confession, just confirmation," said Callie.

Angus jumped in. "He needs this shipment this fall."

"He's right. He's promised it to all his producers for Bloody Wrist shows. Just tell him like three or four weeks. And that he needs to get off my family if he wants his share."

"And if he doesn't cooperate?"

"Worst case, you don't lose anything but a few weeks. If he folds, then we let him think the shipment goes north for him. With me and Ixchel and whoever else is supposed to be hidden in one of those containers. I'll take care of things in Jersey after that, but I doubt he'll care at all about John Slinger. I have one more thing," Callie said.

"You gotta lot of fucking things."

"Was Ixchel already planning to be on the ship?"

"She gave up her spot."

"What do you mean 'her spot'?"

"The spot on the ship she earned when she sold her baby. That spot."

"No baby, no spot."

He swung his precious hair, and banked the plane to the right. "I have resuscitated many Cessnas in my day." He turned up the Dead. Angus groaned while grimacing from his leg pain. Slinger seemed distracted by the horizon. Fires smoked in random places across the mountains and valleys.

"Look at all those fucking ozone murders burning the earth," Slinger said.

"But Ixchel was supposed to go on the ship before all this?"

"Was."

"There's something else going on with Jorge, isn't there?" Callie pressed.

"Do you know what's in those files Rachel sent you?"

"Yes, lists of leather inventory, lists of Latin Leather employees. I think she was worried something would happen to them. And herself."

"I don't think so."

"What do you mean?"

Slinger looked at her and Angus. "It wasn't just a list of employees. It was the list of girls Jorge is shipping north to Hector."

Callie's stomach turned. She stared out the window, down to the endless green blanket of jungle that looked like a plush of velvet draped over the mounds of hills. *Ixchel Cante.* She was sitting in

Paul Paul's office a few days ago. *A list of girls being shipped.* No wonder Mrs. Granger and Ixchel were at odds with each other over the adoption and dealing with Jorge.

"We need to get on that ship," Ixchel had said.

The plane continued over a wide blanket of thick green and rolling mountains and a deep azure sky sewn into a patchwork of unmoving cumulus cotton-blanket clouds. Her head felt slow and throbbed from the mescal and the harsh sun. The hot sun with Dillon. On the fire escape of Angus's building in Philly deciding whether to help Rachel. The brown desert in Iraq. The sky and the earth, the big tease. Her mother sitting in the bland, vanilla crème family room, always afraid to go out at night. Angus patrolling the street at an outdoor coffee shop just before a suicide bomber blew himself up. An infinite space that nobody could touch that cried out to be filled. Inside a Cessna among three disparate dreams. Rachel a pile of waterlogged flesh in a plastic bag beneath them. The old, dead air below them, holding them over three thousand feet of memory below.

They banked in over the shoreline; to their left was the Atlantic Ocean and beneath them estuaries of marsh grass and swamp. The runway looked like an asphalt cut across the sandy ground, and Callie saw two white egrets standing in seagrass. The plane sped past them and landed with a shock-absorbed bump.

Slinger taxied to a halt on the tarmac near the terminal, and cut the engine.

Callie saw two Belizean MEs in government issue t-shirts waiting to ID and record Rachel Martelli's number.

Slinger blocked the wheels and unlatched the luggage compartment, "There you go. One body formerly known as human being number 4.5578 billion. I'll be in a taxi out front. These gentlemen will sign off a release for Belizean authorities. Accidental drowning while boating or scuba diving in a rip current, or some such bullshit. I bought her a one-way flight back to her Maker. Or Philly, whichever is closer to heaven." He held out both hands, waiting for gratitude. "Well?"

Callie didn't know whether to slug him in the Adam's apple or thank him. "What the fuck you want, a medal?" she asked.

"You're welcome." He headed off to wait for them in a taxi.

Angus and she got on one side of the body bag, while the M.E.'s took the other.

They took Rachel's body to a holding room where there was a stack of documentation to sign. Angus stood propped on his metal crutches, staring at the black plastic bag.

"Ready?" he asked.

They both knew the duty required of them. There would be no signing anything—even faked documents—unless they knew exactly who was in the bag.

"Yes," Callie said.

They went over to the bag, and Callie knelt next to the zipper. Rachel had been in the Lake for two, maybe three, days. She had never seen the body of a drowned person before.

She unzipped it and peeled back the plastic.

The stench of decomposition and rotting meat.

The bloated mask of maroon bruises, greenish-bronze flesh, and two closed eyes beneath a matted tangle of stiff black hair. The dead remnants of what was Rachel Martelli waited to return to the temporary dark of the cheap government bag.

She felt Angus's hand on her shoulder for the second time in a few days.

Callie zipped her up into the cocoon of decay, where at least there was no further need of air or light, no suffocating pain, no delusional power of sickening human cruelty.

She turned and asked for the paperwork. She flipped through the few pre-printed forms of death and identification. She found the field CAUSE OF DEATH. Scribbled in the box was *accidental drowning*. She edited and initialed it to read ~~accidental~~ *murder, drowning*. Then signed it and handed back the forms to one of the MEs, and said, "Sign those right now, or I will stick those uniform pins to your nut sack."

He hesitated and looked at his partner nervously.

Angus nodded at them, "I wouldn't put it past her. I once saw her make an Iraqi roadside bomber eat plastic explosive and then bring in a bomb sniffing dog."

Callie knew the story. It was a fabrication they used to let circulate in the military prison.

One of them nodded to the other, who signed it.

Callie shot a picture of it with her phone.

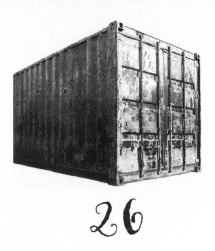

26

Donnie's Marina was at the end of the street, behind a row of scrubby palms, with a large lot full of bright white monstrosities of fiberglass and paint jobs, a carnival of consumptive adrenaline molded into hulls and crammed with twin Mercedes inboard engines. The Caribbean sparkled in the white morning sun.

As they got out of the taxi, Callie could see that Slinger was mentally out to sea, with his frazzled hair blown back at 125 miles per hour while a freighter powered behind in his wake carrying the hundred-thousand-kilo shipment for the medicinal ache of all those lost in pain in America.

Callie crossed the heat-waved asphalt, smelling diesel fumes. What was going to happen to all those girls once they got to New York? A twenty-first century slave trade was happening right in front of her. And Ixchel had known about it the whole time.

They went into the showroom, a two-story room the size of a football field with the latest models polished bright white.

The general manager, Donnie Walker, had perfectly gelled silver hair and wore a Hawaiian shirt, a Floridian transplant. He and Slinger gave each other a handshake and a brief hug.

"Donnie, I need to outrun everything on the water," Slinger said.

Donnie nodded. "This way, speedo."

Slinger looked at Callie. He seemed to have forgotten all about Tony Maul. "*This* is what it's all about." Bright blue and green freedom flew through his eyes into a Bermuda bank, while ordinary mortals slaved in office cubicles.

Slinger said to Angus. "Donnie's been there, he was like us once."

"And what are we?" Angus asked.

"Grunts in a covert war."

"Shit, I was like everybody once," Donnie laughed. "I got more lives than an old cat. 'Nam. Miami mob. I've flipped over more boats than a gator rolls in the water in a lifetime. And they live an average fifty-three years. See my shoes? *Gen-u-ine* F-L-A gator. See the belt? *Gen-u-ine* gator."

Callie wanly nodded. Her heart was still shaken from seeing Rachel's bloated body and learning Ixchel was helping girls toward Jorge's trafficking ring. She wanted to get all this over with and get home to Dillon. She couldn't help her indifference and dismissiveness. "And what about your pants? A *gen-u-ine* gator in there, too?" she said.

She didn't bother to wait for Donnie's reaction. With his leathery, tan face, he looked as though his vain soul had baked to a crisp in the sun. He was a salesman with a hollow, lonesome grin that he bestowed on everyone. She pictured him at home in his expensive cotton bathrobe surrounded by photos of himself standing in front of speedboats like a fisherman posing with his catch. A happy deadness wrapped in salesmanship.

Slinger coolly ogled the boats as they strolled. Donnie narrated. Callie could tell didn't care about the words, probably hearing sporadic bits of every other sentence: *twin 1200 horsepower...jumped the canal going ninety...staggered 525s...Grassig instruments... leather cockpit...gold-plated switches...came down on his head and broke his neck...drunk on the Intracoastal Waterway doing sixty at night before he saw the canal bank...totally custom paintwork in high-end...not damaged at all by the al fresco diners, surprised by a double-shell fiberglass bow in their appetizers...*

"I've helped all kinds of men outrun whatever it was that chased them," Donnie finished. "Now *this* is the one I have for you."

The *Night Slipper* was a midnight blue streak of fiberglass. Slinger climbed up into it without asking for permission. He sat behind the small black wheel and the nose stuck out in front of him like the hood of a Cadillac. He peered over the side and down at Donnie, who was leaning up against the next boat, smoking his cigarette. Donnie was gesturing to him without pause, one sales story leading to another.

"You can check out the compartments. Plenty of storage," he said, knowing how to plant an implication without being overt. Slinger knew men who knew how to discuss unspoken business.

Slinger reemerged, looking down on them. "This is the one, the *Night Slipper*. How much?"

Donnie looked at Angus. "This boat is seven years old. Lucky seven. It's Seventy-two K."

"Looks like he'll take it," Angus said.

Callie rolled her eyes. "Looks more like your big blue phallic toy to me."

Slinger glanced at Callie. "Dread, you better get some suntan lotion. Irish girls like you aren't made for the tropics."

"Thank you," she said.

"I'd say no problem. But you are a problem. You'll see the *Bonita* docked over there. Have a look. She's a true hunk of shit." He waved them off, a mock king dismissing minions.

Callie was staring out into the marina and the harbor beyond the slips and the bright white glare of fiberglass and the fishing towers and radio antennas. She looked at Angus where he had sat down in the heat on an upside down five-gallon bucket.

"When Tony gets here, you have to make the deal sound good."

Slinger came over and sat with his feet over the side of the *Night Slipper*. "Ms. Byrne, I'm a professional smuggler. I'll make it work."

"I'm going with Ixchel and the other girls on the ship. You tell him he gets shit if we get there in one piece, free and clear."

"And why would you fucking do *that*?"

"Because Tony needs to think he has something over me. And he'll think he can do whatever he wants once we're in Jersey."

"I'll think about it."

She nodded, "Of course."

"Hey Cow," Slinger said to Angus. "You going too?"

"Me? Hell no."

"Good. Because I get seasick. I need you on this boat running lead."

"What the fuck you want me for? You just met me. You going to put me out front of a couple thousand kilos of smack? Hell no."

"Because I don't like Jorge's men. They work for him more than me. They put up with me because they have too and because they know I'm connected to Evers. So I need a fucking independent contractor who will do one simple job: drive this fucking boat like he's a fucking joy rider and let the *Bonita* know if there's Coast Guard in the area."

"Fuck off, I'm no trafficker."

"Then I guess Ixchel is staying here with her Uncle Jorge Prick."

Callie looked at Angus now. She didn't say anything, but their eyes met and they were both making their calculations.

"Fuck," Angus said.

Slinger climbed on to the dock. "Well, I thought about it. I'll tell Tony the ship doesn't sail without you and Ixchel on it and safe and sound back in Philly. And I think I'll drive his price up. That should buy some time to see you can get info out of him on Rachel. How's that?"

Callie smiled. "I like it."

"Then you just got a ticket for a one-way cruise on a cargo shitter full of leather, coffee, and Chiquita bananas."

Slinger threw Angus the keys.

Angus's face had turned sour. "Fucking balls."

"Take the boat out and get a feel for her. Then dock it over to Wharf #5. There's a beater car there waiting for you. You can stay the night at the Sunny Mopan Inn and pick up Tony Maul tomorrow."

Slinger had climbed down and did not look at Callie or Angus but was shaking his hair again like a neurotic drummer, walking away.

She and Angus got into the *Night Slipper*. The sparkling blue bow seemed like a mile long, the way the old Cadillacs used to look driven by well-dressed black men in Philly.

"Only one problem with this fucking plan, Callie," Angus said.

"What's that?"

"I grew up in Mahanoy City, Pennsylvania shooting deer in a fucking cornfield. I've never driven a boat in my life."

27

"Well we better fucking learn, eh," Callie said. "I've done it a few times when we went down the shore. Peter had some friends with an inboard. We would hang out and get stoned." She didn't tell Angus one of her Jersey shore memories aboard Tony's boat: she was so hard up for a fix that she stole money from Peter while he was sleeping and let him think it was one of the other partiers on board. He had accused three different guys, and the weekend ended in her pulling him off one of them outside a Wawa convenient store before he choked the guy with a hoagie.

Callie took the wheel on the way out. Then they switched to let Angus get a feel for the boat. It had the power of three Chrysler engines. While he learned the feel of a boat in water, she read him the marine rules of the road. After an hour or so, he was able to make slight adjustments and turns in the light currents. She had a flashing thought of simply delivering the boat and then heading to the airport and leaving with Angus. But there was no possibility now of leaving. Slinger, Jorge, Tony—any of one of them would find her or Angus and head them out on some garbage barge. They were going back to Lake Petén. Each of them felt intertwined, and nothing could be altered now. She was under a "contract" with Slinger to deliver Tony and make sure a boatful of girls got safely to the States and walked away without debts to anyone. Whoever left was likely dead, whoever stayed was likely dead. They had their own separate roles to be played out. A migrating black-and-white warbler flew overhead, mocking them: *Who can't find their way?* As they headed out of the harbor, Angus punched the throttle so he didn't have to listen to anything but the engines. Two cruise ships were anchored just beyond the harbor, a few tankers were tied up to shabby docks.

Callie meditated to the receding wake and the *rrrr-ryyyyyyyyybbbbbbbb* of the ceaseless engines. Rachel and her files. Tony and her. Slinger and his final parade. She and Ixchel. Eddies spun off the back propellers. They seemed to Callie, on the one hand, like B-rate action movie cartoons and, on the other, no different than co-workers in a corporate park, stuck together by random timing of birth, location, schedule—living out constricted lives in a lab dish of someone else's design, amid a flowing history of trysts and exes, people surviving by climbing over those closest to them, the lives of proximal lovers and dead strangers.

They took the boat back in, and Angus was as a close to a smile as his bearded face allowed. A boy and his toy, she thought. As they neared the port terminal, Angus pointed at a warehouse with a black five painted on it. At Wharf #5, where Slinger had said to dock, a few Belizean dockworkers sat in an open warehouse door, looking like they had nowhere to go and suspiciously peering at them pulling up. They motioned and gave a few cryptic shouts to Angus that made it clear he shouldn't be parading himself and his vessel. He gave a small wave to say he understood and reversed out of the cove, nearly hitting the starboard side of the *Bonita*. He punched it forward in time, easing out again into the channel and pulling around to the other side of the Wharf #5 building to slip the boat.

Despite his dead leg, Angus was able to grab the stern line and get back to the wheel. Callie went up front and lay on the bow, trying to reach the dock and do what she could. The men walked around from the other side, laughing, and having a good look at her ass to boot.

"Fuck them," Angus said. He tried reversing to slow the momentum but, having never actually docked a boat, mistimed reverse and slammed into the rickety dock, breaking one end of it into pieces and making a horrible screeching of wood against fiberglass that sounded like fingernails on a blackboard. His cheeks above the beard flushed red.

"Christ, easy!" Callie yelled, looking back over her shoulder.

"Goddamn it! Motherfucking fuck!" he said, and he pounded his fist into the console and broke the tachometer's cover.

"It's okay, go easy on yourself. Didn't you ever hit a corn field when you were learning to drive some shitty pickup?"

"Side of a barn," he admitted.

Up on the dock, the men howled. "Watch out for that dock, man," one said, pointing helpfully. "You want some baby cushions, boy?" another said. And they all laughed some more.

"Callie, why didn't you say something?"

"I did! I said stop the fucking boat!"

"She yelled, man, we all heard her."

Angus didn't answer. Callie knew he hated to be ridiculed. She scrambled to the front and grabbed the line with a hook and held the boat as best as she could against the dock while Angus tied it off.

"We try to tell you to not come on other side, but to go around this side. Slinger told us you come. We didn't expect a captain bear like you, though!" A dark man in sunglasses and a tank top shook his head. "No, man, we didn't expect a fucking Cap'm Crash! Ha!"

Angus climbed down one more time, beet-red mad, and looked at a dark crack and a three-foot scrape of rotten wood against the top of the bow. A sad broken running light hung off the boat.

"Fucking brand new boat!" he said. "Jesus fucking Christ, who the hell made this shitty dock? You can't even reach the lines!"

While Angus unloaded the gear, Callie grabbed her knapsack and marveled at Angus's ability to evade self-responsibility.

"The dock didn't hit you, man, it just sat in the water." And they laughed. "Look, it's nothing but a thing. Don't worry your mind. This boat'll still fly past any Coast Guard boat they got out there. We got you an old car to drive back. Come up and have a toke first, man."

"Thanks," Angus said, calming down, inhaling. "Which car?"

Dark Glasses pointed down the quay toward a small orange undying Toyota with holes in the quarter panels and wire hangers holding the bumpers.

"That?"

"Yah, man, that ramblin' car," Dark Glasses said. "You ramble here, you ramble there."

"You're the crew for the *Bonita?*" Callie asked.

"Yeah."

Angus shook his head.

Callie looked at the cargo ship across the small channel. It looked like a floating salvage yard.

"What you two do?"

"I'll be running scout," Angus said.

"Slinger made part of the deal," said Callie.

The other two men looked unhappy and glanced at Dark Glasses, shaking their heads.

"Yeah, uh-huh, we know what Slinger's all about," Dark Glasses said, lighting a joint and passing it among the others as they strolled easily.

"Get in the car," Callie said. Angus was shaking his head at the sloppy operations.

She wondered if any of this was going to come off, if Slinger knew what he was doing. Evers had blown apartment buildings up, massacred entire small villages to clear things up, drowned people in pools, helicoptered guys into the Peruvian Andes and dropped them in the middle of nowhere from a thousand feet into the trees, stuffed girls into crates and sent them off to landfills. And she was in the middle of this between Tony, Slinger, and Evers? Beth was right: she was crazy.

Angus opened the passenger door to the orange excuse for an automobile. "We'll be here," is all he said.

The three men laughed, and Dark Glasses gave him the finger as they sauntered back into the warehouse.

"Yah, you'll be here. You tell Slinger, the *Bonita* is ready for you. We're friends with whoever pays. You pay, we love you." He handed Callie the keys.

"Yeah, you look ready," Angus said.

"Get in the car already," Callie said.

"See ya soon. And bring da girl!" Dark Glasses shouted. "We love her!"

"Love you, too," Callie waved and climbed into the driver seat.

She started the car, and the afternoon rains started up as they made their way toward town on a rut-infested so-called highway. The rain ran down through the holes in the roof and down the dashboard onto her feet. She pushed the accelerator and the car failed to speed up. No different than Ramona. A minivan and a pickup filled with locals sped around them while Angus was a stubborn quiet. She knew he was irritated being assigned to navigate a boat.

The Sunny Mopan Inn, about a mile away from Wharf #5 in Belize City, was a bright turquoise flophouse on a side street full of t-shirt and electronic knock-off shops. The place was just as dismal as she had expected. There were as many roaches and rats waiting for transport to another land as there were women and men trying to get north to work or reunite with their families or leave their old ones. It was a four-story shabby inn with blue balconies and X-shaped stairwells hanging off a bright white building.

The pulled in, took a room, and waited for word of Tony's arrival.

28

It was late morning, and the TV was tuned into a local news station. Angus lay on one double bed and Callie was sitting against the headboard of the other scanning her phone for a future apartment in Philadelphia for her and Dillon.

There was a knock at the door.

Callie presumed the maid but to be safe pulled Betty and peered through the cheap curtain.

Ixchel with Sylvia in her arms.

Callie unlocked and opened the door.

"What are you doing here?"

"I took the bus."

"You shouldn't have come."

"I didn't feel good sitting like a target at the ranch. They tried to take her once. They will again." She came into the room, wheeling an old ripped suitcase and a worn-out Disney backpack. She went over to Angus. "How is your knee? Can you move it yet?" She touched the bandaged area. "Do you need this dressing changed? Can you move over?"

Ixchel sat with Sylvia next to Angus, and watched the TV news talk about the cruise ship that had docked that morning. There had been a dispute about the ship docking with a case of norovirus on board. Ixchel was calm next to Angus: this American man who had saved her from Rodrigo. Had kept them from taking Sylvia from her. She felt a distrust of Ixchel now, knowing her role in setting up other girls with Jorge's ring. Callie saw her motives a little differently now: Ixchel wanted to get away from Slinger's ranch, but she also came to find *him*. Seemed like just another angle to get to the States.

Angus told Ixchel about identifying Rachel's body, that Slinger had the Lake dragged. Angus had not moved from the top of the polyester bedspread that was full of a loud pink hibiscus. He didn't seem to mind the idea of the baby. Callie went back to writing Dillon another email message on her phone and ignored the awkwardness—as if she were now a third wheel in Angus's and Ixchel's room. *Dillon, where should we live when I come to get you? There is a small apartment in Kensington I saw online. It has a small bedroom for you where I'm going to put up lots of Phillies and Eagles stuff. I'll find my Ramone's poster. I think it's still in the back of Ramona.* Ixchel put Sylvia on Angus's big chest side, and he stared at the creature as if he had never seen a miniature human before.

"I feel so good, like this is all coming to an end. I'm leaving here with you," Ixchel said, looking over at Callie. But Callie had the sense she was actually speaking to Angus. "My baby and I are breaking loose. We're already flowing north on a ship. Like a heavy wet blanket is not hanging on my back any more. Like when snakes shed their skin, right? You know what I mean, Angus?"

Angus was letting the baby girl grab his beard. "Yeah, I do."

Callie had seen something in Angus as they looked at Rachel's body in the basement of the station: he was a man who wanted to change something in his life.

Angus insisted on fetching ice and water for them all.

When he was out of the room, she finally raised what was on her mind.

"You helped arrange all those girls for Jorge, didn't you?"

Ixchel did not flinch from it. "And? What if I did? They want to go. Everybody makes their own decision. All I did was tell them Jorge's terms and set them up."

"All you did? You know they have to work as prostitutes in Atlantic City."

"What's the problem? It's legal in Amsterdam. So what if we have to work a few years to get the rest of our lives free?"

Callie didn't know what to say to that, and Angus came back. It was too big to talk about further.

Angus told Ixchel about the *Night Slipper*, about his role as scout, and how he had never driven a boat before.

"Why are you doing it?"

"Because you and Callie will be on the ship. And I don't want any more women I know drowning."

Callie looked at them both. "I'm not dying in the water. My hair will look like shit."

The boredom and strange intimacy of the hotel room was becoming as unbearable as the bad local TV and ads for deals on roofing for the hurricane season.

Ixchel said the obvious. "If Tony thinks we're setting him up, we're dead."

Callie looked at Ixchel, noting that she had included herself in the set up. "So we better not give it up then."

Ixchel looked at both Callie and Angus now. "I wrote my father an email. I told him I'm coming to New York. And you know what? He wrote back. He said, 'Yes, you come. You will die there with those gangs and drug lords. Here you can work somewhere, and I can meet my granddaughter, and we can go to the park and sit together on a Sunday and drink coffee'."

Callie thought of her father somewhere in Baltimore, probably in a homeless shelter with a jaundiced face and a failing liver.

Finally, she got a text message from Tony.

"He landed," Callie announced.

"I coming with you," Ixchel said, standing up next to the bed.

Angus was up and took one of his crutches and pointed the rubber end at Ixchel's chest. "You wait here. You're holding a baby girl."

Ixchel scowled but sat back on the bed. "Okay. But if the stupid television and these horrible beds make me insane, I'm out of here."

29

She let Angus drive the beater to the airport to get some of his male dignity back intact. As they pulled into the arrivals lane of the terminal, Callie pointed to a man with narrow, sulking eyes and olive-toned skin. He was dressed in black boots, black jeans, and crisp white cotton short-sleeve shirt. His hair was somehow cropped, gelled, and spiked all at once; his skinny arms were covered in tattoos, his ears in silver studs, and he carried a small duffel. He had no luggage. Apparently he didn't plan on staying long.

When they pulled up, he saw it was Callie. He gave her the finger. His almond-shaped, sulky eyes and squared face gave the effect of a permanent indifference and deep disdain for everything around him.

She got out. "You always look asleep. Open your eyes. Welcome to your Central American Dream vacation. We have time shares for all shapes and sizes, even dick heads," she said.

"Fuck off," he said. "Only reason I'm down here is to see Slinger. I thought I told you to fucking stay out of my business. I can't believe you've got the balls to be here let alone be my limo service."

"Slinger only treats guests first class. And I wouldn't have been in your business if you knew how to fucking run it without ruining lives around you. Get in the front."

She got in the back, letting Angus drive and Tony take the front. She wanted to be in the back with Betty ready for anything in front of her.

Angus pulled the car away from the airport, and she had a bad premonition the airport was the last sign of law enforcement she would be seeing until this whole thing was over.

"So, here I am. I heard they found Rachel. Terrible."

Don't even say her name, you piece of shit, Callie almost said out loud. But she caught herself, and lied to him to hold back as many cards as she could. "They don't know how it happened. I found her sneakers on a fence post. Apparently one of the cartel's calling cards in these parts. But you probably already know that."

"Me? I had nothing to do with it. The fuckers down here are obviously not listening to me. Otherwise, why would I be down here to this fucking shithole of brown beach bums and coffee beaners."

She let her silence speak for itself. Angus turned on the radio, and a man droned in Spanish, probably about politics.

He found a tribute to some Belizean Garifuna guitarist. The DJ summarized him: "Andy Palacio. Toiled all his life in music, recorded his masterpiece, and then died of a massive stroke."

Callie wanted to put her head back and close her eyes. The background guitar and melodic ballads of the dead Garifina musician were good for sleeping. The deep voice was like listening to a bedtime story she had forgotten. Tony's head was bobbing right in front of her. She had the flash fantasy of shooting him right there. She was tired of him, tired of herself. She had made Tony think they would give him what he wanted. A music producer turned drug dealer was one thing. A drug dealer turned sex trafficker was just sick. It made her even more enraged not to be with Dillon, not to help raise him into a good man.

As she predicted, Tony couldn't let the silence be.

"All Rachel had to do was pack and inventory some leather."

Neither responded to him.

"So, like I said, here I am. What the fuck's going on?"

"Yeah, I know," Angus said. "I told him there's no reason everything shouldn't work out."

Tony glared at Angus. "And what the hell do you know, Angus?"

"Because I work with Slinger."

Callie liked that. She watched an older woman pushing a grocery cart full of plastic bags down the street, and thought, Well, with his new boating skills, it was true.

"Look, you gotta work with these people. Things move slow down here," Angus said.

"Fuck slow. Where's the ship?"

She continued to let the men face off. Made it easier on her.

Angus drove around three girls on bicycles in the middle of Belize City. "It's over in the port area. But nothing's loaded yet. It's all in a loading warehouse. Slinger's men won't load it until he releases it. Must be five thousand kilos all tucked in nicely between leather coats or inside the liners of the handbags. You should thank Callie here; she's probably packed two hundred handbags for you with the other girls. So don't get all bent out of shape down here, okay."

"Oh gracias, missy, for all the bloody knock-offs. So when do we meet this fucking wanker Slinger?"

Callie thought he sounded nervous, as if already smelling the trap he was being led to.

Callie had forgotten Tony's habit of dropping London punk Britishisms. What a blowhard.

Callie tried to stay relaxed, but she could feel Angus trying to think and maintain his front. "We're meeting him at a resort near the operation. All he wants to know is who he is dealing with."

"I'll pay him. That's who he's dealing with."

"All you gotta do is meet him."

"You know where they found Rachel?" Callie tested.

He answered quickly. "No. Where?"

"Floating in the Lake."

"Like I said, that's fucking bloody terrible."

She had thought a lot about what she was going to say to Tony. She looked out the window at Belize City to maintain her focus. This

All-American Asshole had helped murder her ex-unit MP and was sitting right in front of her as if nothing were wrong. But he didn't seem to know how rare it was to locate the body of a dead woman in Petén or that Slinger might have helped organize the finding.

"And exactly what are you doing here?" he asked Callie.

She sounded like a woman she had never met before, somebody who ran things, who could stroke a man's ego where he didn't even know he needed it. "I came down here to have some fun with Rachel."

"Bullshit."

"Slinger's shipment is ready to come up to New York and work. When we couldn't find Rachel, we met with him. Look, you came from some little city in the country. You built up something. I think you must be a pretty fucking brilliant businessman. Angus told me about all the clubs and bands and venues Bloody Wrist bands have been playing. I told Slinger all about you. You guys can make it work. But Slinger's got his ways. He wants more than money now."

It wasn't hard to sound real about wanting to get the product and the ship to the States. The truck jostled over a curb as Angus took a tight turn to avoid a scooter swerving around a stopped car outside of a touristy beach shop.

Tony looked back at her and then at Angus, "Isn't she a good little coordinator."

She tried to sound sly, trusting, and allied with him all at the same time. "I am. I think ahead."

"She is," Angus said.

She looked out the window as they headed into the countryside. The corn fields were ready for harvesting, and she saw several women with baskets working the rows under hats. The rows went by in flashes of green and brown, rolling over the hills like a blanket being waved at them to crawl beneath the earth and stay there.

The little orange car handled like a bumper car, the wheel loose and ineffective, tires slamming off potholes from one to another, the back trunk rattling and squeaking with the twisting frame. Chickens, roosters, and fowl of countless breeds scattered full of fear and life as they went by.

They got to the border gate between Guatemala and Belize, the docks of Belize City another three hours behind them now.

At the customs window, Angus handed over a set of papers.

The border agent had them open the back trunk.

The agent checked off their passports. The rear doors shut and he was waved on with nothing but a nod. Slinger's network of transactions at work.

She could feel Tony's edgy pleasure as they drove deeper into Guatemala. She thought he was pleased with himself and thinking, *So this is how the big time works*. Tony was openly vain and proud of everything he did, even if it was just taking a shit like every other creature on the planet. Even when he misjudged, he never let it show. She could see why Rachel had first taken up with Tony. He had an attractive greed she imagined a 1920s moonshine runner or a hacker in Queens might have: the alternate beats of bought and sold were in his heart, illicit acts the oxygen in his blood.

Tony looked apprehensive, as if he half expected to end up in a local police station sleeping in a cell with photographs of his mug shot, kilos on the evidence table, and small AP stories about an American arrested on drug charges being picked up by *The Philadelphia Inquirer*.

But the players played their parts, and the script unfolded as Slinger directed.

As soon as they crossed the border, Tony turned back to her and said, "Welcome back to Guatemala. As a sign of my affection, you're getting a call in a few minutes from your sister Beth. And Dillon."

30

With an intimidating military precision and timing, Callie's cell phone rang.

The display read BETH. She looked at Tony and Angus. "You fucker," she said to Tony. She answered. "Beth?"

Beth spoke in a hushed panic. "Callie, what's going on?"

"Beth? Where are you?" Tony was looking at her with a satisfied grin on his face.

"At home. I'm in the closet upstairs with Dillon. Three SUVs pulled up outside the house a few minutes ago! They fired shots through the front window and front door! Where are you? Who are they?"

Callie heard Dillon whisper in the background. "Why are we in the closet?"

"Shhhh, honey, you have to be quiet."

"Call 911," Callie said, watching Tony as she spoke.

"I already did," Beth hissed.

Tony nodded, "The Evers Corporation has a long reach, eh?" He laughed as if he himself had the long reach. "And Angus's friends weren't hard to pay to head back to their holes for a few days."

Angus glanced at Tony, furious. "You don't have to involve her kid."

"And we can visit this Ixchel girl too if you want. I heard she's got the debt of a bloody lifetime." He laughed again.

Callie's thought hard, her head exploding with adrenaline while her MP training reminded her to stay calm. "Stay quiet, Beth, I'll stay on with you."

For a time, Beth said nothing.

Callie said nothing.

Two women on the end of a digitally networked world with an anchor to nowhere.

There was an awful emptiness of breathing and dead closet air.

She could hear Dillon asking in a hushed voice, "Why are we in here? Who is coming?"

Beth whispered quickly. "Callie, why is this happening? What did you do?"

"Nothing! It's Tony Maul, Peter's old boss. Just do what they say if they find you. Don't answer me, just keep quiet."

Beth didn't answer.

Callie listened to the dull echo of the Claro cell company somehow connecting her to Verizon in Philadelphia. Between there and here, Tony sat right in front of her. She thought of pulling out Betty and putting it to the back of Tony's head.

A younger Callie wouldn't have hesitated. But the sober Callie skipped over the emotion and went to the strategy: he was delivering a message. Let him think it was heard.

As long as Beth and Dillon were okay, she would wait.

She muted her phone. "What do you want?" Callie asked.

Tony nodded. "Let me call Slinger, and we'll see."

He dialed Slinger on his speaker.

"So, Tony Maul the A-hole," said Slinger.

"Why don't you explain to our little crappy car load what's going on," Tony said.

Slinger said, as if he knew what was happening, "He wants you to know what he and the Evers Corporation can do." He made it sound like Tony now had some say in the Evers network.

Tony said, "Very good."

"So what do you want already? Beth, just hold on, okay," Callie reassured her.

Tony calmly laid out his proposal, all the while pointing out his open window. "You want to get home to your son? I hear this Ixchel wants to get to big New York City? Okay. I can do that. It's all there for you. Two beautiful girls like you. Opportunity, right? Start a new life? Who gets to fucking die in the desert? Who is a piece of shit refugee drowned like a rat in a smuggler's tin-can boat overstuffed with bodies? And who gets to fuck some Johns in Atlantic City for a while? Pay off your fucked up debts? Who gets to do that, eh? You can. Up to you. Your life is a goddamned red carpet spread out before you."

"You want to sell us as prostitutes? Fuck off," Callie said in disbelief. Before they even negotiated with Tony to have them on the ship, he already did it.

Beth said quietly, "Who is that? What's he's talking about?"

Slinger chimed in flatly, "Callie, you should agree, given the situation."

"What?" Callie said. "Fuck no." Angus was shaking his head. She could hear him in her mind's ear. *Never negotiate with terrorists.*

Her heart was trained on Dillon. Her conscience was channeling Ixchel's exodus with Sylvia, the fragile hope that held Mrs. Granger fast to her lost ranch, the dead soul of Rachel under a foreign lake. *You think anybody fucking cares about the mothers or girls who get raped or killed here? Civil war. War on Leftists. War on Drugs. War on Cartels. And nobody blinks. Murders every day of this gang or that cartel arm fighting Evers Corporation or whichever kingpin shot the last guy. And we stay here and do nothing? No, we live black-market lives because that's how the world is. You can do what you want, but I'm fucking going. I'm finding my father again.*

"Listen to Slinger, maybe he's a sensible dickhead after all" said Tony.

Callie tried to play it off, but her tone revealed her worry and helplessness. "You're a slave trader."

"You know what? I'm nothing but a Sam Walton of smack and music. Slinger and I have our businesses. Hector has a good business. America has its low business of depressed men in casinos. The business of the fucking lonely in a crazed country. America is nothing but a country consuming itself in ten thousand different highs and lows. That's my fault? Millions of dirty beds to be made. Empty cocktail tables to clean. Trash to collect. Toilets and shit to clean. In a few days, twenty-three girls who paid me go to New York and Atlantic City to help that fucking muddy superpower turn over. And you know what makes me American most of all? I operate with motherfucking freedom. I've organized my customs. I worked with Evers shipping lines. I do all the fucking work to make something. And what have you done, eh? Bring democracy to Muslim tribes of barbarians? Arrest some soldiers drunk off duty in a mosque? Well, why can't you get your next mission and do what all the fucking working girls do? You fucking clean shit or suck cocks until you and your family are clear. Then you fucking disappear or die. We don't give a fuck. But one thing is damn true: people fucking pay for the filthiest shit human beings create. So, tell me—now that you came down here and found your girl Rachel—what's the harm in fucking global fair trade? Beth, what do you think?"

Beth's voice sounded broken, torn between resigned survival and despair. "Please don't hurt Dillon. If your men want to take me, that's fine."

Callie was shocked at her sister's courage, and her mind raced with a flashing vision: *Slinger on the other end of Tony's phone, scribbling in a notebook to himself, like a child immersed in a fantasy world.*

Tony laughed. "See, she knows. This is how business works." He wagged his finger at Angus now. "You think you want to meet them too? All twenty-three girls? And 'save' them from whatever you think they have here? Okay, so you'll join them. See they already know they have nothing here now. And they decided to leave and work for Hector and make the fucking Great American Dream-Come-True. You see for yourself—number twenty-four, or my guys can go inside and say hello to your sister and son. Your choice."

This had been a military operation precisely planned and timed, and all coordinated within twenty-four hours across two continents of operatives. Callie still held the phone to her ear, reassuring Beth again, Dillon right on the other end of the line, staring at Tony, feeling Ixchel back at the Sunny Mopan Inn, waiting for her. Seeing all of the names and initials from Rachel's files again. The name *Ixchel Cante.*

And as she sat back against the small seat of the beater, she realized now in a new light what had happened to Rachel. She had discovered what the list was when she got down to Slinger's warehouse. Had she tried to convince the girls to not go? Or she was trying to set up Tony too? Something had happened to her after she met up with Ixchel.

"Rachel should have minded her own business," Tony said. He pointed down the valley. "Too many American bodies in Lake Petén are bad for the environment. I could use an American girl to keep the other girls safe. You're experienced. Hector needs high-end people at several of our upscale clubs. Help take care of the younger girls. What's another tour of duty? You want me to call Evers security or let them clean up the mission?"

She felt the branches of a hundred palm trees swaying high up in the canopy. The clouds looked like refugee children who had lost their homes, blown and scattered into an unforgiving sky. The only security she had was the illusion of control that she came from already booking her ticket with Slinger.

"Okay," Callie said, simultaneously faking an acceptance of and recognizing his threat.

Tony smiled at her.

"You hear that Slinger? Two more."

"Yeah, I heard," he said. "I have to go take a swim in the Lake. Meet me at La Lancha Resort tomorrow. I haven't agreed to anything yet." He hung up on Tony, who just laughed again.

Tony made a call and blurted commands. *No mas. Enough.* He turned back to Callie. "Tell your sister the weather should clear up outside. You can let me out in another few minutes. I have a real car waiting."

She took a breath, and then unmuted Beth. "Beth, I can't explain but see if they're gone."

In a few seconds, Beth said, "Yes, they're gone. Callie, what the hell's going on?"

"I will explain when I get back, Beth. That's all I can say right now. Please take care of yourself and Dillon." Beth started to object and curse her. Callie paused. There was no way to explain. "Just please take care of Dillon—she ended the call.

In a few miles, a bright red Ford Mustang was sitting on the side of the road.

Tony hopped out. "See you guys at the resort tomorrow. Can't wait to share an exotic brunch with a couple of loser security guards with bad hair and watch the peasant brownies pretend to like us." He slammed the door, gave a finger back at them, and got into the passenger side of the Mustang. It took off in a growling of valves and road dust.

Callie got out of the back seat and came up to the front. She saw a small quetzal sitting on a tree branch. Its head snapped back and forth manically. Small beads of sweat had formed on Angus's forehead.

"What's wrong with my hair?" He rubbed his thin male pattern. "Why'd he pull all that?" he wondered.

"Insurance," she said.

"Insurance? On what?"

"There's a fifty million dollar shipment sitting in a dock warehouse and a fucking beater cargo ship. And a lot of necks on the line. Out of nowhere two women and a bodybuilder show up in quick succession to "help." In case you don't read the news, cartel security teams do not fuck around. Somebody told him what to do and helped coordinate. It's too professional for Tony—this ain't hiring ex-vets as security for punk concerts. So as far as I see it, they now have three insurance policies against interruptions. Rachel's in a bag on her way home. Ixchel's daughter is on a permanent *Kidnap the Baby* list. Now Beth and Dillon."

Angus nodded following. "So that just leaves a couple of old Kistlers and two herds of dairy cows to visit up in coal country."

Angus turned on her, as if she had miscalculated, as if she could have prevented something. "I thought you told Slinger we were here to get Tony out of his hair. I thought he was the one to worry about."

"I thought so too, at first, but it's Tony and Jorge we have to worry about."

She felt like an agent whose cover might be broken from either side. She called Slinger back.

He answered and said, "So that went well. Glad you brought him down here."

"Rachel was planning on doing something with the girls, wasn't she?"

"Look, Callie, I know she met with the girls, including Ixchel the day before yesterday. I don't think she realized what the fuck she was doing."

"With Ixchel? That can't be." Ixchel hadn't told Callie that the meeting included all of the women.

Slinger hung up.

Callie said, "Let me drive. I can't sit on the fucking helpless side."

They switched seats, and Callie started the car, punching the gas pedal toward Lake Petén and not letting it up.

"Slow down," Angus said. "Pounding this shitter into the dirt is just the illusion of doing something."

She let off the gas. She realized she had been speeding to get to Dillon. There was nothing for miles but gentle palms swaying in the breeze.

Back at the ranch, Callie retreated to her cabana and lay down on the bed. She was worried about the ship and Tony. But she wasn't going to let Dillon get caught in the crosshairs again. If Tony needed insurance policies, so did she. If he did it once, she knew he'd try to use Dillon and Beth again. But for several hours, she came up blank. Her mind was tired from one of the longest days she could remember since Mosul. Then with her eyes closing, she heard his voice in her mind. *Ad novam vitam.* The man who had risked his life with underground information to undo decades of perverted behavior disguised as ministry. Father Tim was resourceful in exercising hidden power. He knew clandestine protection.

She put in the call.

He answered.

"Father Tim, Callie."

She briefly filled him in on her time in Petén.

"I need some help."

"What kind of help? You know I will if I can."

"I need you to pay a visit to a Hector Perez in Atlantic City."

31

Callie and Angus wound their way up a curvy mountain road getting glimpses of the Lake between breaks in the mid-morning jungle sun. The meeting with Slinger and Tony was scheduled for eleven o'clock.

Large black gates were open into the drive, and they drove the beater between two tastefully appointed stone mason entrance pillars, both inset with bronze plaques. One on the left read *La Lancha Resort and Spa*, on the right read *Private. Guests Only.* Callie was surprised there wasn't a customs check point. Security cameras here probably grew in the palms themselves.

They entered the lush eco-tourism resort through black gates that drew back automatically and stopped under the front portico. Valets were waiting and opened their doors. Volcanic rocks topped dribbling fountains and pools. A manicured pathway wound between bougainvillea and lilies, and trim shrubbery led down to a private beach and dock lined with bright red kayaks that stood out in the silvery rain. Cascading terraces housed a set of pools and waterfalls. Callie could see thatched roofs of guest cottages—probably frequented by German engineers, Canadian stock brokers, or Silicon Valley lawyers. Entering this first-class place after what had happened in the last few days disturbed and displaced her. If she had entered a club on the Hamptons, she couldn't have felt more duck out of water. The place was a cocoon of status for those addicted to their importance.

"Ah, home away from home," Angus was saying, waving his arm in a mock panoramic sweep.

"Tony got a room *here*?" Callie said. "Bloody Wrist shows must be selling out."

"More like Tony who is selling out. Some punk promoter he is." Angus said, holding up one of the monogrammed *LL* towels stacked on the pool bar. "Ixchel would have liked the bedspreads here, eh? You think Ixchel and her father would visit us in Philly after we're back?"

Callie stared at him, picturing the scene of the makeshift "family" sitting on the dumpy bed in the dank and depressed Sunny Mopan Inn. Was this really the "single forever" Angus Kistler speaking?

"Visit *us*? Who knows," she said.

That was enough between the two of them. He would get what she hadn't said, just as quickly as if the situation were reversed. She was torn between her respect of Ixchel's grit and her ability to cover up this meeting she and Rachel apparently had with the other girls. So at the moment, the spark of Ixchel Cante was more like the taste of an acidic car battery.

"She lied to us."

Angus said, "I'll take a Bloody Mary," he said to the bartender.

An elderly man in a summer linen blazer with a massive watch on his wrist was reading a copy of *Le Monde* at one of the tables and did not bother to look up. He looked to Callie as if he had been propped there in his ego since the 1930s as old world décor. He said good morning in a French accent.

Callie watched Angus walk across to a table beneath the tallest, upright palm in a small covered patio.

He sat down in the shade, like a polar bear looking for snow.

She followed him.

"She didn't lie to us. She just omitted information. Let's see why before we hang her."

"Sister Greta Catherine used to have us sing, 'Sins of omission go against God's mission'!"

Angus changed the subject. "You know who that is over there?"

"Who? The natty dude?"

"Yeah, Frenchie."

"No. He looks like an exiled Nazi."

"You mean I got one on Callie Byrne? He's Gerard Michel Purrell, the actor and director. He must know Coppola."

Callie shrugged. "Or he's here to act like he's Gerard Michel. Can I ask you something?" Angus didn't bother answering; he knew she would ask anyway and just waited. "Why did you come with me?"

The waiter set his cocktail down with a dark blue umbrella. Angus picked it up and held it over Callie's head. "I would never turn down giving cover to you and Rachel."

Callie picked up a knife from place setting. "Thank you."

He nodded and leaned back and a drop of his cold drink lingered on his beard. In her day, she would have ordered ten mojitos and licked the drop off his beard just to screw around. But she hadn't felt that kind of playfulness ever since her OD. Maybe she was in Guatemala infiltrating drug and sex traffickers, but nothing really made the pain of her failures subside. Other than a few occasions when she could beat people like Hector or Tony.

They waited for Slinger and Tony to show for half an hour. The anxiety of the upcoming meeting was only exacerbated by the luxurious slow pace of the poolside and the spoiled leisure of a has-been French actor staying in a resort owned by Francis Ford Coppola. It was the kind of place where the staff's jobs depended on their secrecy. You had to admire that system: Want a job serving the richest tourists, then shut your mouth.

Somehow it was the waiting for Tony here that made her reanalyze the alliances she knew and realize the whirlwind that had blown through her life by involving herself in this network. At what point had she crossed the border? It was difficult to tell. All of the steps were just simply following one-foot after another: using, finding dealers, the addiction whorl, ODing, cleaning up, and leaving the Grave that night with Rachel's flash drive and note.

"So after we went to Hector's, he told Tony we were coming, eh?"

"No question." His tone implied he was holding something more back.

She hoped Father Tim had made Hector see the light. Then it hit her. "So if we hadn't come—"

"I don't know, Callie, we can't think like that."

Yet she was thinking like that. Coming here could have been the tipping point in the decision to have Rachel killed. Maybe Tony didn't even know that Rachel and Ixchel had met with the other girls? Angus was looking down into his drink. She got up and walked around the pool, her bare shoulder brushing the wall of plantings and unnamable tropical flowers that exploded with oranges, pinks, and reds, an overload of Georgia O'Keefe stamens and petals. The landscapers must have spent a fortune maintaining the lush blanket of artificial nature. As far as Callie was concerned, they might as well have been plastic.

"There ought to be labels on all these fucking flowers," she said., as if the earth had grown a mysterious complexity just to create an intense confusion.

Angus waved his hand at her. *Full of Byrne nonsense again.*

Just then she heard boot heels clicking on the patio cement. Slinger came bobbing into the pool area.

"Bonjour, Monsieur G., top of the morning. I'll have your case squared this week, I swear," Slinger said as he passed.

Gerard flicked *Le Monde* at him, but did not look up. "I shall believe that next week when next week is last week."

Slinger pulled his hair back off his neck, and let it go behind his shoulders. His untucked plaid shirt, jeans, and sandals somehow seemed appropriate as he crossed the patio. He sat down and immediately started talking, nodding back at Gerard. "Clever asshole. Stays here for months at a time to escape the Paris summer tourists. So. We get this shit sorted out over a stiff Guatemalan coffee with shots of mescal and a shot in the head if need be to start the day. Jorge and a few of his men came along with me, but I made them stay outside. They are concerned of course. Francis doesn't really like us here, but what can we do? We go where the business is."

"So before Tony gets here—" Callie said.

"I haven't had my coffee, yet," Slinger held up his hand. "I can't listen to anybody else in the morning unless I have an hour of complete silence and three coffees laced with mescal. Sometimes with coke if I'm feeling tired and have to fly. But never milk. Lactose intolerant. Which is funny because growing up we lived most days on milk and fucking peanut butter on Wonder Bread."

Callie looked at Angus quickly. *This is the guy we're doing business with to get Tony?*

Angus did what he always did. Shrugged with the barest minimal movement and sat back to sip his cocktail.

Then he arrived.

Tony stood in the entranceway to the pool, and scowled at everything in the bright sunshine.

32

Tony clearly would not have been anywhere near the harsh light of day if he could have helped it. He wore a Bloody Wrist logo black t-shirt, a Hawaiian patterned bathing suit, and his perpetual sulky expression. He carried a towel draped over his left hand, and Callie knew Tony was a lefty. He definitely would have a pistol under the towel, just in case.

He sat down opposite Slinger and between Callie and Angus. "What are they doing here?"

Slinger didn't respond, so the four of them sat.

A waiter approached. Tony flipped him the finger (his second favorite appendage). The waiter showed no surprise and retreated no differently than if he'd served a table of grandmothers.

More idiotic male stand-off followed, until Callie just couldn't take it. "You two want me to get a therapist? Because we don't have all day. I booked a kayak and a massage, and I'm not going to miss it."

Slinger said, "He's the one wants product. I have no need to change one damn thing. So go on. Impress me."

Tony seemed frustrated that even though others had now spoken, he was somehow on the spot. He squirmed in his chair and puffed out his chest and folded his tattooed blue arms for a minute. "Twenty-twenty."

"Of what? The shipment? You can go fuck yourself."

"No, I'll pay twenty percent more than your present regional guy for twenty percent."

"And why would you do that? Why don't you just buy from somebody who likes you, although I can see how that might be a challenge for you."

Tony looked at Callie now, enjoying the pleasure of showing off his business acumen. "Because in addition to Atlantic City, I'm getting into Hollywood."

"And we care because?" Callie said.

"Charlie Sheen."

"What the fuck are you talking about?" Angus asked now.

Tony looked at Slinger and smiled. "I know a guy who supplies Charlie Sheen when he's in New York. So I called him and asked if they needed a supplier. He called me back. They're in. I called Hector and Slinger figuring we have ourselves a fucking party! Charlie been taking heat again in the media. He wants to get out of LA for a while. How about that fucking idea, eh? So he's going on the down low in Brooklyn. I supply fucking Charlie Sheen, and he comes to some of our shows and rages. We'll sell more shit that entire ship can carry. So we're going to straighten this shit out."

Callie couldn't believe the delusions of celebrity Tony had about himself. She had tried to tell Slinger, but there was nothing like seeing it firsthand. She and Angus waited to see where this would go. It was just crazy and high class enough that maybe it was how things were done? The punk club circuit was no Charlie Sheen Tiger Blood of media obsession, drugs, and liquor.

Slinger sat back and laughed. "You have got to be fucking kidding me? That's all we need is an actor freaked out on a bender. Too bad you didn't supply Philip Seymour Hoffman and get snatched up by now."

Tony tried to hold his poker face, but his forehead scrunch was a tell that he had turned defensive. "I tried to sell to him, but the fucker died."

"Warm sentiment," Slinger said.

"Well, okay, this was before I heard everything that happened down here. Look, a fucking Hollywood celebrity should calm you down. They feel like God's generous to them. We get a party started. We make friends. We let past shit glide into a happy fog. Tony Maul, music promoter. Backed by you, a guy who knows the Evers network inside and out. You want to move product to some fucking piss-poor fuckers who gotta steal from their mothers to get a fix? It's business. And in good business we all make a shit load of money and be fucking happy. And we all get too stoned and naked to care." He smiled at Callie, but his eyes said, *Don't say a fucking word, or I kill Dillon and Beth.* "We do this deal, Tony Maul and Slinger are goddamned bragging to everybody that we're LA's New Dealers of Choice. It's fucking brilliant. Just try to find a fucking problem."

"I like a man with delusional ambitions. Traditionally, you know, that's the perfect customer of Capitalism," Slinger said. "But I'm not selling you shit unless I get something out of it besides your twenty percent."

There was a long pause, as she tried to absorb the semblance of a plan that now involved Charlie Fucking Sheen in addition to her supposedly being used as pawn to keep her quiet.

Callie looked at Slinger, reading his face and the hand he was playing.

"I tried to tell you," Callie said to Tony.

"And what would that be?" Tony asked.

Slinger sucked on a cigarette, looking around the table, his eyes puffed open, peering at Callie and Tony, trying to figure out if Tony knew he was being played. He exhaled and spoke at the same time, "Okay, Callie agreed to go to Atlantic City. So she and Ixchel are going with the rest of the girls. And her baby. But they get there free of charge. Or you get shit and I'll have Evers schedule you for an ocean-going barge ride."

Tony looked at Callie. He couldn't believe it. "Fuck off."

"Ixchel and Callie make it to the lovely port of Newark and back home to Philly, then fine, you'll get your cut. I don't care who the fuck you sell to. That's your problem. But those are my terms.

Callie Byrne and Ixchel Cante, free and clear. They get off the ship. They stroll on their merry fucking way."

Tony looked at Callie. He was pissed now.

"I don't know about that."

"You got no choice, Agent to the Stars," Callie said.

"Why?"

Slinger answered. "Because somebody—meaning you—is going to fuck this up like an amateur. And I'm not done. I think you should have to ride with them. That's why I'm not moving product anywhere unless I know where everybody is when I do it. And the best way for me to know where everybody is, is to put all of you inside a cargo container and not let anybody out until my shit is over with. Except him." He pointed at Angus. "He's going to run decoy. If he learns how to navigate, he'll make to Florida. But one way or another, every one of you needs to get the fuck out of my life. And what better way than to ship you stacked up like fucking sacks of coffee."

Despite Tony glaring at her, Callie did not flinch from the truth. She really had no idea who was her friend and who her enemy beside Angus. But she could feel her pride and anger on her face at being treated like a piece of meat in the middle of two dogs.

Slinger nodded at Callie. "What the fuck did you think would happen to you when you came down here for your friend? So now you can help smuggle a bunch of girls north and get the fuck out of here at the same time." Slinger was good, she had to admit. "Everyone has to break into America somehow, even Americans."

Across the pool, A tall man wearing a trucker mesh style POW baseball hat entered the pool area hobbling with a metallic cane and a spine that looked twisted from decades of sitting behind truck wheels and bar stools. He wore faded denim jeans, an American flag t-shirt, and dusty construction boots. A thick wallet chain hung to skull-shaped outline in his back pocket. His thick, gray walrus mustache twitched, and his close-cropped hair was classic American Legion.

Slinger waved him over with a flick of his hand.

"Who's that?" asked Callie.

The POW man walked up to the table behind Tony. Tony didn't know who to look at. The man swung his cane as quick as any lead-off hitter for the Phillies. It crushed into the side of Tony's skull with a bony *clang!* and Tony fell forward over the table. Then POW grabbed Tony's hair on both sides of his head, and before Tony could do anything, POW was smashing his face into the pole of the table's umbrella. Tony struggled to twist out, but the man continued to smash Tony's head into the umbrella. Blood ran from his eye socket and nose and was splashing into polka dots on the white painted wood.

Slinger started asked him repeatedly, "You had Rachel killed? You had Rachel killed, right?"

Tony tried to nod, between pole smashes.

Slinger looked at Callie. *Good enough?* Callie nodded. It wouldn't be good in any court of law, but she had enough for some kind of justice.

Finally, Slinger waved his hand. POW took Tony and flung him back down into his seat. His face and head were mashed up pretty good, but nothing fatal. He was still conscious.

Slinger had not changed his expression at all. He reached over and picked up one of Tony's teeth and dropped it into a water glass. A root floated up in a swirl. Tony was dazed and saying "fuck" repeatedly between his pain. He grabbed for a napkin to cover his face.

Slinger nabbed it first, and said, "This is the gentleman who will be in Jersey when you get there. A fine member of the Teamsters Longshoreman union. He calls me that my shit is clear, and Ixchel Cante and Callie Byrne have returned to their regularly scheduled lives, then, you, you piece of shit punk, you get five percent of the shipment. After that, we'll see what the future holds. Half down, then I schedule departure."

Tony garbled through the blood, spit, and his hands holding his head. "I want some kind of insurance. Or I will blow your fucking head off right here."

"Insurance?" He threw the napkin at Tony. "Your insurance is that you can put half down—that's two hundred fifty grand. Or you can shoot me, and Rikert will knock you out, put you in his favorite convertible Mercedes trunk, and deliver you to the Evers security network so they can have fun with you before they tow you out to sea. And if that happens, I will personally make sure Bloody Wrist Productions becomes the property of Callie Byrne. You try to think about it for a few days. I have all the time in the world. You're the one with a deadline that nobody but you gives a shit about. Because I do things lockdown tight. I mean so professional that nobody knows the difference between FedEx and Evers Shipping Corporation by the time we're done. Now, why don't you find the ice machine and hobble back to your room. I would like to have brunch with my team here."

Callie noticed that Gerard, the pool boy, and the bartender had disappeared.

Tony got up, grabbed one of the *LL* towels, and left holding it to his face.

Angus looked at Slinger, "You're going to sell five percent to him?"

Slinger spit an ice cube into his glass, and swung his hair. "Hell no."

33

Slinger got up to greet the POW. "Now to proper introductions. Callie, Angus, Mister Mitchell Rikert."

Mitchell flicked his cane at them. His voice sounded like a desert cactus with emphysema. His mouth was covered by the biker mustache hanging over this lip. "Pleasure." The trucker let himself fall into a chair and hung the cane off the umbrella braces above them. It swung in Callie's face with remnants of Tony's scalp stuck to it. A rain started to fall in large, sporadic drops.

"Well, that was an entrance, there Mitchell," Angus said. "I think Tony got the message."

"So who was that?" Mitchell asked in a distracted way as he surveyed the resort, his good leg bursting into a jackhammer of restless quivering. He spoke in his throat cancer rasp. "Why we out here in the fucking rain, Slinger?"

"We needed some privacy."

"Privacy? What the fuck's that?" Rikert scoffed. "Crime is the only privacy left."

"So you two are apparently old friends," Callie said, more making a joke than expecting an answer.

Rikert took out a cigarette and tamped it with admirable flare, as if opening a court session. "Nine years ago. I was driving a load of mattresses from the port of LA to Vegas. They also happened to be fucking chock full of Evers Shipping Corporation grade-A crackie coke. On my way, one of my guys called me. He had a bulk order to a VIP in the Palm Casino, said to bring the delivery there first. When I got there, there was one dead drunk and stoned John Slinger. I told him what I had, and we hauled three mattresses up the freight elevator and into the middle of the Sky Villa penthouse living room. He made me help him and three strippers set them up like a teepee. You know, balanced against each other like this. Damndest thing ever in my life. Then he made us all sit under them while he slit each of them with a bowie knife. I never left that night. My truck sat with a couple hundred drive trains. The next morning, I took all of them with me, we delivered the load, and then I took them for a three-hour ride in a friend of mine's Uncle Sam Bammer, a monster truck designed from the Betsy Ross flag and fucking three-story wheels. Been with him ever since."

"See, I told you. Even Americans have to break into America. But that was a three life times ago. I was a stupid fuck. Now I'm middle manager ready to cash in my pension and disappear, preferably alive."

Callie just tried to absorb the absurdity of what was happening.

"Drink?" Angus offered.

Rikert nodded quietly, then hacked his larynx out and blew smoke at the same time. The little circle of men was getting that claustrophobic pressure around it.

Angus waved at the pool boy, who had miraculously reappeared. "Callie?"

"No, thanks." She didn't want to be around anybody. Everyone seemed to be living in an international police state with a vast network of informants. The arrival of Tony and Rikert had made everything worse. The gated eco-resort seemed an immaculately tended façade of posh corruption, as if every business were blood money. She could have been one of the beautiful, savvy staff. But right now her soul was heavy with the lives she had hauled around inside her, like a broken down fishing boat that sat off shore, stalled, low in the water, and covered in fish guts, stink, and old nets. Maybe the Catholic nuns working the slums of Philly or Rio or Mumbai were right after all—serve the poor and love the god that made the crappy world they were born to. She just couldn't do it though.

"Why are you protecting me and Ixchel like this?"

Slinger had taken out a black notebook and was scribbling. His head looked to be in a minor convulsion, his hands battling the shakes.

She reached out and with two fingers, gently pinched the top of his pen to stop his writing.

He looked up. "I like your hair. And because Ixchel will be useful to me some day. And because you asked for my help, I'm hoping you'll be useful to me too."

Callie knew that would be all she got, and it was plenty.

"I'm going down to the Lake," she said, getting up.

Angus and Mitchell moved themselves under a cabana of sofas and pillows for lazing and drinking. Between the cane and the crutches, it was like a senior home for hobbled cops and robbers. Callie watched a pool boy lay out towels for three of the ugliest men she had ever seen in her life. Mitchell lumbered down onto a lounge chair, a giraffe navigating doll furniture, a stretched example of the human male. Angus propped himself up for an easy afternoon. Slinger, the contradictory specimen of a careless, mad, and manic human race, sat beneath the umbrella still scribbling away at whatever crazed phrases rattled in that half-fried mind.

Ignoring the gentle rains, Callie headed down the winding path to the dock and walked to the end. There was an attendant in a booth. She pointed at a kayak, and he pointed at the skies but waved that it was up to her. She picked up a life jacket, threw it in the front compartment of a red kayak, and climbed down into the seat. She pushed off the dock, and began paddling with powerful strokes, pulling the water as hard.

She paddled toward the middle of the Lake as the pellets stung her face. Her arms burned after several hundred yards, but she continued to pull, pushing herself into a sprinting pain. Finally, when her lungs were bursting and her back, shoulders, and arms exhausted, she let up. She sat back and the kayak glided to a stop. The afternoon rains poured down on her. Rain ran down her unmoving face, and she felt her dreads heavy behind her head.

Rachel had sunk somewhere in the Lake beneath her. She knew now Tony would be calling Evers Corporation on John Slinger, and who knows, Slinger may be calling Evers about a problem with Tony. Either way, there was a deep lake beneath her and mountains on all sides.

Low, meager waves slapped the boat from the west side in the late day wind as blankets of rains were fine gray curtains up the Lake. The kayak rocked. She thought how easy it would be to roll over into the airless desperation into the unknown. She could feel the sad threads of a heart that used to be Callie Byrne. But her torso remained physically balanced. How can grief and failure have no gravitational pull when they feel so dead heavy? Her legs stretched out in front of her into the bow. There were extractions to be done, lives to be disentangled, a cycle of desperation to break. She just couldn't see where any of those lines were headed. They were like the criss-cross bungee cords laced across the red plastic in front of her.

She needed to stay above water because Dillon was still in the world with her, because Rachel and Ixchel deserved somebody to care what happened. Because she deserved somebody to care about her. Because she had to get in a cargo container and make some good come from all this. As the water streamed down her face, she remembered Angus holding the tiny paper umbrella over her head.

She pulled one of the bungees as far as it would stretch, and snapped it back on her own hand.

"Jesus, Callie, you can't avoid reality sitting in a fucking kayak."

She picked the paddle up resting across the cockpit, and turned back toward the dock.

34

It had been almost a week since the La Lancha meeting. Like the still tropical air, nothing had moved. Slinger had received no wire from Latin Leather in New York, and Tony had apparently gone into rehab to get his face back and lie low. Ixchel and Sylvia were in hiding somewhere. Father Tim had emailed that a friendly visit had occurred at Hector Perez's apartment and Angus security had been told not to leave until further notice from him. He also faithfully emailed three times a day with security updates from Angus's detail: Beth and Dillon were safe at home and all quiet. But it only seemed a temporary a calm.

Callie spent her days inside the leather warehouse doing nothing but hauling dollies loaded with leather bags from one finishing station to the shipping room, where there was a team of Jorge's men sewing packets of heroin in scent-proof packing into the linings.

As she loaded one dolly toward the end of the day, a local woman who spoke no English walked by her, locked eyes for a split second, and with a graceful sleight of hand, slipped a small slip of paper into one of the bags outer pockets.

She just as quickly removed it and slipped it into her jeans.

Meet me tomorrow at The Happy Market in town. Ixchel had finally emerged.

The next day was a local holiday, and the warehouse was operating with a few of Jorge's men. It was ostensibly closed to keep up appearances. The streets and houses were flying blue and white flags. Mrs. Granger had said there would be parades of little smiling cheerleaders marching.

Christ, how perfect, a celebration, Callie thought as she and Angus drove into San Olvidado to meet Ixchel.

Mrs. Granger was relieved. "Thank the Lord, she's at least still alive."

"She's a survivor," Callie said, thinking of the meeting with the other girls and Rachel. She needed to know what happened at that meeting. "But yes, it would have been nice if she had given us some clue where she's been for a week."

The Happy Market was a bodega on the corner of the block draped in blue and white crepe paper, strands of lights, and garlands for the holiday. Underneath a large wooden sign that read in Spanish, *Grandfather Speaks, Nobody Listens*, three old men sat wearing bright blue button-down shirts for the holiday but speaking as casually as they would have any other time of the year.

Ixchel was holding Sylvia sitting on the front steps. Callie could tell Ixchel was annoyed by the far off fireworks celebrating nothing but a history that didn't matter to her. "Can you hold Sylvia while I go get some things?" Ixchel said. She seemed distracted and depressed.

She handed Sylvia to Angus, who sat down on the step outside to wait. Callie watched Angus's face. He looked like a terrified bear holding a bag of eggs for the first time in his life. She saw the old men stare at Ixchel's body, groping with their eyes. Through a flimsy screen door, Callie followed Ixchel down a narrow aisle of brown Formica flooring. They picked up diapers, toiletries, three cans of beans, and a cake.

Ixchel explained, "We're going to my mother's grave today."

Callie nodded. She was confused but said, "Okay."

Ixchel sensed her unspoken question but left it unanswered until she picked up some plantains. "I won't be here for the Day of the Dead, and I never liked Independence Day parades. Usually you make fiambre salad for the grave. But she liked cake better than salad. And I like the Day of the Dead better than Independence Day. So I'm getting her a cake. And we're going now."

It made Callie think of Beth and her mother sitting next to her at the pool. Her mother was waiting for news other than that Rachel was dead, and she had nothing to tell her yet. Callie had never bought a cake for her live mother let alone for a dead one.

The four of them walked together out of town quietly while people shot off more small-time fireworks and got ready for the town parade. Men were busy trying to finish off painting psychedelic mosaics on giant kites along the Lake front, the wind gusting and flipping the kites so that the boys had to hold them while the men worked. They happily yelled for Ixchel and Callie to come look at their big kites, pointed to their creations, ghosts of joy spun into intricate star-shaped patterns of reds, oranges, purples, and bright blues.

They walked down a long dirt road across a pasture, the hills looking brown and uninspired next to all the celebration in the little town.

They arrived at a cement-walled cemetery, plain, with a simple wooden gate. Inside, Callie saw plots of painted plaster humps, pure white crosses, mums and garlands and wreaths hanging from painted gravestones and body boxes; lumps of sea foam, eggplant, and azure grave markers made the ground look like a jigsaw puzzle.

"On the Day of the Dead, we come here with picnics, and we fly these big kites in the sky. We serve peppers and beef on a stick and all kinds of food. I won't be here and I wanted to show you her place."

Callie saw short dirt humps that appeared fresh.

Ixchel walked around them indifferently.

They arrived at a plain, unpainted cement headstone with an archway and shelf shaped into it for offerings. For the quickest of moments, Ixchel prayed—one sentence, perhaps—and then she placed the chocolate cake on the shelf next to a bundle of yellow flowers that had been left by some other relative.

"Slinger says the government killed her."

"Why?" Callie asked, confused.

"He says Teddy Granger told him that a PNC car ran him off the road into her, that some of the local military were always threatening him for helping the guerillas and locals kill some of their men during the war," Ixchel said. "He killed her, and it wasn't his fault."

"Was your mother from this area?"

"No, she came to Petén after the dictator Montt started the genocide of the Ixil people in '82. They killed her entire family and buried them in mass pits. She fled to the mountains and then got to Petén by going village to village for six months. She just kept going north. So I'm even lucky my mother is here in front of me."

Callie read the name: *Sylvia Cante* written in marker on a simple yellow cross. She wanted to ask about the meeting with the girls, but it seemed the wrong time. There was some kind of intimate trust Ixchel had opened by bringing her to this spot.

"Is this why you don't want to be in San Olvidado?" Angus asked.

"Partly," Ixchel said. "But the rest is some life I can imagine but don't have here."

"Do you know what your father does in New York?"

"Last time he wrote me he was digging ditches on a new golf course He uses false papers to work up there. He is scared they will deport him."

Angus wondered, "Why him and not millions of others?"

"You tell me? Your friend Rachel was a desaparecido. We have thousands we will never find."

"I know, I'm sorry," Callie said.

Ixchel didn't react at all, as if she expected as much. "Lots of people come to see Slinger, and he has tried to help them even though he works with Evers Corporation. But I don't think they find anybody either. Sometimes people find old clothes in the jungle but no body."

Finally, Callie needed to confront her. "Ixchel, I know you and Rachel met with the other girls before Rachel disappeared."

Ixchel's full brown eyes, her scarred face from Jorge had a kind of unbreakable hope, but she looked at Callie with a settled sadness. "We were smoking a joint at the ranch together on the first night. She had come to me on the front porch of the house. She told me that she knew I was supposed to be smuggled with other girls by Jorge somehow. She asked me how we were supposed to go—a bus across to Mexico? Walking over the border in Texas? She was worried about us."

"I know, but why didn't you tell me?"

"Would it matter?"

"Knowing the truth matters," Callie said.

"I didn't want to admit to you that maybe what I did got her murdered. I thought you would think I was to blame."

"Did you know that holding a meeting with the other girls would be risky?"

"Yes, of course. Jorge would try to burn the rest of my face off if he found out. But it was Rachel's idea. She said that if we all found a secret location and met and talked together, that maybe she could help. She wanted to check everybody's names and get photos of us all. She said that if we wanted to, she would help us try to get asylum instead. She would go to the FBI when we made it to the States and try to get us out of prostitution."

"Where was the meeting?" Angus asked.

"We met at an old fishing camp that is not used any more along the Lake."

"So how did Jorge find out?" Callie said.

"One of the girls."

"One of the girls? Really?"

Ixchel was rubbing the dark hair on the soft skull of Sylvia. "Yes. She tried to trade the information in return for having her entire debt wiped out when she got to America. She went to Jamón's one night."

Callie and Angus were quiet for a few moments.

"Do you have lots of money?" she asked Angus.

Angus was sitting with his back against a grave marker. "I work security. And been hooked on painkillers for three years. No, I don't have money."

Callie had never heard him admit he was addict before. He had just said it aloud probably for the first time.

Ixchel went over to him and sat with her back against the other part of the grave.

She lifted Angus's head, which was staring at the grass between his legs.

"It's okay. Isn't there a place in Philadelphia to get help?"

Callie pictured her room at the Mercy House, remembered her own sessions in the rehab unit, and her own regimen of methadone.

Angus gave the smallest nod.

Callie looked down at the Lake. It was a beautiful blue. Perhaps because of the colorful markers around them, it looked alive with blue. She could see wooden skiffs far out, sitting still, fishing poles leaning into the sun like plants. Callie could feel Ixchel's hopes hanging on the other side of the Lake, in a mist of never-going-to-happen over the mountains.

She felt Ixchel's heart thumping through her slender limbs and her hopeful mind, saying, *I'm going to live in New York. I already live Not Here.* She was no different than other grunts from a unit shipping out, who had walked around the base in Mosul one day with a directness and connection to every movement on the base, even the MPs. But the sooner they got to shipping out day, the thicker the glaze of distant absence became. They were lame ducks who didn't care.

Ixchel shook her head at Callie and, it seemed, at the Lake itself. "I'm sorry I helped do that meeting. I thought it was a chance to get out from Jorge. I didn't mean to get her in the middle of it. I just don't want to make blankets on the street like Lita Ruez and my mother and those women and do my wash in this awful Lake. That's all I can say."

"It's okay, it's not your fault," Callie said.

Ixchel looked at Angus. "Do you understand I hate that Lake. I hate this town. I hate Jorge, Slinger, and all the big invisible men running this little country. That's what I told Slinger. The same thing. And you know what he said? 'It's just a question of how the world will humiliate you. At least you know me!' And he laughed, flipping his long hair around the way he does. He's right, I do have other friends, too. The other girls packing leather. We can weave in the streets with our grandmothers or take our chances.

Callie didn't say anything. She just leaned forward with her arms crossed on her knees. Ixchel picked up her dreads and examined them with her hands, tenderly straightening them.

"Colocha," Ixchel said. "Mestiza Colocha." Curly half-breed. Ixchel let Callie's hair drop against her back. "Some of us have to take what we get, Colocha. Even break the law to live. Or we'll be sitting in a front doorway generation after generation weaving the same pattern until the end of time. And some women can live under that blanket, and others will go insane if they don't throw it off."

Callie let Ixchel wind and unwind her dreads behind her.

She watched Angus in front of her, staring into the twisted grasses between his knees, as if the gnarled and matted ground hid an answer about how to untwist a Mobius strip of made of yourself, your desires, and your slow, dying life.

Ixchel suddenly stopped, "Angus, you should take us dancing."

Angus looked up, "Dancing?"

"There is a club here. Open to 4 A.M."

"Why me?"

"Because. My mother loved to dance. And you look—what is the expression—light on your feet. Even on crutches I bet you can dance."

"You were in hiding for over a week, now you want to go out to a club?" Callie asked. "That doesn't seem smart."

"It's not smart, it's defiant. Let them come for me if they want, at least I will be dancing when they come instead of hiding in a closet underneath the stairs."

"You were at the ranch the whole time?" Angus asked. "I was all over the Department looking for you when you weren't at the inn."

"Mrs. Granger fed me and I would sit in the parlor and look at Vogue while everybody was gone." Ixchel was smiling. "I know how to live in hiding—right where they will not look. But you know what happened?"

Callie finished her thought. "You started to talk to yourself in solitary confinement, and you realized you're too crazy to listen to."

Ixchel pulled her dreads, and kissed Callie on both cheeks. "Exactly."

Callie struggled with a cruel dilemma that seemed to plague Ixchel: how do you live your life if you can't find the beginning?

35

A week and how many hundred leather jackets stuffed with heroin later, Tony still had not paid, and Slinger seemed to waiting for a neuro signal in his brain that had not fired.

But an hour ago, Tony sent Callie and Slinger a text.

Center of Flores. Basketball court. Noon.

Slinger and Callie drove up a narrow side street in Flores, while Angus and Ixchel stayed at the ranch with Sylvia.

He stopped at the end of the street where the plaza started. A large palm tree in the center of the plaza appeared to be melting into the barren cement walkways through the palms. A basketball court between three worlds sat empty in the center plaza of Flores, next to the Nuestra Senorita church and a long colonial-era building.

Slinger nodded casually. "I feel civilized here, don't you? Between God, the law, and the three-point line. What could be more Catholic? Reminds me of Saturdays at St. Helena's gym and the smell of sneakers and wood polish."

"You see him?" Callie asked.

"We're here first. I always make sure I show up first to business meetings. Tony said noon, and he doesn't strike me as a man with much foresight."

"So Ixchel came back from Belize," Slinger said, putting his truck in park to wait.

"How'd you know that?"

"Because Angus went back to the Sunny Mopan Inn a few days ago, and the room was empty."

Callie didn't attempt to bluff. "Stubborn girl. Just couldn't wait it out where it was safe."

"So where is Shadow Girl now?"

Callie looked at him. "I don't know."

"Liar."

"I don't know. But if I did, I wouldn't tell you any way. Who knows what you'd spill if they hooked up car batteries to your balls."

"I know what I would say. Goddamned everything I could think of. But you better realize I'm on your side. I'd be happy as you to nail Tony Maul. And I just met him the other day for that wonderful brunch of Bloody Marys with umbrellas."

"So if you're on our side, how do I know she, Sylvia, and I aren't going to end up with Hector when the ship gets to New York?"

"You don't. But that doesn't mean I want you to." He was tapping the wheel with this fingers impulsively.

"I will get Tony out of my son's life if it kills me. And if I do that, Ixchel can go where she wants."

"Easier said than done."

"Tell me about it. I'm here with you aren't I?" she said. "What did you mean when you said Shadow Girl?"

"Ixchel. Mayan for Mother of Shadows. Sylvia. Nice name. Sylvan wooded glades of dreams. Callie, Calliope Crashing. Should I keep going?"

"Nah, I got it." Callie remembered how she had named Dillon after her great-grandfather, a brick layer with the Kelly of Grace Kelly business. She looked at this expat crazy and tried to avoid thinking about how Dillon and Sylvia's lives were dependent on how he handled Tony in the middle of the Flores main square.

"And you, Slinger of Darkness."

Slinger started reciting, "'This is the first account, the first narrative. There was neither man, nor animal, birds, fish, crabs, trees, stones, caves, ravines, grasses, nor forests; there was only the sky.

The surface of the earth had not appeared. There was only the calm sea and the great expanse of the sky. There was nothing brought together, nothing which could make a noise, nor anything which might move, or tremble, or could make noise in the sky. There was nothing standing; only the calm water, the placid sea, alone and tranquil. Nothing existed. There was only immobility and silence in the darkness, in the night.'"

"What's that?"

"The Popol Vuh. From the Mayan creation myth. Whether we live or die, ordinary earthly business continues as it has for eons. Government payoffs to file, shipping agreements to be made, family squabbles between exes to fight. In my opinion, Sylvia has joined one really long bad story."

"Maybe we can change that." Then Callie saw him. "There he is."

Tony was exiting the same Department building where she and Ixchel had met Inspector Piñada.

What was he doing in there? Paying off Piñada?

He looked like an American insect that had flown in with the late summer locusts in the same white cotton button-down shirt, green pants, alligator boots, and two bulbous aviator mirrors for eyes peering out. He was anxious enough that he lit a bud to ease his mind. He halted. She could see him *issssshwoped* in a deep toke. He was pretending to idle casually. Even the way Tony carried himself grated on Callie, with his self-importance, as if he had just swallowed a *Rolling Stone* article about himself or a tabloid photographer was going to sell a picture of him to *People*.

Tony saw Slinger's truck up the alley and nodded to them toward one end of the basketball court near the palm.

"He wanted us to see him coming out of the police building. Let's go see what over complicated bullshit he has concocted this time," Callie said.

"Let's go see if he has a face," Slinger said.

They got out and crossed the square.

As Callie approached she said, "You like basketball? Or is this place in Fodor's *Guatemala!*"

Tony turned around, a disgusted curl in his mouth, his face still a set of large polka dots of blueish-purple bruises and a cut lip. "You're lucky I don't shoot you in the head right here," Tony said to Slinger.

Slinger walked passed Tony and started circling the palm slowly, hands behind his back.

"I feel lucky."

"You got my money, right? I'll go along with your deal, okay, for fuck's sake. So I wanna know when the ship leaves."

"No, I didn't get your money."

"I fucking wired it this morning to the account Hector gave me. I came all the way down here, and you have some sucked out string bean with collapsed veins beat the shit out of me. I didn't kill Rachel. I can't help it what Jorge did down here. Now I've paid you what you want. You in this to do business or to fuck people over?"

Tony sat on the decorative wall around the court, and the hot stone burned through his pants, so he stood up again.

It was the perfect moment to get on with the plan she and Slinger had talked over on their way. The key was to keep Tony's manic mind guessing and spinning.

"I'm wondering the same now too. You know who killed Rachel," Callie said to Slinger.

"You *know* nothing," Slinger said to her.

"I know you're dealing with the same people who have been drowning uncooperative women in the Lake down there."

Tony took a swig of water, watching them carefully, wondering where this was going but starting to show some relief that Callie was falling in line. "Good to see you know now who is helping take care of Beth and Dillon."

She wanted to say something to Tony like, *You touch Dillon and I will blow your dick off. And I have a set of files listing every girl headed for Hector's escort service in Atlantic City sent to me by a manager working in Latin Leather inventory who stumbled across*

*it. She met with these same girls and the next day comes up missing?
It's good I've backed it up in twenty places with five different people
I know, with annotated notes.*

Instead, she said to Slinger, "He's right."

Slinger got irritated and Callie had no idea if he was playing
it or serious. "What did you want me down here for, Tony? To talk
about Rachel Martelli?"

Tony was shifting on his feet now. He sounded deliberately
cloying. "No, I told you. I wanted to tell you in person that I'm
good with your deal."

Slinger paced slowly around the court, like an asylum patient
around an obsessive vision. "I have a ship full of tight leather chaps
just for your Latin Leather regional sales. So you want to make a
killing, eh?" His voice sounded like a bird of paradise was blooming
in his mind, an orange and warm idea that looked beautiful and full
of life. Callie could see it made Tony enraged to think an old hippie
stoner like him was blowing up his scheme, his face grim and exhausted, purple, red, and enraged from the sun.

The three of them stood, conspicuous and cocked. Callie really
did have no idea at that moment which man might be more of an
enemy.

"Look around, Promotor Tony Maul. This plaza's full of people," Slinger said, low and smooth as he could. "It's laid back down
here, man. Relax. Your money made it. I was just shitting you. We're
going to put it to productive use."

"Then why the hell didn't you say so? I had to leverage everything I fucking had to get you that money. I don't turn some product
over, they'll throw me off the roof of one of their nightclubs."

"Because you have put two years' worth of networking and
operations at risk of being jettisoned into the fucking ocean like a
pile of fucking garbage. And I don't deal in garbage. I wanted to see
what I thought of you in person. I'm a visual learner, Tony, I don't
deal well with aural communication methods over fiber-optic lines. I
wanted to see the man who wants to ship girls to the States with all
the sweat of fifteen hundred Argentinian and Guatemalan coca and
cattle farmers in the Evers network."

"Here I am. Out for a fucking stroll to see the dirty Sanchezes."

"Is he always this pleasant?" Slinger asked Callie.

"Yes."

Slinger was around the other side of the palm tree, walking one foot precisely in front of the other, as if walking a meditative maze. "If you don't like my ways of doing business, you can always head back to New York and wait with all of the other bungholes for somebody else's shit to get to your music clubs."

Angus came crutching his way across the plaza out of nowhere.

The three of them just stared at his big oafish guy swinging himself toward them, toking a half burnt joint at the same time. He spoke through a tight chest and clamped mouth, then let out the smoke, "Afternoon. Having a party?"

Tony looked at Angus, scanning quickly for a weapon and his hands.

Callie had told him to arrive after ten minutes. She was glad he was there, but immediately worried about Ixchel and Sylvia being left alone. She could sense everything around her now, as if her skin were attached to the garden plot, her bones part of the palm, her hair a flower where a hummingbird poked and reversed, thrust and pulled back, dove and escaped around a bird of paradise that looked like a punk drummer with dyed spikes and a long nose. A mutt was trotting off toward the lazy Lake Petén Itzá his tail hung like a spent member.

"So that's it then. We've all met. We've had our fun. So you just let me know when the ship heads out." Tony said to Slinger, then glared at Callie with a *you're mine* squint.

Slinger continued to peer at the ground in front of him. "If you want your shit moving any time soon, why'd you go see Piñada right before we met and right in front of us."

She saw Tony do a quick assessment of his position. "I needed to be sure the police were on everybody's side, not just yours. What's wrong with that?"

Slinger paced like a slow robot, thinking. "You're getting your five percent. And this beautiful creature, Callie, you're going on the ship and back to Philly to buy a minivan, right?" Callie looked at Tony. It was not hard to sound angry and resentful, with a coating of compliant. "I don't have a fucking choice."

Tony grinned, "Thanks for the ride from the airport."

"And my goddaughter, Ixchel, right?"

Goddaughter? Callie and Angus immediately pretended to know this fact.

Slinger continued, "Two smart ladies. I bet they'll develop nice franchises in Atlantic City. You and Hector have made quite a little play up there, haven't you? And there goes a girl I've looked after all my life. She has ideas of modeling in New York, and now I know somebody in the fashion industry. How about that? So you're getting your good deal. I don't see any need to involve children in the world of import/export, do you? Why don't you show some professionalism and leave Dillon and Sylvia out of the shitty life you've made for yourself?"

Nobody had planned on the palm tree or this plaza or a basketball court or Slinger's bizarre maze walking. It was surreal and slow. Callie looked at Slinger. Had he really helped cared for Ixchel since the Granger accident?

Tony started imitating the same walk as Slinger, but coming up from behind him gradually. "I think I could do that. I don't like kids involved either." Callie watched Tony's enraged face, not taking her eyes off him. *Fuck you and your pretense of alpha.* As he approached Slinger, Callie and Angus both went for their weapons.

The two men were circling on the other side of the tree's base wall.

"Let's keep it calm, boys," Callie said, so they both knew they were on alert.

They came around the palm tree and were just about to Callie, when Tony pushed Slinger into Angus and jumped at Callie. She felt Tony twist Betty in her hand and heard a shot blow a hole in some part of Tony, who went down.

"Aww, jesuschrist, that's my fucking foot!"

She jumped on top of him and tore one of his arms behind his back. "Well you don't listen very well," she said into his right ear from behind him, trying to get a grip on his neck. Tony reached into the front of his pants and lifted his own handgun at Slinger, the first target he saw, who had easily bounced off Angus and smoothly continued behind the tree. Tony shot the decorative wall encircling the palm tree between them. Somehow the bullet ricocheted off it and hit a demented pigeon that had been turning helplessly during the meeting.

Callie pulled his other arm behind his back, rolled forward, driving her knee into his kidney and grinding Tony's face into the cobblestones, and pinned his gun hand down, smashing his fingers into the rock. She took his gun and slung it quickly over to Angus, who leveled it at Tony.

Tony growled like an injured, trapped animal. "You're all fucking dead trash to me. What the fuck is so wrong with my money?"

"There's nothing wrong with your money. I'll take it. And a one percent BSC. That's Bunghole Service Charge. It's you I hate. But nice shot," said Slinger, who reversed direction again on the other side of the palm tree. "You specialize in taking creatures out of their misery. Keep doing that, and we'll take out a few of these gawkers. I'm impressed MP Byrne, you didn't forget much did you."

"Jesusfuckingchrist, my foot's shot. You gonna let me sit here and bleed to death?"

"Maybe," Callie said.

Several Guatemalan women saw four white Americans in a fight and hurried on their way. Three elderly men sat having coffee under straw cowboy hats, and the whole scene looked like a low-budget western movie called *Tropical Injustice*. The men didn't move, sitting beneath a pock-marked, graffitied wall with *Fuck the World Bank!* scrawled in dark blue swirled letters across it.

"I'll fucking kill you all," Tony said through his mashed mouth, flesh of his cheek pressed into the stone.

"No you won't," Slinger said. "Somebody kills me, all my product goes to Evers and evaporates into the world as easily as a few puddles. You think I do all this shit without my protection? It's simple Mister Maul. You get your foot taped up and you get yourself on a fucking plane back to New York. When the ship gets in, you'll know. You wire the rest of the payment, you do whatever the fuck you want with the other girls, but you let Callie and Ixchel have their cruise, let them on their way, and we'll never see each other again."

Tony groaned loudly, and tried to roll Callie off his back but only got a knee further into his kidney.

Slinger walked over. "Having trouble speaking with the dirty street in your mouth? You had a problematic brunch at what is ordinarily a first-class resort. Now, you've had a very unpleasant stroll in Flores. Do you want to go one more time or do we have an agreement, Mister Maul?"

"Fuck off," he said.

Slinger nodded at Callie, "You're right, he's always impolite." She hopped up and down with a clean, sharp WWE move and heard the crack. Tony screamed as one of his ribs cracked. She saw two boys watching her from the basketball court. They walked away. Slinger slowly took off Tony's boot and his bloody sock. "I don't think you'll be much of a salsa dancer now. If you sit up, you might be able to wrap that foot with that sock." He flung the sock on the street next to them.

Callie let Tony roll over. He was breathing short, holding his side. He reached for the sock. Callie picked it up just before he grabbed it, and stood up, dangling it over him. "Dillon, Sylvia, Beth?"

Now he nodded, but didn't say anything.

"Now, if you sit here long enough, one of the nice local 'Dirty Sanchez's' will call an ambulance for you. Don't go anywhere now," Slinger said, heading for his truck. Angus and Callie followed.

"Jesus, I hope he's gone now," Angus said.

"We're all gone after this," Slinger said.

Desaparicedos, Callie thought.

As Callie climbed into the truck, she said, "Thanks, I owe you one."

"One what?"

Callie understood. "One of everything."

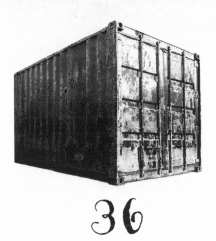

36

After the face off with Tony, they headed to Slinger's house.

They pulled up outside a stone bungalow painted in a turquoise blue.

When they pulled up the lane, his bed and furniture were scattered in front of the bungalow, tossed out of the window.

He got out of the truck, surveying and trying to cover his panic. "Lucky I didn't like my décor."

Lina came from around the back. "Jesus. I got here an hour ago and it was like this. Evers has to know. You're a walking dead man," she said. "And where the hell have you been?"

"Of course, Evers knows what I'm doing. You can't move this much stuff without him knowing. But that doesn't mean he knows *everything*."

"Tony set us up to meet in the plaza," Callie said. He had finally called Evers.

"Looks that way," Slinger said, looking at Callie with suspicion. "But that's fine, because I told Evers about Tony. So we'll see who he believes more."

"You called Evers? If you get your head sawed off, I'll kill you," Lina said.

"You're a fucking magician with conditionals," Slinger said, walking across the road into the eggplant-colored house, climbing over the sliced mattress folded up across the path. "Angus, can you keep an eye on her?"

Callie had never really seen a destroyed place before. Sloppy, yes, but not the angry chaos of *ransacked*. She felt Tony's reckless presence.

"My notebooks," he mumbled to himself. "My books."

She saw a copy of *One Hundred Years of Solitude* torn in half.

She picked it up, the two halves hanging by horse glue. "I'll get you another copy," she said.

Slinger crawled on the floor, turning over detritus, deflated by the violation that surrounded them. "Forget it."

Somehow she understood the recycling of disaster that had blown through the room. "Slinger?" He ignored her. "Slinger?"

He stopped for a second and looked up from all fours. "Yes, if you insist on dialogue?"

"You need to get out. This is going down, and you need to disappear."

"It's too late for out. There is no out. Nobody gets out of this business once you're in. And yet I live and spin toward the Big Exit. Now you, you have a chance, and if you'd stop interrupting me, I could locate your ticket to Out."

"Fine, don't let me get in your way or anything."

Whoever had done the job—and it had to be Evers's men—had torn off and through everything: the refrigerator, shoes, closets, storage boxes, the bookshelves thrown on the floor, books ripped into shreds of pages and covers, the glass coffee table smashed into the wall and hanging by one leg like a poor sculpture installation, pieces of the bathroom mirror scattered on the tile floor. The only thing that hadn't been ripped apart were Slinger's clothes, which had already been on the floor. They had knifed open any box that might have contained coke, money, or any sign of coke and money.

Callie looked at his stringy hair and tousled shirt and his drawn face as he stumbled across the apartment.

He ripped off a panel of wall behind the faucet pipes of the bathroom sink.

"What are you looking for?" she asked.

"The keys to my plane for one thing. My peaceful disappearance. Pfffft! And one fucking incredible bag of biblical accounting. My life's work."

"Won't they come after you?" she asked.

Slinger threw one of Lina's shoes across the room, crawling on the bathroom floor.

"They? Probably *they* will, yes. But if the satchel's still here, you can do whatever you want with them. They can forget Mrs. Granger the Missionary, and Jesus will come again."

Callie suddenly had a sickening feeling. The Ranch.

Angus was pacing, looking out the window at Lina. "He's going to push us out of that plane probably."

"Not a bad idea," Slinger said.

"Look," she proposed to Slinger, "After we get Ixchel and Sylvia, we'll take the truck to Belize. You'll never hear from us again."

"It's quite apparent that we will not communicate again after today." Slinger was crawling half into the wall now. "If you would cease the hapless theories, I will be able to think through the mescal and recover the realities that will matter substantially to the rest of your lives. If you are to have them, of course."

Callie looked out the window. The street was quiet, the Toyota, the clothes on the ground like the house had blown up. Angus had gone outside to wait with Lina by the truck. Lina was grousing, unable to bear any sight of ugliness or the chore of cleaning. "This is a friggin' mess," she yelled up at them. "I'll be in the truck. Slinger, I need to eat soon, so don't make me wait!"

"You'll wait until I find what I need!" he yelled back.

Callie bent down and picked up a napkin she saw on the floor. RED ROCKS, COLORADO, 1976. Slinger seemed to write down every scrap of thought he ever had. She picked up a cooking recipe for making cheese bread scattered on the floor next to it and put the napkin in her pocket. "Cheese bread?"

"My grandmother cooked it with Polish sausage back in Chicago."

"Can I have it?"

Slinger looked up from his knees, pulling out boxes of tools and hardware. "You can have whatever the fuck you want. I don't need anything here except the keys. And this particular satchel."

She took off her black shirt, leaving her tank-top undershirt on beneath. She realized it had been a shirt she'd had since first meeting Tony. Why hadn't she trashed it before now? *Ramona. A pile of her clothes in the back seat. Empty flat ghosts.* She threw it on the pile of strewn clothes on the floor.

"Thank the fucking Mayan gods."

He pulled out an old cardboard Gallo beer case. He stood up, dangling a set of keys strung off a Mayan braided necklace. Then he reached into the beer case and pulled out a thick brown leather satchel, cracked and worn.

"Our keys to the sky, baby, our keys to the sky," he smiled and his gap tooth looked as lighthearted as a sunbeam slipping through a gray layer of stratocumulus. "And your documents of passage to your new life." He handed the satchel to Callie. "Here. You're taking this."

"What is this? Why?" she said, the full weight of it hitting her shoulders.

He paused and looked her straight in the eyes. "It's my final say. Somehow, I think you'll figure out what to do with it. I'm done. It's your turn."

He sounded as if he had just been given the news that he had a terminal illness. Then he hunted for another few minutes for his favorite leather boots, cursing the whole time and mumbling to himself and finally commanding them outside.

He shuffled toward the door. "Time—the unseen, relative dimension with which we war and lose. Every day, every night, battles and détente, birth and death, golden planets, black holes. Goddamned reincarnations."

Callie followed him. "Does Jorge know that if he touches us on the trip north his share is done?"

"He knows that."

"I could kiss you."

He stuck out his puffy hand, and before she could dodge, he planted an unavoidable wet kiss on her veering cheek. "You and Ixchel should be fine," he said. She wanted to be rid of this complete lunatic, a library of contradictions, a criminalian creature with a strange code of his own making, which only evolution and constant running could breed. But there was something about him that was undeniably authentic.

"I'll come find you if we aren't, even if I'm dead."

"Such an American woman," Slinger said. "Think you can do it all. You have to fail somewhere, you know, it's just a question of where."

"I've already done that," she said.

She wanted her life back, as messy as it had been, but she couldn't help feeling an ominous thrill from the entire clandestine operation that had emerged to turn Tony's and Jorge's necks.

They went out to the truck. The sun was still high in the midday sky. The street was quiet, and Callie had that eerie sense when a bungle of disloyalty was in the works, that all of San Olvidado, even Flores, had become a deadly place. Angus ran next to her, and they climbed back into the back of the truck.

"I've been *waiiiiting*," Lina said.

"Sorry," Slinger said. "We were matching up all your shoes."

Callie laughed. Lina flashed a look. "You have a problem? Don't mess with me, honey."

"Mess with you? You're already a mess."

"That's enough out of both of you or no dessert for you tonight!" Slinger said, driving through the small streets, nervously looking at every car moving and every man on the street underneath a hat.

37

Slinger drove them out to the airstrip. They passed some of the leather workers in their jeans and boots and t-shirts, walking in vain down the road to the plant that would likely close without Slinger. Would Evers's men be at the warehouse waiting to erase them all? It was a sad scene, men walking along the dirt road outside of the town, toward a hope and future that had already disappeared.

Lina rolled down the window, yelling, "Está cerrado! Vete a casa! Vete a casa!" *Go home. Go home.*

Callie thought she was trying to tell them Latin Leather didn't exist anymore. But they didn't understand what she meant, looking back at her tiredly. The truck stirred up the road dust behind them. She saw the workers continue to walk toward the warehouse that would soon be the same ghost building of Roberto's Bananas that it had once been.

Slinger said, "They'll survive, they always do."

"No, some will, some won't," Angus said.

The dirt road bounced them around as they made their way out to the airstrip. The old white-and-red-striped Cessna sat on the dirt. "So you're gonna fly to California?"

Callie pictured. *Coast of the Pacific. Ventura Beach. Slinger and Lina sleeping on a blanket in the middle of the day.* Slinger laughed. "In legs, yeah. We've got three Evers strips between here and LA.

He looked around paranoid—saw something move up in the trees. But it was just a howler in the canopy.

Lina looked at the plane. "There better be a toilet in that thing."

Slinger wagged the pistol at Calllie and Angus. "Don't think. Don't fuck with anything. There isn't a thing out of place. A perfect little revolution in motion. You call me when you're safe, okay? I'll be at my undisclosed location in the La Jolla hills in a hot tub."

"Okay," said Callie.

He started walking across the dirt toward the plane. "C'mon, Lina, it's time."

She hopped in her heels behind him. "What about my things?"

"No time for things. When that ship gets to Elizabeth, New Jersey, then we'll have the rest of our lives for things."

He turned around. "Take a last look, MP Dread and MP Gimpy, because when I get to LA, I have an appointment with a plastic surgeon. A new face for a dead soul? Callie Byrne lives on, but—pfffft!—John Slinger will cease to exist."

"Slinger?" Callie said.

"What?"

"You remember Rule Number Three?"

"No, never heard of it."

"Nobody gives a shit if you're dead."

His forehead scrunched in thought. "Yup, never heard of it. But still so true."

Picking up his duffel, Slinger started to the plane.

"It seems like I've been down here for years," Callie said.

He looked at her intently. "Yeah, we all came down here for something or somebody, Callie Selassie. And at some point those reasons just don't exist anymore. What do we matter when gods war with gods, eh? Read that shit in the satchel I gave you before you're at the bottom of the Lake too."

Angus and Callie watched Lina's flying black hair bouncing across to the plane's steps and Slinger slouching his way behind her.

"You can keep the truck," he called back. "And whatever else you want. I have a fifth of mescal behind the seat if you want it for the road. Pfffft! Read that shit. I spent ten years of my life on all that. And I'm giving it to you, Callie Byrne, you understand, I'm giving it to *you*." He didn't turn around, but he flopped his arm and waved carelessly. "Adopting the burdens of your friends is love."

"Let's go. He's right," Angus said.

"One second, I want to see the fucker take off in that thing."

Angus leaned against the truck. "That sounds like a bad idea."

She grabbed the satchel and pulled out a stack of notebooks. Scribbled across one of the first was, "Read the blue one." She flipped quickly through the pages expecting exotic ramblings of an ex-hippie drug-running operator, but as she skimmed and flipped, it was unexpectedly clear and detailed.

She pulled out an old photograph, bent around the corners. She stared at it in disbelief.

Across the way, the prop on the left engine started slowly circulating. Up in the cockpit, Slinger opened the pilot's window and looked around. He looked like a drunk driver checking to see where he was. The engines started and soon they couldn't talk over the chop-chopping of the blades.

She held up the photo to him. She thought he grinned at her from the past.

Lina sat in the copilot seat, looking like a mannequin at Bergdorf's who had just joined the Marines, a headset over her hair and her face turning in all directions. They could see her mouth moving at Slinger, her mind whirring with hot air like the props. She leaned across Slinger as the plane turned its nose out onto the runway and gave Callie and Angus the finger. She was a special one. Her mouth ran like the plane's engines with angry expletives, a black hole of entitlement in the universe.

Callie squinted behind her sunglasses as the sun made its way down the sky. Her bare shoulders felt like parts of the jungle and she saw Slinger looking across the strip, like a grand marshal of a parade. He waved at her and laughed and swung his hair back in the window and slid the pilot's window closed. The plane's props whirled. A brown cloud flew behind the engines and the palms and underbrush bent back as it started down the runway like a running hippo trying to escape a gator, then rumbled out of the Lake Petén Itzá jungle in a propellant of dust.

Climbing over the trees, the plane disappeared quickly behind the thick canopy.

And then it was quiet. A howler yakked to himself. George-in-the-Bush's cousin probably.

Callie stared at the photo and back at the airstrip of tropical clay. It practically shimmered in the sun with the layers of earth on top of layers of earth.

"Let's go," she said, respecting the revelation that had just passed. "We need to get to the ranch and pack. Ixchel and I have an undercover cruise to catch."

"What's the photo of?" he asked.

They were speeding down the jungle road. He asked her again. She shouted over the open windows and wind. "It was Slinger. Probably in the Eighties, judging from the bad hair. He was posing with three other men. You know where they were? In front of a DEA building in DC. All of four of them with badges on their belts."

She looked at Angus, wondering if she knew who anybody was.

"Slinger is DEA?" Angus repeated.

"Is. Was. I don't know."

They both sat silent driving back past Roberto's warehouse. There was nobody on the road now. It was as if all the locals knew something they didn't.

38

Callie and Angus sped along the valley road into evening. Despite watching Slinger take off, or maybe because of it, the tires themselves seemed to spin with a freedom that led back to Dillon. One way or another, she and Ixchel would be leaving on that ship. She skipped the brake, just taking her foot off the gas enough to swerve through the winding turns and around the divots and potholes. Dillon and Beth were waiting for her.

"You know where we're going?" she asked.

"Where?"

"Home."

But she knew what stood between her and home, and it was probably waiting at the ranch. A bright sunlight poured over the Lake and the farmlands and seemed to put the innocent world behind a glass case, but one that was possible to break when they had removed the layer of Tony Maul's filth for good.

She passed a man on a bicycle, hunched over, and she wondered if it was the same man she had seen on her first morning. Where was he going? Who was he? What changed for him in the last few weeks? How was he still pedaling along as if nothing had happened?

As they arrived at the Guadeloupe Ranch, five black SUVs were parked across the river at the top of the hill near the main house. She could see a team holding semi-automatic assault rifles—AR-15s from the look of it—fanned out around the main house and the school building, a confusing buzz, like dragonflies moving in slow motion. There were about ten men wearing bandanas over their faces, skullcaps, and a mishmash of fatigues and government-issue, army-brown shirts.

She slammed the car in reverse and backed it out of view onto the main road.

She looked at Angus. "Yup, Tony went to the Evers network about Slinger."

He nodded. "Wonder if we'll ever get to see Philly again."

Callie didn't hesitate. "Hope so. I figured this was coming eventually. Tony would have turned on Slinger the moment he left the pool with a broken nose. Call the police. Ask for Inspector Piñada."

"And tell him what? That part of Evers's security force is at the Guadeloupe Ranch for a fucking trail ride? Let's go, there's nothing we can do up there. We're only two people, and they've got at least twenty."

"That's only a ten to one ratio, not bad. No, tell him that Slinger fucked him over."

"Slinger? What's he care about him for? The guy's probably in Mexican air space by now."

She looked at Angus. "I'm betting Piñada's in a shitload of trouble without Slinger's operation to cover him. Maybe he's on the hit list too, who knows. But we need some men from somewhere. If Pinada thinks Evers men associate him with Slinger, maybe he'll choose not getting killed by Evers's guerillas if knows Slinger has bolted."

He thought about it. She saw his eyes squint with the stress. "Okay. And what're you going to do?"

She tried to reassure him. "Go on. I'll be fine. You think I can't handle myself or this gun," and she flipped the pistol so the backstrap of the handle hit the flesh of her palm and aimed perfectly at Angus's head. "Don't worry, the safety's on. You stay with Slinger's satchel in the truck and wait for the locals. I'll drop up the road from the gate. I'm going in through the bush and will text you with the intel on numbers and locations."

She had slipped back into MP talk. *The beige cement walls of Mosul. The Tigris winding around them.* Angus didn't say anything, but he nodded. There was no talking her out of this.

"What's your plan?"

She kissed him on the cheek. "See if they're are open to some negotiation."

"Negotiation? What the fuck do we have to negotiate? They're only going to be into open firing."

"I can think of a few things. For one thing, what if they don't know where Slinger's product is? Go blackmail some local policemen, would you? And head down the road slow until you get out of earshot. Don't fucking announce me."

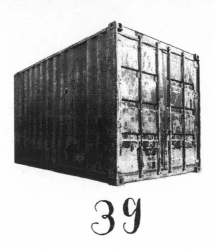

39

Callie waded across the shallow part of the stream, and headed up the hill in the brush to the left of the main house. She wanted to have a view from the open end of the yard that would put the ranch house to her left, the yard in front of her, and the old school house and barn across the way, and their SUVs to her right.

She hurried as much as she could without making noise in the underbrush and the ground cover of dried palm fronds, branches, and weeds until she had a location with the vantage point she had envisioned in her mind.

She saw Tony on the porch with a gun pointed at Mrs. Granger, who sat in her wicker chair. Mrs. Granger appeared to be pointing at the sky and talking to it. The SUVs were circled professionally so that the driveway was blocked and facing the house in a semi-circle. Across the yard, against the wall of the old school building, she saw three of the ranch workers and stable hands with their backs against the light blue cinderblock wall. An Evers soldier was tying the arms of the third man. They could not have been here very long. Probably just the time it took for them to leave Slinger's and see him off at the airstrip. She did a quick count. Angus had guessed right. Five vehicles with four per truck was twenty total.

Callie could see Mrs. Granger sitting as if her shoulders were nailed—sharp, unforgiving—looking down from the sky and straight at Tony. Then she looked skyward again, as if seeing Jesus's bearded face in the fuzzy green of the treetops waiting for her.

One of the narcos pulled the first ranch hand out to the middle of the yard between the main house and the school. She heard the man offering the narco money. She didn't know much Spanish, but the high stress and intense pleading on the word *quetzals* was easy to pick out.

Tony yelled out, "One of you is going to tell me where Callie Byrne is!" He spoke as if he had deputized himself into Evers' team. "Or we're going to start popping off people. We know this is Slinger's ranch. And been hosting her. You've been getting locals organized against them. We want her and Slinger." He held up his phone and raised his voice, as if addressing her. "And if she's here somewhere, we're going to have a showing of Beth and Dillon here on ShootYourFuckingFaceTime."

She processed the facts. Tony had informed on Slinger as she'd anticipated, tried to cut him out, and had some kind of deal with Evers worked out. She went quickly through her possible moves. He would try to use Dillon again. He would likely try to kill her for the info on Slinger and his ship. Unless Hector had turned on him and Evers showed up and believed Slinger.

Mrs. Granger said to nobody and everybody at once, "Callie Byrne is gone. She no longer exists. Ixchel Cante is gone. She no longer exists. Sylvia Cante is gone. Teddy Granger is gone. Sylvia's—"

"Shut up," Tony yelled, pistol whipping Mrs. Granger on the side of the head. Callie could see a red gash open on the side of her silvery hair. But she remained in the chair somehow, holding her head up, defiant.

The narco in a black head mask held the ranch hand in the yard by his hair. He knocked in the back of his legs, putting him to his knees in the grass. They shouted and threatened to find out where John Slinger was, where their product was. She saw, then, the full extent of Slinger's operation: it truly was his own rogue shipment. He wasn't just skimming a portion off the top, he was completely shutting Evers out. They really didn't know about the *Bonita*. They didn't know where fifty million dollars of their heroin was going.

There was a long pause.

The choices diminished. Stall, just stall as long possible She fired off two quick shots, one at the front porch door near Tony and the other into the dirt near the narco in the yard.

Then she shouted, "Okay. You made your point. There's fifty million in product waiting. Slinger's gone. I watched him fly out. So looks like you're the man now, Tony. You're so big, I'm sure you can get whatever share these guys agree to. So I'll come out if you let the woman and the ranch hands go."

She saw the rest of the narcos looking in her direction. Then they pointed toward the area of jungle concealing her. A barrage of bullets hit palm tree trunks about her, and she saw three men running toward her. The one behind the older ranch hand swung his rifle butt like a baseball bat across the man's head, then the *pauw pauw pauw* of three bursts. The right side of his skull and brains burst into the grass. Then a second set of rounds hit the side of the schoolhouse, and the two other bound ranch hands slumped to the ground dead.

She ran toward the back of the main house. She came into a stand of palm trees at the back corner of the house and saw the three narcos fanning into the jungle near her old location. She broke for the house and jumped through the back porch screen, ripping through it and rolling onto the floor. She scrambled, hunched over, and ran into the kitchen and toward the front parlor.

As she passed, she opened Ixchel's stairwell closet-room. It was totally dark. The hall light revealed a shadow on the far corner of the bed. Ixchel was crouched with a bottle in Sylvia's mouth to keep her quiet.

Ixchel whispered quickly, "That crazy old woman went out to meet them. You understand? She went out to meet them." In the glare of the dark, Callie could hear Ixchel was crying.

"Stay here."

She moved up the hallway, Betty drawn up toward the front parlor and front door.

She had to get Tony to get up from the porch and come in to the parlor somehow.

The only way she could think of was to use herself as bait.

She was about to say the simple words, "Come inside, Tony." Then she heard vehicles coming up the driveway. She took a quick look through the front windows past the bleeding head of Mrs. Granger and Tony and the SUVs. The local police had sent cars, and they were pulling up the hill toward the SUVs. Evers's men turned their attention to the police and there was a barrage of automatic fire from both sides.

Then the rib-hobbled and bloody-footed Tony dragged Mrs. Granger by scalp out of the chair. He was heading inside for the front parlor. He came through the screen door past Callie, typically sloppy and oblivious. She could see his bandaged foot, and he walked holding his side from his broken rib. Callie gave a left to the rib and then pistol-whip on his head, and before Tony knew it, her pistol was at the base of his neck, his left arm was half way up his back, and she was kneeling into the same broken rib cage she'd cracked a few hours ago. Tony was groaning in excruciating pain, but she didn't let up.

Mrs. Granger had picked up his gun. "Mrs. Granger, would you—" but the old woman had already opened a front window screen. She had her pick of Evers's men, who were occupied by the firefight with the police. She started firing off shots and then she ducked down. A volley of bullets came crashing through the windows and exploding into the walls behind them.

"Ranchers have plenty of time on the range," she said to Callie with a nod. She had glass in her hair.

Callie was busy keeping Tony held down. "Let's just keep your skinny ass right where it is, or I will blow a hole in the other foot."

She rolled Tony over, pointing Betty at his head. He started to speak—"You're killing Dill-"—she punched him in the mouth with a strong right hook, and dragged him up into the armchair. *Ixchel*

Cante reading a glossy mag, pregnant. Ixchel's father sitting with a little girl, leaving for Florida. Now an interrogation chair for Tony Maul.

"Say another word, and I'll start breaking more ribs."

"I want my fucking shipment or your son is dead," he growled through his bloody lip.

She shoved the gun barrel into his left ribs. He howled in pain. Callie played her part, letting him think Dillon and Beth were being held. "Who's got Dillon and Beth? I want to know right now, or I will shoot the other foot for a start. You're going to call them and tell them to stand down."

He looked at her with a demented satisfaction. "Hector Perez. But this isn't the army, you dumb bitch."

"You fucker. So what do you want me to do?"

"Which fucking ship is his? If it doesn't move, they'll be on a fishing boat tomorrow headed into the Atlantic."

Mrs. Granger went up for another round of cover. "Three more. I think we're down to a dozen, maybe fourteen."

"Mrs. Granger, you have scissors? Would you cut a few of my dreads please?" The old woman quickly retrieved them from her quilting desk, and Callie felt a pulling behind her. Mrs. Granger presented three long dreads. Callie took them from her and gagged Tony with them. "We'll see about that. Eat my hair in the meantime."

With Angus and Piñada's men blocking their exit, and Mrs. Granger popping them off from the ranch house, several of Evers's men retreated into their SUVs.

One in a skullcap shouted at half the men, and they turned back and covered the house. She saw Angus's pickup truck and Piñada's men pull further up the lane in their black and gold pickups and SUVs. There was more shouting from the police through vehicle speakers. From two of the lead vehicles, police in riot gear spilled out and were now trained on both the Evers SUVs and the main house, unsure who was located where.

Everybody held their positions.

Callie ignored Tony now. "Mrs. Granger, cover me."

The old woman gave a short nod, "Oh, I got him. He moves and I'll blow his middle leg off." Mrs. Granger saw Callie's surprise. "I've been expecting them for a while."

She looked out one of the blown-out windows. She could see Skull Cap, Piñada, and Angus. The world seemed to slow into a still life of the ranch hand's head splattered in the grass.

Callie yelled out one of the front windows.

"So, who wants to talk? Is there a smart businessman who knows how to fucking deal with reality, or are you all stupid thugs who want to shoot this out until we take as many of you with us? At least five or six police cars aren't going to let you drive out of here now."

She saw Skull Cap glance at the lane blocked by Piñada's men, who apparently had listened to Angus and believed their fates had crossed with Slinger's and now needed to fight Evers's men for the time being to survive this year's alliances. Skull Cap glanced down the hill and back toward her in the house.

Nobody moved or spoke. George-in-the-bush screeched off in the jungle behind the main house.

Then in the back of the second SUV, a window rolled down. There was a calm voice. Skull Cap looked up at her window and nodded at Callie. He walked casually to the SUV. Everybody held. There was a discussion with a man in side. Then out of the vehicle stepped a man dressed in a full length leather coat, silk tie, and neatly trimmed black hair. He looked like a night club owner from Buenos Aires. Callie knew him immediately, a man who seemed air conditioned at all times. Manual Evers. *Slinger flying back from Bolivia. Storage rooms of heroin and coke getting packed between slabs of leather fabric. Slinger sitting with Mrs. Granger in her parlor, buying the ranch, housing all of his men.* All of Slinger's operation in Petén under Latin Leather had undercut this man, and when Tony called in fifty million in operational betrayal, that indeed got the attention from the CEO.

Evers nodded at Piñada. Piñada nodded back. And in just that gesture they seemed to agree to some unspoken terms.

"Why is Piñada talking?" Callie turned to Mrs. Granger.

"Because he knows if he takes him in, every one of his men here will be targeted and killed."

Evers turned toward Skull Cap to accompany him, and the two of them approached the front porch.

40

The Bonita sitting at port. She, Ixchel, and Sylvia inside the container. Evers wanted to know where Slinger's shipment was going, and she wanted to get to Elizabeth, New Jersey, in one of the ten thousand containers in the vast port.

"Welcome to the Guadeloupe Ranch, Mr. Evers," Callie said. They came inside the front parlor. Mrs. Granger and Callie both pointed to the open sofa, and the dapper man looked at Tony —shook his head at him—as he sat down, as if he had arrived for cocktails.

Tony's face strained with rage and humiliation, hoping for an ally now that Evers himself had arrived.

Evers spoke with excellent, educated English. "I heard your little speech. I respect a woman with a head on her shoulders. I'm sorry about the gentleman who no longer has a head."

"I doubt you're sorry."

"There are a million ways to do business. I can make entire villages into good places to live. When I do, people love me."

"Can you get my son and sister out of this asshole's hands." She nodded at Tony. His eyes and face struggled with her gag. "I think they're being held in an apartment in Atlantic City."

"Is what this man says about Slinger true?"

Callie knew what he meant. And she knew there was no other way at this point other than the absolute truth.

"Yes."

"And you were helping him?"

She thought about that for a split second of doubt, and she could see a seething anger beneath his coiffed veneer. She had in fact helped pack leather coats and bags for weeks. "No," she said. "I was only here to help a friend of mine. But she's dead. Then I was helping Mrs. Granger's foster daughter try to get to the States. I worked for Slinger for the last few weeks because my friend worked for Latin Leather when she came down here."

Evers looked at Tony, then back to Callie. "He says you were trying to interfere with the shipment, that you're ex-US Army. I'd like to know where Slinger's product is. I will find it sooner or later, but sooner is better."

Slinger and Lina flying over the jungle toward the Mexican border. "I'm *ex* US army. And I told you. I don't care about the shipment. There's a million people in my state who want fixes and want to get clean at the same time. So I'm fine helping you with your big problem if you help me with my little one."

He folded his hands over his knees, "Really, Ms. Byrne? You are making demands of Manuel Evers."

"You said yourself, there's a million ways to run a business. And no, not demands." She knew which way to play him. "I'm coming to you to ask for a favor. For my family. I would never be here if this asshole hadn't gotten an innocent woman killed. And who is threatening my sister and son. You have three daughters, Mr. Evers. I've read about you. What would you do if this punk-ass pisser couldn't tell the difference between a dog and your daughter or between a deal and his own ego? I'm asking for your help. I'd like my life in Philadelphia back, with my son and sister safe. And I want Ixchel and her baby with me. That's it."

"You know Slinger's already dead. He can't help you," Evers said.

Callie didn't know if that was true literally yet, but the odds of Slinger and Lina making it to California and new identities before Evers tracked them seemed longer. She looked directly at Manuel Evers. His eyes were a deep brown, his jet-black hair gelled.

He seemed as composed as a CEO of an oil company. "You know Slinger also told you about him. You probably know I only just got here a few weeks ago. I came down here because my friend was in some kind of trouble. She accidentally saw that Tony Maul and Jorge Mercado were trafficking girls to Atlantic City. Tony has my son and sister kidnapped just to get me to help Slinger undercut you. So, you have fifty million dollars of product on a ship somewhere in the Caribbean, and all I want is safety for my family and a one-way trip to Philadelphia for three."

"Very well advocated and argued, Ms. Callie Byrne." Evers nodded at Skull Cap.

Skull Cap got up, and pulled a knife out, sticking the tip onto Tony's Adam's apple. "Let's just check on some of this. Where's your cell phone?" Evers asked. Tony's eyes motioned to his right pant pocket. Skull Cap retrieved it, and sat back down. "Passcode?" Skull Cap pulled his dread gag out a bit for him to say some numbers. Evers hit the numbers, and scrolled through phone calls. He hit a call, and was then on the line speaking Spanish to somebody for a minute. He sounded like he was issuing a death sentence to whoever he was speaking to.

Callie was watching Mrs. Granger, Evers, and Tony. Skull Cap had positioned himself at the door. Mrs. Granger was still holding her gun, and she crossed herself with her other hand, looking at Evers as if she was in a shock that he was in the flesh in her parlor.

He spoke again in Spanish again for a minute. Then hung up.

"You are right," he said to Callie, and then crossing his legs and cutting his sharp pant creases.

"What's right?" she said, waiting to hear if Father Tim's threats were going to hold.

"Hector told me exactly what you just did. Tony ordered him to kidnap your sister and son, and he has them in his apartment bedroom."

So Hector had turned: he had lied to Tony about Dillon and Beth being taken and he had lied just now.

"I don't lie about family or money," she said.

"Callie Byrne, neither do I anymore," he smiled. "I only do one thing now."

"What?"

"Conglomerate."

"What did you say to Hector?"

"I asked him if he's more interested in staying alive or keeping Tony Maul alive. How about that Mister Maul? You know what he said? He wants to live. Sorry for you. Because whether you knew it or not, you were trying to buy a lot of my product at a discount rate and trying to take over some of my biggest markets."

"In twenty minutes, Hector Perez will leave them on the Boardwalk in front of Trump's Casino. They can walk away. Unlike some other souls here." He looked at the wide eyes of Tony Maul. "So? Now. Shall we complete this business?"

Callie looked at Evers, feeling her entire scheme coming to its finale, and continuing the pretense of being under the leverage of Hector. "How do I know they'll be freed?"

"Because I just said so."

"What about Ixchel and her daughter? We're getting on the ship."

"Si, doesn't matter to me who gets on a ship. That's your travel choice."

She and Dillon were in the pool. A squirming bundle of small ribs and laughing in her hands.

Mrs. Granger nodded at her. *Take the deal.*

Callie said, "Okay. Then thank you. The shipment is on the *Bonita* in Belize City. Wharf #5."

41

Evers loosened his dark red tie, and he looked past Callie at the books on the shelves and seemed lost in thought. Then he said with a firm clarity to Mrs. Granger, "There is one reality in which I torture you and shoot up this place." He looked at Skull Cap, then went to the window and surveyed the yard full of tense ex-military awaiting word. Callie thought one nod from this psychotic and it was over. He turned around. "But I like Petén. This is a place where we can move a lot of product. Slinger has developed this region, no reason to trash it over one deluded, dead distributor and a stupid dealer from New York. I don't want any attention. Locals like your ranch. You should have your school here again. And Mrs. Granger. Although I do have men like Raul here"—a proud wave at Skull Cap—"who would enjoy killing you, I prefer to buy people. It's better business. So my product and your girls must be separated."

Callie stared at Mrs. Granger, "Your girls? You were working with Ixchel and Jorge too?"

Mrs. Granger was still pointing the gun around the room, and then she sagged a bit and felt at her bleeding, swollen face. "Whatever it takes. They're dying here. These girls have no hope here anymore. I only help them get set up with their passage money, their fake passports, buses or vans over to Costa Rica. From there who knows. Tent cities. Florida if they're lucky. Jorge is just another conductor on a slave trade, an underground rail, whatever. I know he's a monster—but he is the man who gets them there."

"But do you know that he makes them work off their debt in prostitution once they get there?"

"And what else will they do here? Get raped or killed by men like these animals? They have taken my whole life. They took my ranch, my husband, my school, my missionaries. They took me. Took it all so that I'm just a freak from a gone time with nothing left. But I can help these girls get out. And I tried to help Ixchel too, but she was too proud. She always wanted to do everything by herself. She's an unforgiving steel rod."

Mrs. Granger's whole being wept and shook from the pressure of the attack on the ranch, her men dead, but also from the years of loss and slow disintegration of a threadbare remnant that once was the fabric of her life.

Ixchel stood in the doorway with Sylvia. "You never were anything but an old dry leaf. The other girls do what they have to do. But I don't just *want* to do it myself. I am all by myself."

Evers stood up.

"I'm not scared of you," Ixchel said.

"You should be, but I admire that."

"You see my face? Half of me is old volcanic rock. I am as old as the earth in my heart. My soul is the fucking night sky. So, when am I going on that ship? Me and my Sylvia are going to New York. And the rest."

Evers smiled. "And you save a bunch of nameless girls? Women do take care of each other, don't they? Where's Slinger?"

He and Lina arguing, giving her everything he had done with his life.

Callie felt strangely torn. He had tried to investigate the hit on Rachel. He had helped her get Tony down here. And gave Ixchel a chance at what she thought she wanted. And in his way protected Mrs. Granger. At least up to now.

"No, he You're getting all the product. What else do you need?"

"I don't need anything. But my business needs him dead. So, his location. Or I can just as easily blow up this place and send all the girls back to their villages." He took three quick steps right at her. "Now!" he shouted for the first time, grabbing a fistful of her dreads and wrenching her head back. He had ignored her Beretta. Skull Cap had his gun on her. She tried to relax. *Let him feel in control.* Manuel Evers was staring directly into Callie's eyes. *A psychopath's brain neurons were firing as quickly as hers.* "Which do you want?"

Tony Maul, of New York City, of black clothing, one foot mangled, in the middle of the desert. She remembered the confession by the pool, and the fact that she had no evidence other than that. What had he said? "Who gets to die in the desert?"

"I want you to drop Tony in the middle of the Mexican desert so he can shrivel up and be eaten by wild dogs."

Evers, apparently impressed with the dark place her imagination lived, stepped back and let go of her hair. "I can arrange that."

Tony muffled a plea, eyes wide.

"Good luck out there," she said. "It's a dog-eat-god world."

"End of talk. Slinger?" Evers said, straightening his tie in the mirror.

There was nothing else to be done. Slinger would have to take his own chances. She had played all the cards she held and was lucky to even be alive. "Slinger and his girlfriend are in a Cessna. Left within the hour. Said he was headed for LA. I don't know where. He said he would let me know when to call him. I don't know which airstrip."

"Thank you. You passed. I already knew that from my air recon."

"Then why do all this."

"Because now I know what matters to you. And because if you had said anything else, you'd be dropped with him in the desert." Evers invited her out the door with him. "Come wait in my car. Skull Cap, grab the New York shithead."

Skull Cap picked up Tony by his hair, yanking him across the floor as Tony grunted.

"Callie," Mrs. Granger said. She seemed to be saying goodbye and come back at the same time.

Evers nodded to Ixchel, "You coming with us? You want to go to New York, right?"

Evers, Ixchel, and Callie went out the front door.

The group stood on the front porch steps, covered by Evers's men. Evers waved a special hello to Piñada.

"Okay, everyone hold your places," Evers said coolly. "We're going to be here for a while. We have arrived at a deal to end today's unfortunate conflict between international fair trade and local farmers. However, the details will take some time to finalize while we get in touch with John Slinger. These two will be visiting with me until then. We are going to be sitting in my vehicle. Anybody moves, I will shoot one of them in the head and roll her out the door. Piñada, tell your men to reconsider their professional opportunities here in Petén. That is, if they listen to you at this point, you fucking piece of dirt. You were messing with the wrong man, and we will have to discuss that."

Evers led Callie by the elbow towards his SUV.

She could see behind one of Piñada's vehicles Angus with a gun trained on Evers. She could tell he was waiting for any signal she would give to take the shot.

She gave the quickest, slightest shake of her head: *No.*

42

Evers opened the door of the SUV and Callie, Ixchel, and Sylvia slid across the back seat. Evers got into the front. He shut the door and his driver locked all the doors. Callie did not let him see her worry. What incentive did this man have to keep his word? Was he going to turn the ranch into a blood bath after his men were done with the *Bonita* and Slinger?

"So I'm calling Slinger?"

He pulled out his phone and didn't answer her.

She listened to him make a call with the *Bonita's* location. It was nearing noon, and Evers's men would have all day to unload a year's worth of Slinger's product, pile it into their trucks, and drive it toward Mexico.

After a short conversation, he hung up his phone and pulled out a laptop.

Ixchel gave a quick, desperate look at Callie. *What do we do?*

Callie made a *stay calm* motion with her hand.

Callie could see Tony trying to squirm against Skull Cap outside the vehicle. Skull Cap picked him up and pile drove him into the ground. The squirming stopped.

Mrs. Granger was about the only one who did not move, never taking her sight off of Skull Cap. He let Tony lie on the ground, and some other narcos started kicking Tony in his head and ribs.

Angus stood with Piñada, and for a time, Angus seemed to be attempting to persuade Piñada to do more. He kept pointing to Evers's SUV.

Evers finally said to her, "Have you ever been to Mexico City?"

"No," she said.

"Do you want to go?"

"Not today."

He frowned, as if it was insignificant whether she wanted to or not. "Do you understand that I can do whatever I want to you?"

"Doesn't seem that difficult to comprehend." She glanced out the window at the first ranch hand lying on the ground. The right side of his head was blown off in the back, and he had bled out into the scrubby grass. "But I don't think you will."

"Why not?"

"Like you said, more people dying here today is bad for local support, and local support keeps the flow moving."

"Smart lady."

"Have you ever been to Philadelphia?" she asked.

"Yes. I met once there with officials at an international finance conference. I know many bankers. We toured Independence Hall. American freedom, Ms. Byrne, I love American freedom."

"Do you want to go again?"

He didn't answer, but she thought she saw a small grin. "I know you came down here for your son and sister."

She thought about that for a long moment. *Beth, sitting by the pool in her judgment.*

"Yes. And for my son and Rachel Martelli."

"Everything in life is about loyalty."

"Not in America anymore. Everything is about money."

"That's a shame," he said, shrugging.

Ixchel asked him with a firm confidence, "Does Jorge Mercado work for you?"

He pointed with a scarred index finger at her. "He does right now. But I have a future prediction for him. I predict he will be arrested in New Jersey. He'll be taken to a Federal prison. Maybe to

Ryker's Island or Upstate New York, maybe Colorado. And then, one day, one of my men in the yard will cut out his liver and his tongue and his heart and put him in the trash incinerator, and he'll be smoke in the atmosphere and rain watering my compound's gardens."

"Good. I will plant some roses then too," Ixchel said.

Evers said, "We'll sit here until all my product is off the ship and out of the wharf warehouse."

Callie only said, "Okay."

43

"Where are we?" asked Lina.

"Over Mexico City."

"Looks like a cancer that won't stop growing," she said.

Slinger looked ahead at the sky and drank a swig of mescal.

A few hours later, after a fuel stop at a small airport, the old Cessna 340A was over the Sonoran Desert. The plane was at six thousand feet, and the ground looked like a brown patchwork blanket rumpled on a bed.

Lina sat in the copilot seat, hunched down, licking a chocolate bar's melt from her fingers and arranging a mirror on her lap to cut a line.

"It's a blue and white world, baby," he said quietly.

"I want to live in LA," she said.

"We'll live in LA"

"Everybody's in LA now."

"We'll swim in LA"

"In our pool," she said.

"Where's the pool?" Slinger asked.

"Behind the biggest fucking villa up in Beverly Hills."

"Pacific sunsets galore," he said.

"With a fountain spitting at the world all day and night."

"So you can hear it splashing from the bedroom."

"And French doors made of cedar," said Lina.

"Cedar?"

"I like how it smells," and she drew her face downward, snort-ing the line. She looked at herself in the hand mirror. Her mouth hung half open, and her funny round face winked at him.

The plane rumbled, and he checked the map. He scanned the horizon. All he could see were white clouds of payoff, his stomach turbulent with anxiety. Now that she sat across from him, he was glad he wasn't alone, which was not the same as being glad for her company. Even if the entire plan flamed out, she was willing to venture, and he had to give her that. She helped with nothing practical, but she did help with something significant. He had done something he'd never done before; he had organized other people to act, to take what they could before someone else took it. And what he looked forward to enjoying was simple: a beautiful woman who would appreciate what he had done.

He remembered how she had ridiculed him for being scared of Evers, for jumping up at every command to make a run, go where he was told, for having no balls to do his own thing. He had endured the dull abuse until he was sitting one day outside Jamón's at a table by himself, his head swimming drunk, and his eyes falling asleep in the afternoon sun. Lina was off having her nails done by a woman who doubled as a psychic and had told Lina she would die fantas-tically rich. In the sun and the glare, he fell asleep at the table and dreamt of an Evers killing on the TV news, men lying dead next to a car in Guatemala City with wads of money sticking out of their mouths. When he awoke, it was late afternoon. The streets were quiet, and he picked his heavy head up, peering down at the Lake. A long rowboat looked like a floating book, and he saw the entire vision in front of him. He was free. He could sit here, fearful and drinking himself to death, or he could attempt an operatic exit. And here it was. Fifty million headed to the Port of Newark. They just had to make it a week.

He heard giggling next to him. Lina was curled up in her seat, putting her face up to the instrument panels. "The little arrows are fun to watch! Ha!" she said, and giggled. "Don't you have an auto-pilot? I want you right now!"

"I'm not fucking this up on the last run. Just sit down."

She pouted with her golden-brown, bug-eyed Hollywood sunglasses hanging perfectly false on her face.

Two flashes of gray and afterburners of circular flame suddenly burst just off the tips of the wings, missing them by a few feet on either side.

Lina screamed and flew up against her seat. "What the fuck is that, Slinger?"

"How the hell should I know?" he yelled, adrenaline jumping through him. "But they're Mirages."

The two planes were doing a coordinated turn back, banking in large arcs and moving back behind the Cessna, probably to come up alongside him, Slinger guessed. Mexican Air Force?

And they disappeared behind him.

He saw two blips circling on his radar.

There was a long wait, as a condemned man might have felt sitting in the electric chair after the guards had closed the door.

Finally, the jets glided like hawks along either side of the Cessna. He could see the black visors of the pilots. Slinger scanned the planes and their markings. Nothing. But the letters had been painted over. Colombian Air Force, the FAC. He turned to Lina, and there was no sign of Hollywood in her face, but rather some aghast mask, like a bad horror movie still, staring at him, waiting for him to do something.

"They're Evers's planes," he explained.

"Evers has fucking jets?"

"He's got everything."

"What do they want?" she asked, sucking her lip and thinking hard with nothing to work with.

"You're joking, right?"

"What?" she asked, confused.

"I'm trying to think," he said.

"I want to be in LA"

"The odds of that just went way down."

"You better do something!" she commanded.

"I'm trying to think—if you would shut up for two seconds—"

"You should be able to think whether I talk or not," she said to the window, looking at the jet to her right.

The two jets stayed just feet off either wing, like two marshals walking a prisoner, hands locked on either arm. Clouds roiled by in the air like fugitives attempting to scatter in all directions. Down below, patches of Tijuana's transient slums and the toy-glass office towers of San Diego fanned out into eternal dirt, crossed with irrigation ditches. He saw an indifferent, oak-paneled, immense courtroom of earth.

The pilot to his left signaled a frequency to him. He adjusted the radio and waited.

"Buenos tardes, sirs," Slinger said, smiling and tipping his head in both directions.

The two men peered at him, their sun visors covering their faces.

"You will follow us. We're going to bank west."

"And if I don't?"

There was a long pause as the engines rumbled and the two jets both set off air-to-air missiles that shot into the distance in front of them like fireworks until they disappeared in the sun and dropped into the desert.

The left pilot gave a wave to the left, to the west.

"We're going to bank to heading three-four-four, on my word. Nice and slow. Understand? These aren't requests."

"Okay, okay, I'm a flexible man," Slinger said, despair pumping into his heart. "I understand." And he desperately made eye contact with both left and right black visors. He really didn't want to be knocked tumbling out of the sky like a rag doll.

The two jets moved to eleven o'clock and two o'clock, and he followed their lead as they banked slowly left. The setting sun swung around into their faces.

Her headset off, Lina's mouth moved like a fish in a bowl, still talking and gesturing. Slinger was grateful for the silent movie.

"I guess you know I'm hauling some valuable product on this plane?"

No response.

They were over the Baja Peninsula, Slinger calculated. Maybe they were taking him to Tijuana.

The two jets were gray triangles hanging in front of him, and Slinger pulled out a bootleg Dead from the Fillmore East, February 14, 1970 and put it on the boom box behind his seat. He needed something familiar, some old Uncle John's Band in his head. He'd been in a lot of deals and done thousands of runs over the years, flying by himself at night, landing, lighting the plane, and walking away, as scheduled, as he was told. But this was clearly different; this was the end of a big story. The two gray crosses with tails were immovable in front of him, steaming nihilism in their exhaust. While behind him, pallets full of the white dreams he'd cooked were packed tight. He wondered whether the *Bonita* had sailed.

Lina now seemed sullen and angry. She had thought of herself as an unknown queen to be obeyed and remembered. She turned into a woman with her own frustrated plan. She stopped speaking, a Colombian stone statue.

He remembered when they made out in Ipanema underneath a café umbrella, indifferent to the tourists and the locals and the waiters. They were straggles of hair falling around each other's faces and covering up nothing but each other's ancient, dark mouths. She had loved him. His plan and her plans had seemed like adventures that had joined into one tropical storm crossing the cities and jungles of Central America. It seemed they had it all to themselves.

Now he watched her face. They were trapped in this plane, and she wanted no part of any plan that was not hers.

She had already cut him loose while they sat there, separated only by the engine throttles.

The four of them, Left Visor, Right Visor, Slinger, and Lina, flew like that for two hours into the twilight.

At around seven-thirty, Slinger started rambling into the radio: "We all could have been Mayan emperors in another age. Or howlers. But what kind of lot is this? We can't fly, but the Wright Brothers prove differential lift? We can't know the Big Bang, but we can see the remnants? We can imagine what we could be like but can't make it real? You love someone but lose them in a fog? And where does it go? Beneath piles in the attic? Underneath tires? Downwind, rushing out to sea? Why is Leftie sitting off that wing? Following his orders. Can you hear that guitar wandering? Headwind, tailwind, where is the human race going? How far before we just circle around again, eh? Evers guessed our flight path? No, how would he know? Jorge? The fucker. Who would have known? Callie, Piñada? Somebody will look into your business, that much is certain. Where's the goddamned pioneer cabin in the woods? It's a condo complex of creepers and helpers, gossip over the grass, and chatters in checkouts next to the tabloids. I mean, fuck, how the hell can a man make his kilo of life?"

The Visors sat unmoved, their gray birds migrating with cold calculation. "You bastards think you can take me down? I'm a host of atoms; I'm a bundle of earth and strands wound into a helix of desire, and I'll just wind around until I come back, you bastards. Tell Evers I have $100 million worth. I'd like him to know the exact amount. Why does anybody need one hundred million of anything? Hell if I know. Ambition is addiction. And I once thought it was all so funny. How much New Jersey relies on Latin America! If they only knew. The contented have scruples to keep them safe and sound. It's an empty ocean beating in here, fuckers. That's where real life starts, out past all safety, where the moon and deep come up and go back to wonderful nothingness, over and over again, A-fucking-men."

Slinger finally stopped talking.

Lina said, "Did that mean anything?"

"No, just been talking myself to forever."

She looked at him now, tears rolling down both cheeks, "We're not coming back, are we?"

He saw her black eyes wet, looking at him for some answer he did not have. He looked at her as seriously as he had ever looked at any person in his life. "No, baby," he said. "We're little pieces of eternity on a one-way flight home."

"But we have thousands of kilos we could give them. They could have anything they want. Why don't they just take us down!" and she yelled out at Right Visor.

Slinger pulled his sweaty hand through his hair. His operation was a bungle, but at least all his files and maybe the *Bonita* were on their ways. There was no stopping that. He looked at the horizon, and he listened to the Lockheed engines whirring. An hour later the trinity of planes was twenty-seven miles off the coast of southern California. The strip of coastal lights had faded behind them, and Lina and Slinger were sentenced to the black night and the two unresponsive jets.

Lina was crying, "Just turn the fuck around … just turn around … just turn the fuck around. Oh god, we're not coming back. I'm not going to LA I never should have counted on you. What a mistake. I'm only twenty-seven, for fuck's sake, and look at you, a sloppy old man. A fucking dealer who tries to steal two thousand kilos! I want to get out! Turn the fucking plane around!"

She had talked herself into a terrible state, and no amount of stomping her feet would get her what she wanted this time. She had lived her life tantruming for what she wanted and manipulating men around her. Her hair now fell around her face—for the first time—with a frizz of failure and defeat and sadness. She didn't want to die young, and she was scared of what was coming next, of hell, of her sins giving her no luck in the next life, of falling in terror. She loved small rooms and beds, not the awful Pacific and this awful night and his stupidity.

"You never should have talked to Callie. She did this," said Lina. "That fucking girl did this somehow! I know it."

He thought of Callie Byrne and knew she would get all his files to the States. He had done that at least.

Slinger turned up the Dead, an electric guitar wandering everywhere. The night and the jet engines in front of him burned like the rings of cigarette lighters, and their tail lights blinked incessantly and became hypnotic flashes of inevitable red and green, stop and go and stop and go. In the musical waves of the night, he was debating whether to turn around and try the missiles and end in fire or to watch the navigation plot and the fuel supply as they approached the point of no return, when they would run out of fuel over the swallowing Pacific even if they did turn back. At least he had a choice about how to end it.

He recalculated the point of no return and stared intensely at the joints of jet lit up in the night in front of him. And he let it go, like revolutionary guerillas laying down arms, burying their wasted friends, and heading back to their villages. He programmed the autopilot. He looked over at Lina, her eyes smudged with tears and black mascara.

Finally, the point of no return passed, Slinger kept it to himself, and nothing remarkable happened. The engines rumbled on. Nobody asleep on the North American continent could fathom the depth of anti-climactic silence that came after the Point, like arriving home at the end of a long journey and nobody caring that you made it. He climbed out of the pilot's seat and held out his hand to Lina, and she shook her head stubbornly. He climbed back in the plane and pulled out a blanket and laid it on the floor in front of the rear seats. He lay down on it, his hair bunching up uncomfortably beneath him. So he grabbed an old sweatshirt he'd brought and rolled it into a makeshift pillow to rest his head on. Then he lay on his back and folded his hands over his chest.

"Lina."

"What?"

"Come lie down."

"Fuck off!"

But after a few minutes of sitting up there alone and the black windows, she got up and came back.

It had been about ten minutes since the Point.

"They're gone, they turned around."

"I know."

She had apparently figured out the situation.

"They took us out too far, didn't they?"

He nodded.

"But we could try to land on the water?"

"We could. But we have no life vests or anything. I didn't expect to be over water."

He thought about it. What if his calculations were wrong? What if the Point was off and they could make it? Maybe a fishing boat would pick them up if they did a water landing? "You like sharks? Or drowning? Or being knocked out?"

She lay down. "Knocked out," she said.

He got up, turned the plane back toward the coast, and came back. "It's just math," he murmured.

He thought about how many tortured ways there are to die. He was tired of attending to himself and the mess he'd made of his life. He moved beyond Evers and felt the atmosphere above the plane in his soul and forgot everyone, forgot Hector, Jorge, Callie, and would have forgotten Lina if she were not in his arms. But since she was, he held her and waited.

The Cessna's red and green strobes accompanied a black indistinct shadow moving out across the Pacific until finally there was a sputtering and choking and seizing of pumps and windy props spinning intermittently in vain and a dropping into Slinger's vertiginous mind and Lina's whirling belly and the ceiling of the sky knocking into their heads until they finally met the surface and split into pieces and waves of oceanic currents that carried the remains of Slinger and Lina into a sea chock full of refuse and debris.

For about three days after the crash, a waterlogged paperback title published by the University of Guatemala Press, one of only thirty-seven copies sold, *Central American Black Markets: Civil War, Organized Crime, and Peasant Politics*, floated until it finally dropped into the fathoms, with a corner turned down to a page with a footnote citing a dissertation from the 1980s on social survival tactics among rural poor men by John Paul Slinger, A.B.D.

The FAC Mirages had returned to a private airstrip near Culiacan, Mexico. The two pilots headed off for an early breakfast of sausage, salsa, and dark coffee, and then off to sleep through a sunny afternoon.

44

Finally, around nine o'clock, Evers took a call.

When he ended the call, Callie said, "Can we go now? I have a son and a sister to go see in Philadelphia." *Dillon sitting on a bench on the Boardwalk, waiting for her.*

"Yes, you can go now. Miguel, unlock please. Drive to the ship. If I hear your name again, you and your family will be dead." He said it as if he'd order a pizza for them, and smiled that strange smile again.

"I understand." *Slinger's notebook sitting in the truck.*

"You said you wanted Maul in the desert?"

"It was just an idea," Callie said.

"You decide. You throw him in the back yourself or leave him be. You put him in. We'll put him on a truck headed through the Chihuahuan Desert."

The locks clicked up. She and Ixchel got out of the car and crossed the yard. She felt the entire ranch watching her, the woman who had just negotiated a ceasefire with Manual Evers.

She saw Mrs. Granger on the porch, sitting in a chair, watching her. Ixchel walked to her, heading for the safety of the house.

Skull Cap was standing over Tony, his assignment.

She dragged Tony up. She stepped on his bloody foot, still with a bullet in it. He was half conscious and groaned through the hair gag, in shock.

"You don't fuck with an angry mother."

She pulled Tony by his armpits to the back of the SUV. She was taking out everything she could on him—she knew that even at the time—and she knew it went against all of her police training. But she rolled him into the back of the SUV. She looked at this terrible face a last time.

She nodded at Evers. She closed the door on Tony Maul.

Evers had Miguel start the SUV. Then his window smoothly descended. He surveyed the ranch, and he yelled over to Piñada, "San Olvidado is going to receive many blessings from me. Inspector, this is over now, you understand?"

The Inspector nodded.

It was dead quiet. Then a woman's voice—Mrs. Granger's—her tone low, but firm—"Jesus is the Lord and Savior! Jesus Christ Our Lord, Our Savior!"

It happened so quickly. She tried to shoot Manual Evers. The shots ricocheted off his bullet-proof car door.

In the dark of the yard and through the bright headlamps of the vehicles, it looked like a staged show.

Callie heard Piñada say, "Drop it! Vera, no!"

For a moment, testifying and sacrificing, Mrs. Granger was low on the porch, transforming the entire standoff into a desperate prayer.

Ixchel screamed, "Vera! Stop! They're leaving."

Then Vera Granger stood up. "What else? What else do you want? You want to come kill me? Kill children? What else? I'm more than glad to go with you! Heaven welcomes lost souls!"

There was a burst of gunfire from Skull Cap, and Mrs. Granger's torso became a gaping hole of open blood and flesh as she fell backward into Ixchel and Sylvia and fell in a heap, dead before she hit the ground.

A police man fired at Skull Cap, who went down.

The other soldiers circled, firing at the police.

Ixchel picked up Mrs. Granger's weapon and broke for the interior front parlor. Callie dove beneath one of the police cars.

She saw the Evers SUV fly by her and crash through one of the police trucks. *Angus*. She heard a few bullets hit the SUV, but it continued off, and Evers and Tony disappeared down the driveway. The police fired back on the narcos. Callie aimed toward the men near the porch to cover Angus.

A few narcos had pulled the SUVs in front of the school building. Others retreated to their SUVs and drove through the opening Evers's driver had made. One of the policemen was pinned under the car as it slid over his leg, screaming.

And then it was over.

Skull Cap and nine other narcos were dead on the ground near the silent black SUVs.

She heard nothing from the ranch house.

Three policeman were wounded or dead to her right. Callie ran toward the porch. She heard birds in the jungle, creatures still alive, breathing in the dead air that now hung over the terrible ranch. Piñada looked pale and resigned. As if he knew all this was going to happen eventually. A few police rushed to wounded colleagues. She saw one of them deliberately ground his foot into the wound of one of Evers's men.

On the porch, Mrs. Granger's face was frozen with an expression of defiant anguish and enraged faith. Callie would never forget her eyes—they peered at the world with an eternal certainty. She looked like a broken-open doll, splayed awkwardly against the front door of the house.

Angus came up behind her. Ixchel emerged from the front parlor with a blanket, and covered the body. Mrs. Granger's blood and parts had splattered against the wall in a chaotic pattern.

For an indeterminate time, they sat in a dazed shock under the front porch light, moths crashing into the lamp glass.

Eventually, Angus, staring out at the blue police lights flashing endlessly, attempted, "You did what you could, Callie."

She could feel his hand holding hers, sticky with blood. Adrenaline and defeat alternated in her pulse. The shrouded body of Mrs. Granger under the blanket was like an anchor of grief. Angus said it again, "You did what you could, Callie." He was saying what people who loved you said. Callie didn't respond. It felt like a lie that would take years to believe.

45

It took three days of bureaucratic reports before Piñada and the local prosecutors would clear them to leave the Department and arrange a burial for Vera Granger. She was buried in the same cemetery as Ixchel's mother. It was unclear what was going to happen to the ranch after the police released it to Mrs. Granger's estate and her daughter in Seattle. It seemed headed for a sale or, maybe, a boarded-up abandonment and gradual collapse. Mrs. Granger's daughter seemed hopeful that an NGO or Catholic aid group might want to carry the mission forward in honor of Mrs. Granger's life.

Callie filed her statement, mentioning nothing of the satchel full of Slinger's documents. She had started going through them in the last few days and had seen enough to know there was a maze of intricate details and documents on the Evers cartel operation.

Angus had turned to Callie at one point during the statement process, looking up from his forms. "I think I'm going to go into social work. Or maybe law school. I need a steady job."

"We need a steady life," Callie said.

Ixchel had Sylvia in the front wrap, and the baby girl looked as comfortable as she could be hanging from her mother's shoulders, completely innocent in the room where Callie had set Rachel's sneakers on the table. Ixchel was refusing to supply a statement but was waiting patiently for Callie and Angus to finish. Ixchel did have a story, though. She told her questioner that they were flying to New York to visit Ixchel's father for an American Thanksgiving holiday.

"After all this, you're still getting on that ship?" Angus asked Ixchel at one point when Piñada was out of the room.

Ixchel didn't hesitate. "Because of all this, I'm still getting on the ship. You think I'm going to leave Jorge's men with twenty-two women on a trip that I helped arrange?"

After word of the Evers massacre, Jorge had fled. Already, the air seemed to feel lighter, the streets safer, the world temporarily humane.

During the three days before the ship left port, Ixchel organized the other girls' transport out of San Olvidado and Flores in three Latin Leather Suburbans. Callie could feel the emptiness in the village. They were done with a life of laying leather, done with boredom, done with dreams of grandmothers, the police, and the church, done with old women sitting on the pavement smiling and weaving Mayan blankets for tourists.

While at the Flores Department building giving statements, Callie had received a text message from Father Tim, *Dillon and your sister remain fine. Hector cooperated as promised. Everyone believed it? You okay?* Nothing would ever be *okay* again, Callie thought, but she wrote him back it was.

Before they left, Piñada stood with her at the door of the Department. She was overlooking the square and the basketball court. *Slinger walking in a circle around the palm with Tony. The basketball court. The Cathedral hovering over Angus as he walked through the square.*

Piñada said to her, "You're leaving, right? You are safer in the States, but La Cadena will be coming for you."

"I made a deal with Evers."

"And you think that will matter to him? He will make sure his men know what he wants. And he wants this entire story disappeared. Like it never happened. Believe me we know about disappearing history here."

She looked at the Inspector, and saw a man who had no choices left. "What if he comes for you?"

He said, "I don't know. We will have to see what things look like then. We hoped Slinger would be here for a long time. I thought he had made arrangements. He had a philosophy. More like a farmer just doing the work."

When they got out of the police building, they wanted to return to the ranch one last time, to somehow reclaim it if they could. The front yard and parlor were taped off, but they were allowed to use the cottages and the kitchen. Sitting on the back porch having a dinner at the ranch, Ixchel suddenly said to Callie and Angus. "You don't have to come."

Angus looked at Callie, "She's right. Tony and Jorge are gone."

"Hector's not. The girls are not. I'm not."

Angus didn't push it and neither did Ixchel. If they had learned anything about each other in the last month, it was that once one of their minds was set, it was set.

She had thought about it, though. "My sister said the same thing when I called her. 'Why do you always need to choose trouble? Those girls are not your responsibility. Come home. Dillon wants to see you'. And the like. And I spoke with Dillon. And I do want to go get my son and never leave him again. But you can't tell me that some of this isn't my fault for coming down here. Especially Rachel. And you can't tell me that it wouldn't be helpful to act as a kind of marshall with the girls and try to finish this thing. You want me to let twenty-four girls go into the sex trade in Atlantic City? You want to leave Ixchel and Sylvia to get into a cargo container for a week, or worse, leave them in Petén with this madness?"

Angus stroked his beard and shook his head. He knew she was right. "But I don't know what we do when get to Jersey."

Callie looked at them both. "We'll have all the evidence we need when they get there."

It was late, almost midnight, before they drove Slinger's truck to the Sunny Mopan Inn. Ixchel got out with Sylvia, "Maybe Angus is right? Maybe we can never get out of this debt?"

Angus came around to help Ixchel carry her bag. "If things go wrong, I'll call you, and you can head into the center of town, and we'll go back."

"I don't go back," Ixchel said. "Sylvia never goes back."

They headed up to the third floor where they would join the others. The *Bonita* was supposed to sail at six the next morning, and they would board in the middle of the night. The girls waited in a few rooms in the dark, watching TV, waiting for the morning to come. Ixchel paced. The rest chattered about blankets, food, and water, and how they would live with one small bag of luggage in America. The girls were nervous arguing. Sylvia started crying. "Shut that baby up, Ixchel. What you bring her for?"

Ixchel ignored the other girls, who sneered at her.

Playa, a thin fifteen-year old, looked at the annoyed girl. "You can't shut a baby up. They talk when they want."

"You talk too much yourself."

Callie took a turn and bounced Sylvia on her arm. She laid her on the floor and looked at her dark hair against the white tiles. She wriggled on the floor with a pink face scrunched up in need.

Ixchel, though, was exasperated. "What the hell do you want? A nipple, a bottle of milk, a clean piece of cloth? We're going to New York, Sylvia, so you can't just sit here crying."

Sylvia continued crying. Ixchel said, "I want to see the ship before I go."

"We can't leave here."

"I'll go where I want." She needed to be outside before they were shut into that box. Handing Sylvia to Playa, Ixchel walked down the stairs to the street. Callie caught up with her. "Okay, okay."

"Colocha, get on the handlebars. We'll put it back when we're done." She climbed on a red-and-black beach cruiser leaning in a doorway. Ixchel and Callie rode through the dark streets that during the day were full of women shopping, buzzing with reggae, with clothes, shoes, leather belts, blouses hanging off flimsy racks on the sidewalks, and young men on the corners sitting on banana crates. Callie dreads flew back into Ixchel's face as they wound their way through the streets, bump-bumping over speed humps on the empty road.

Ixchel leaned up to Callie's ear. "You feel it, Colocha? This is the world Sylvia's in now. And then—poof, we'll be gone, new people."

They rode into the port area. A night shift was on, and they could hear men hooting at them, tools clanging on the floors of the warehouses, and men driving forklifts of pallets wrapped in metal bands. Callie pointed them toward Wharf #5. Callie saw the number three painted on the side of a large warehouse and knew they were getting close.

They jumped off the bike and snuck down to the end of Wharf #4. They stood behind an old crane, looking out the narrow channel that would shoot them out to sea—the Black Out There. Dilapidated fishing boats sat low in the water with a few sparse running lights in their docks or moorings.

They saw across to Wharf #5 to the *Bonita,* although the chipped *i* on the port bow made it look like it was the *Bon ta.*

"I don't like that ship," Ixchel said. "It looks like a prison."

They both wondered the same thing: how many other girls had been kidnapped or smuggled on a boat like this? They both understood that if their plan failed, all the girls at the Sunny Mopan were headed for indentured, invisible lives of beatings, sex trade, and a hopelessness that might not end.

"You really think we can bring this whole thing down?" Ixchel asked. "There are mothers in Petén who make their girls hide in holes in the ground when they come into a village. What if they come back for your son?"

"I don't know."

"Where will you go? Here they kill the police that try too hard. I think they will treat you the same."

Callie picked off a sliver of rotting wood from a creosoted dock pylon and flicked it into bobbing foam of dirty port water. "I don't know."

"Who else goes down beside Jorge if we pull this off?"

"Jorge's guy in Atlantic City. Hector. He had lists of girls' names and next to them were cities. New York, Houston, LA, Miami. We're here. We're the only ones inside this."

"I won't be shipped right back?"

"I don't think so if you become a government witness. They'll need you as evidence; they'll need your testimony. You should be able to get a deal."

"We'll see," Ixchel said. "We're gonna live in one of those?" she asked, and nodded to a rust-red container that said *Hapag-Lloyld* on the side. "It looks like a toy box or something. And we're the toys."

"Jorge gave you the idea that you should model in New York, didn't he?"

Ixchel nodded, "When I was around ten years old. Told me there's a big Latino market for pretty girls like me. That I could be a supermodel if I worked at it and was willing to be with the right people."

Callie took out a tightly folded piece of paper from her jeans pocket and handed it to her. "I thought you'd want to see this."

Ixchel unfolded one of Rachel's lists.

"You see all these codes. Here's you. IC/10g/96. That's you. Their plan is to move you—move us—around. Jersey, Carolina, all over. We don't do what they want—they'll beat us or threaten to ship you to back here or to Mexico or chain you up for a few days."

Ixchel looked at the ship floating in the water. Callie saw a leaky vision of America, a New York of speckled towers of light, the determined sense of Out of Here, the prospect immense and significant, like the Atlantic Out There, a world of engines and computer navigation and satellite radios.

Down the dock a stevedore in a hard hat started waving and shouting at them.

"Everybody plays with us."

Ixchel asked again, "Why do you think Slinger helped us?"

Callie thought about that, "I don't really know. I guess he he drew a line somewhere in that crazed head."

"I don't need any more fucking help from men. There's nothing to do now but go, eh?" She meant that she and Callie were tied to each other. She could tell Callie thought the same.

"Take pictures of what you can. The Sunny Mopan room. The other girls. The ship. What happens when we get there. Take this card. My cell phone is on it. Memorize the name and the other phone number. It's a bar in Philadelphia. The Grave. No matter where you end up, call my cell or this number any night. If I'm not there, I put two other names. Father Tim. Or Symington Wandreth. They both know people in power."

Ixchel took the Grave card but seemed to ignore it. "I like Angus. I want to see him in Philadelphia."

Callie smiled "I think he wants that too. Let's go see him."

They rode down the wharf to the slip for the *Night Slipper.* Angus was on board putting in supplies. He smiled at Callie. *I told you so.* Ixchel went down to the dock ramp, jumped on the speed boat, and asked Angus if they could meet in Philadelphia. Angus had come down here under the illusion he had the life he wanted. But then he got here and saw his life was missing ordinary things he didn't know he wanted in it—a woman, a job he cared about doing well, which he had not had since leaving the military.

He said yes they would meet in Philadelphia. As Ixchel climbed back on the dock, Angus was not smiling anymore.

A longshoreman started walking up the dock but hadn't seen them yet.

Ixchel climbed on the bike. She felt a renewed hope. "When I get to the States, I'll see for myself whether that big fucking country is bigger than me."

Callie hopped on the handle bars. Ixchel pedaled them back toward town. Ixchel stopped and asked a lady walking a side street with her grocery cart, "Ma'am, which way do you go to get to old?" She meant it with all seriousness, but the old woman took it badly.

The old lady picked up a gourd and held it like a gun, shouting, "Proud girl! Proud girl! Proud girl!"

"Proud old lady!" Ixchel said.

"I'm sorry," Callie said, trying to diffuse the situation.

"Proud old lady! Which way to America, which way to get old? Which way to be young?" The old lady pushed her cart, ignoring the two insolent young women who were clearly out of their heads.

They rode the rest of the way back to the Mopan, returned the red-and-black bike. Callie saw Ixchel to the room on the third floor balcony. Before Callie could say anything, Ixchel shut the door to room number 337 and turned the deadbolt. Callie stationed herself outside on night guard duty.

A few minutes later, Ixchel came out with a Mayan blanket folded in her hand, "I want you to have this. My mother made it, Colocha. She used to sit outside our house with the loom tied around her back and to the cross she nailed into the rotting boards. I have one from my grandmother."

Callie could hear the murmurs of the girls inside mixing with the sound of the surf from the tide along the barrier beaches outside the city. Between the buildings, the lights of a cruise ship anchored in its own self-contained world of sixteen decks of distraction and coral destruction. It might as well have been a ship from Mars.

16

Callie tried to sleep outside on the balcony on a makeshift blanket, but it was no use. She ended sitting up against the wall, waiting. Angus returned, and they shared a joint to try to break the tension, elbows on knees. Callie had Ixchel's blanket draped over her legs, the orange, black, and red zigzags taking on a strange glow from an iridescent streetlamp across the way reflecting onto the Sunny Mopan's passageways.

Finally, around two-thirty in the morning, a white van pulled up on the street.

"Here we go," Angus said. "You sure they won't just shoot us and dump us overboard?"

"No," Callie said.

"No they won't or no you're not sure?"

"Both." She reached in her purse and pulled out Betty. "But if we need it, I have my own head protector."

They went in the dark room and woke the girls. Ixchel hugged Callie with one arm and took her place behind the other women but in front of Angus.

Two men came to the bottom of the stairs.

"Tell them to come," one of them said.

She couldn't see the face, but she recognized the voice. Jorge Mercado had returned.

"We'll be down."

Callie waved the girls out of the room in a line, as if she had been sex trafficking for years. Then came Ixchel carrying Sylvia, and behind her, Angus.

Jorge smirked at Callie. "Once they board, they're on their own."

"Evers and I have a little arrangement for these girls—one of them is touched, and he'll move a few hundred thousand from your bank account to mine."

Jorge scowled and looked confused by the threat. Evers did control banking access and security access in the dark web. "That's a lie."

"Believe whatever you want, but I don't think you're in a position to do anything else but do what you're told if you want to live more than a few days." *He'll be arrested and sent to prison, and then in a yard, one of my men will cut him up and throw him in the garbage in the Atlantic and he will rain on my garden.*

They all boarded two vans and moved in the night through the small streets and out along the shore road to the port where Callie and Ixchel had ridden the bicycle. The inlets and docks were filled with boats, like a traffic jam of fiberglass and fun. But the warehouses looked like abandoned military buildings.

All of them were quiet.

Dark Glasses, one of the ship's officers, pulled up next to the *Bonita*. Wharf #5 was dark; the *Bonita* had a few running lights still on, which bathed it in subdued pinkish light. "The first open container across the deck."

The night air was damp and black. Callie thought she saw the silhouettes of Slinger, Lina, and Angus on the railing up on the bridge, but it just mind tricks. A crane was completing the loading of containers. Dark Glasses appeared to supervise, while the crew operated the crane and forklifts, signed paperwork, dealt with fuel trucks, and worked the guide lines.

Angus paced nervously next to Ixchel.

A crew of merchant seamen—an unlikely collection of Belizeans, Russians, Filipinos, and Mexicans—loaded the cargo containers, moving back and forth as the crane's cables slung up and winched pallets full of Slinger's operation into the air, swaying gently back and forth as teetering blocks of leather-bound cocaine hovered over the dock.

It reminded Callie of operations moving between Bagdad and Mosul, how bigger things than you led to finding yourself in the middle of incomprehensible, inane bureaucracy. Callie had the same feeling now as she'd had learning basic Arabic, trying to see through generations of local conspiracies, and layers of deadness. She felt she should pull the hawsers and undo all the twisted knots of this operation like a magician, but they were just too large. She had a new respect for undercover agents, trading their way up crime organizations, performing frauds and lies for some kind of poor justice. She reminded herself she wouldn't be here without Tony forcing all this.

"How many days in there?" asked Ixchel.

Dark Glasses walked off, not answering.

"Slinger said it would be about a week," Callie said.

"A week inside that?" another girl said, worried.

"Who's going to meet us?" said a third.

Ixchel and Callie caught each other's eyes, and Callie said, "I have people."

What if the plan didn't go? Where would they end up? Dispersed like car parts, out to basements and boarding houses.

The girls got out on the wharf. Dark Glasses waved them on. "C'mon, move your little asses. Nobody wants you here, and nobody wants you there." His face was as secure as a dirty cop's, insulated by layers of fat protecting a biologically rigged system of corruption.

Ixchel and the girls walked up the dock.

Ixchel stopped and looked at Callie, who understood what she was thinking.

There should be some other way, the world a different place than this. I just wanted to start a new life in New York, and now I'm going to bring down Hector Perez and Jorge Mercado?

Ixchel said, "If I stay? Backstrap abuse. And if I go? Abuse on my back."

Callie didn't know what else to say. They had made their plan. Callie felt an immense responsibility, and Ixchel was asking an equally immense answer from the world. Neither had any idea what waited at the other end. Their individual pasts seemed to separate and bind them at the same time. They'd both tried to escape their lives; both had taken wrong turns to find new lives.

Ixchel, waving her baby bag of formula, said, "I'll be like a can of beans in a tin can," she said. Callie watched Ixchel climb up toward the deck with the other girls. Sylvia's head bounced on Ixchel's shoulder as she walked up the gangplank, which was clanking and shaking like a metal fire escape on the side of a slum building.

Another crewman looked down from the deck. He waved for Angus to leave.

She looked up at the pockmarked blue ship and saw several men with machine guns strapped around their shoulders.

She started climbing the gangplank behind the girls.

"Callie?" Angus called behind her.

Jorge pointed his gun at her, waving her back. "Aw, Christ, Jorge," she yelled up to him, "I'm not going to do anything. What the hell you think I'm here for?"

The girls climbed slowly ahead of her, and she could see the containers arrayed before them like a prison cell block. Slinger's and Tony's containers filled with nothing but leather, extortion, and self-delusion stacked atop each other. Callie reached the deck. Dark Glasses backed Jorge off.

Angus stood on the wharf watching her.

Dark Glasses came over with a friendly smile. "So you come wid us?"

"Yeah, I'm coming. Slinger told me to ask for you. I'd like to know exactly how things are going down up there?"

"It's pretty straightforward. Hector pays the freight. The *Bonita* goes up the Narrows, docks as planned in the Port Newark-Elizabeth marine terminal. Our Teamsters local does their crane work with Latin Leather Group fine leather jackets, coffee, bananas, and handbags. The girls' container is off first, before Customs arrives. They'll be on the Jersey Turnpike in no time. That's it."

She said, "That easy."

"That easy. It's like everything else in life. Timing."

She nodded, "Okay."

She followed him out into the running spotlights as the crane motor spun and another container dropped on top of the girls' container with a metallic thud.

Below, she saw Jorge harassing Ixchel. Sylvia's dark head of hair against Ixchel's white shirt bounced like a buoy as Ixchel waved her hand and twisted her torso to avoid Jorge's face and words and commands.

Ixchel had something almost old-fashioned and noble about her, standing on the deck of this dilapidated ship with her large, fragile eyes looking both empty and determined to fill them with a new life.

"Let me talk to Jorge," she said to Dark Glasses.

"Sure, I don't care. No little fits, though. Hugs and kisses, off we go," he mumbled.

The ocean wind blew through her. She went down from the bridge and over the deck to Ixchel sitting inside the container with Sylvia. The place looked like an industrial-strength slumber party. The girls arranged blankets the best they could, nervous but making jokes. The container smelled like urine.

She ignored Jorge, "Ixchel, how about I take Sylvia for you?" Sylvia stared up at her with wide brown eyes and cheeks like ethereal flower bulbs: brown, perfectly smooth, ready to bloom. The child of an unknown father.

"Nobody takes her. Not even you," Ixchel said.

Jorge pointed a pistol at Callie's abdomen. "Or maybe I'll shoot to keep the population down."

"I'm having a conversation here. I know speech is difficult for you, but some of us still use words."

Jorge moved to grab Callie's arm, but she twisted away and leveled her gun right back at him.

"Nope, he just can't do it," she said to everybody. "A fucking rabid dog right here. I think we have to put him down." She felt her temper in her trigger finger—furious at Jorge, at Slinger, at Ixchel for her stubbornness, the ease and responsibility of the trigger up against her finger.

Total freedom and justice opened at the mouth of the dark cargo container.

All she had to do was pull.

It would be for Rachel and Ixchel and Sylvia at the same time.

Then she saw Angus at the top of the gangplank. Several of the men came running over, AK-47s drawn at her. Then she heard a shout and discerned amid the commotion of her fraying mind that it was directed straight at her.

"Christ, we all have a fucking job!" Dark Glasses bellowed, "We all have a job. I get paid, everybody gets paid. Now get them into the container."

Jorge stood in front of her, tapping one of the rifle muzzles, as if he'd won. He nodded at two of the men with guns who gripped Callie's arms and made it clear she was heading into the cargo container.

The other girls gathered around Ixchel in a chorus:

"We'll all take care of you."

"It's okay, Ms. Byrne, we paid our money!"

"Ixchel will be good!"

Jorge spit a mouthful of sunflower seeds on the deck at her feet.

The last thing Callie saw as she climbed into the container was the eternal black sunspots of Dark Glasses high above them peering down over the high railing's edge, his white teeth in a wide smile of genuine Caribbean joy under the industrial running lights on the bridge.

We all have a job.

47

In the dark cargo container, Callie's mind was haunted by thin men cutting trees. Through the blackness, green sunlight and the sound of chainsaws and the men in their toyo hats outside of town cutting back the jungle became more real to her than when she had cleared brush herself or stood watching them with Slinger. The metal container's stench was urine, moldy blankets, and salted rust—the smell of humanity passing through a crypt. She heard men outside shouting every so often. She could feel the rumble of the ship's engines beneath her, making the hard sheet metal beneath the sleeping bag vibrate and the sidewall at her back shudder. None of the other girls said anything. Thank god they had finally shut up.

But she could hear their presence in the dark, the nervous breathing, the restlessness. Sylvia was sleeping now, seeming to join in the slow, bittersweet act of leaving. She felt a significant bump of the tugboat pushing the ship away from the dock.

"Here we go," Ixchel said.

And somehow now, Ixchel seemed the only woman who understood her. They were both trapped in this, and hoped the other knew what she was doing.

The ship slid sideways, so slowly that it seemed impossible it would ever get anywhere. It was moving away from all Ixchel knew. Callie felt like Ixchel was the soul of a rare, migrating butterfly.

The slimmest cracks of Caribbean morning light eked through the seams in the container's doors. Out there, birds and monarchs were migrating north with her, an entire Atlantic, a completely foreign and endless sameness that separated continents and families. Ixchel cradled Sylvia closer, kissed her head for luck, and let her drop back into her lap. Until she had Sylvia, Ixchel had been a lone thing. But from what Callie could see, when Ixchel became a mother, it was as if she'd given birth to every living thing.

Callie's cell phone was safely hidden in the blanket Ixchel's grandmother had made.

She'd already taken several dark pictures and texted them to Angus while cell service was still in range.

The *Bonita* quivered underneath them.

She would take more pictures in Jersey too.

She'd get pictures of Ixchel, Dillon, and Sylvia in Philly. More and more pictures of her future.

In another week, if things went to plan, she'd be cutting an immigration deal with the Feds and putting the man who collected these girls, Jorge Mercado, away for life.

Time was difficult to endure. Her cell phone at least showed the time of day. Callie guessed the *Bonita* was probably off the coast of Florida by now. Angus and one other go-fast boat were somewhere out there, preceding the cargo ship and running along the coast with nothing else but power and speed.

Then the engines stopped.

She heard a loudspeaker and a voice coming over the water and into the *Bonita*.

Then she heard shots fire. Orders coming through a PA for all crew to stand along the rail with their hands over their heads echoing from the cutter's loudspeakers.

More warning shots fired.

The engines ground into a vibrating reverse.

The ship finally stopped after hundreds of yards.

244 • JOHNNIE DUN

Ixchel climbed past several girls, Sylvia in her arms. "Something's wrong." Callie could hear in her voice: *the plan I have awaited for years is going wrong for some unseen and unknown reason.*

"Ixchel, stay calm," Callie said.

Some in the group whispered harshly for silence, still hoping for a smuggled destination. Others naively thought they were just going to be let out for their daily break. But Ixchel knew the hopelessness of the law's labyrinth once you were in it. Nobody wanted to be discovered like this and sent back. They were here to move to a new life, even if it would be a debased one for a while. At least they would be poor and debased in New York.

In the pitch black, with all the flashlights off, Ixchel picked up Sylvia and three cans of beans beside her. Callie heard yelling across the deck, and boots stepping on containers, clanging door handles, squeaking hinges. Ixchel put the cans inside Sylvia's blanket wrap.

Boots and voices scattered around the deck. Other containers were being opened. Callie could hear the door levers and hinges.

It happened in slow motion, like a car wreck happening to you.

She felt tense, dejected bodies around her.

The metal door opened and flung around.

Bright midday sun exploded into the container. A crew of Coast Guard seamen were on deck.

Callie and Ixchel made their way with the other girls out of the container in the direction of one of the seamen.

Callie saw a suspended container, half over the deck and half over the ocean water below. It was like a child's building block ready to tumble. It looked like Jorge had tried to dump the container on top of theirs, hoping to get to theirs before the Coast Guard had approached. Had Angus told Jorge they were coming? Had he missed them altogether? How did they know about the shipment?

Jorge squinted through his dark sunglasses at three clean-cut Coast Guard seamen wearing blue baseball hats, orange bulletproof life vests, and blue coveralls. The boarding officer, who looked like a shaving commercial model, was ordering them all to stand down, to listen to every order he gave, and declared that he was now in command of the ship until further notice.

Callie heard men's voices talking with firm, trained control.

The boarding officer ordered the seamen to start opening and searching other containers. Teams fanned out as the crew stood, hands on heads, their distant homes now pointed at by their elbows.

The seaman next to her was in discussion on the deck about getting lines and getting the girls processed. Ixchel stood in a stone cold indifference. It was as if she were not there. The Coast Guard cutter was tied to the ship. The shiny glints of water twinkled and vanished in the punishing sunlight. The dark blue shadows of US maritime law were shining flashlights into containers and searching the one the girls had occupied.

The group of women stood on deck with nowhere to go.

Ixchel said nothing in response to the courteous but firm orders to remain where they were. Then she looked at the seaman next to her. He seemed like a boy in a movie.

"We came from the jungle, from a little town," Ixchel said. "We have nothing back there but murders and drug gangs," she said. "We need asylum."

He replied, with a respectful military courtesy, "I'm sorry, ma'am. We are just upholding US law. We do not determine asylum."

"And you beat us with your laws, don't you?" She squinted back at him, bitter at his polite and clean-shaven face.

Ixchel looked around at the ship, shifted back and forth on her heels.

Callie was feeling all the conflict in Ixchel: her home in Lake Petén Itzá, pieces of herself in the ranch front parlor and the jungle, lifetimes packed together, Slinger getting them out of and into this all at the same time. Whole fields of coca sweat and sunburn seem doused with pesticidal wilt and a tidal, biblical flood of ocean.

The officer looked at her. "Please follow me. We will get you to land safely."

She saw Jorge with the cutter's officer.

Another boarding Coast Guard officer was taking photographs of the leather lying in the boxes and ripped open like slaughtered cows. They were peeling back the leather and finding nothing. An officer near Jorge took out a knife, ripped the liner. He held one up like a fish. "Just leather." He said it with disappointment, hoping to have one-upped the DEA. Evers had denied them that satisfaction.

Callie watched Jorge as they searched. He watched Ixchel and the women across the deck, the colors of their shirts and brown faces and intense eyes all trained on him. He had arranged Slinger's cooks, the transportation, and the operations for nothing. He had worked for two years to set up the packing with Ixchel and the women, for nothing. He looked at the white cutter and the blue uniforms heading around the ship, at the women down on the deck, government blankets and wraps around them. He had a face of arrogant cruelty. He would have killed all of them if he could have.

48

"This vessel is under US command now," the officer said to the girls through a megaphone. "We will be taking you down one at a time, and the girls will be disembarked to the cutter *Reliance*. You'll receive food, water, and medical attention. You all will be processed at Customs and Immigration."

They repeated their instructions in Spanish and the girls behind Callie and Ixchel were silent. She saw Sylvia's eyes were closed.

"She's asleep. Better not to see the world," Ixchel said.

It all seemed surreal in the middle of all this water, a Coast Guard cutter crew prowling over their things, changing the journey itself, carrying records and shooting photographs and marking containers while the ship floated in odd silence. Callie knew she had her cell phone with the pictures of Jorge and the other men on it. The wind carried wafts of damp sea air, brine, burnt diesel, and garbage. Ixchel seemed to be running plans in her head like a maze, back and forth, ending in a dead end on this deck.

"We're not going back," she whispered to Sylvia. She heard the seaman say something to her, but it didn't have any meaning to it.

Callie was afraid of what Ixchel might do. There always had been a black, hopeless freedom in Ixchel, yet she gripped Sylvia tightly, her eyes like a rabid dog's, ready to bite anyone who tried to come for her.

"You're not going to do anything to us, right?" one of the other girls was saying.

"Not going to do anything? That's what people do. They do things to us," Ixchel said.

Callie just kept wondering who had informed on the *Bonita*. Had Angus changed plans? Evers? Whoever it was had been specific about the ship and its destination, because they had found them with ease. So much ease that the whole plot seemed foolish. If she had been military or law enforcement, they would have known about the undercover operation, would have bided their time to make the case airtight.

The women behind her were being escorted through the hatchway to the white cutter, the ocean swishing back and forth under the blue sky.

Callie heard a seaman asking for Ixchel's name, age, and her place of birth.

Ixchel Cante. Nineteen. San Olvidado, Guatemala.

She said nothing though.

The officer asked if another seaman could hold Sylvia while they processed Ixchel and lead her to the gangway between the cutter and the ship.

"No, I will hold her," she said, a demeanor like a boxer, face to face.

Ixchel looked out at the water's glare in the distance. Callie followed her gaze, trying to see what Ixchel saw. But it was just the expanse of the Atlantic waters.

Sylvia turned toward Ixchel's chest; the three cans of beans were heavy inside Sylvia's wrap.

Ixchel held out her cell phone to the officer. She looked at the phone. It seemed to be getting messages from *Callie Byrne, Callie Byrne*. "Take this," she said. "Put this under my name. It's evidence that that man ran this trafficking ring." She nodded toward Jorge. "Will you let me stay if these pictures help you? I want to be a witness. I would like to request asylum in the United States because my life is at risk back home. If I go back, they will kill me."

The officer took her by the elbow. "You will have a chance to make all official requests once you're handed to US Customs."

"That man there, Jorge Mercado, has kidnapped girls, killed people, smuggled people into the US, forced girls on this ship. I have pictures on that phone. You better arrest him."

"Yes, ma'am," the seaman said neutrally, reaching for Sylvia. "You'll all be safe. We'll give her back to you shortly, but we need to get you out of here."

He was so polite. Trained polite. Programmed to "deal with them." Callie felt Ixchel's disillusion: a universe of indifference and disregard. He hadn't listened to her. He didn't believe her. She felt the recklessness welling up in Ixchel—the last straw in her soul. She felt a fear of a military man taking Sylvia, of a government confiscating her child while she cried, shipping her where they wanted, keeping her where they wanted.

Ixchel looked suddenly broken and tired of men around her holding everything.

She twisted out of the grip of the officer, gripping Sylvia to her closely.

It was little more a defiant spin. She stepped off like walking down the beach of Lake Petén. She tumbled toward the water below. It was roughly a four-story fall to the water, and it was a long time down, during which her body was no longer hers. It tilted sideways and forward. She held Sylvia somehow.

She heard a cry descending into the hard floor of water that Ixchel and Sylvia smacked into like a jumper into cement.

She became Ixchel in the water.

Her head throbbed.

She struggled to breath in the deep cold around her.

She and Sylvia were in a gray deep, and she saw a blurry daylight far above her.

She wished for Angus, felt a deep pressure in her chest. She had tried to hold Sylvia to lessen the impact, but now realized her arms were struggling around her, grabbing around for something, for Sylvia. The Atlantic freeze had woken her entire being. Her eyes and lungs were full of salted, metallic water. She saw a blur. Her arms grasped at shadows. Was that the disappearing bundle of orange blanket around Sylvia? Three cans of beans taking her down instead of both of them. The orange smudge disappearing into a black, airless depth.

There was shouting and a large splash. And then another. Floats flew in the sky and slapped down on the water somewhere nearby.

Everyone's heads bowed and strained, looking at the patch of water, a small whitecap just merging back into the dark black and blue. Ixchel heard the officer yelling and the crew scrambling above.

The two hulls were like canyon sides rising above her.

Two seamen made the leap.

She couldn't see any orange blanket. No orange blanket.

A circle of men stood at the railing and looking down at Ixchel, several giving terse commands and pointing.

An arm wrapped around Ixchel's midsection, an arm forcing her to lay back and stare up.

A second seaman was diving down repeatedly looking for Sylvia.

There was a long tension. The diver came up after several minutes, his head nodding, gasping for breath, holding his head above the currents and waves between the ship and the cutter. He held Sylvia. The immutable wind gusted, and the face of the sailor was calm, business-like, exhausted.

It took twenty minutes to get her, the two seamen, and Sylvia hauled up to the deck of the cutter, wrapped in blankets, clothes tight and wet, hair hanging in her face.

Ixchel looked over the horizon and its cold routine of choppy waves filled with the drowned and the dispossessed. They would not give her Sylvia after the attempt, and a female sailor took her to the cutter to get warm.

She saw Jorge chewing seeds, smiling, dead calm in plastic handcuffs, far above the abysmal ocean floor where he belonged with ugly pre-historic fish.

She had lost something to him that she might never regain.

Ixchel had never seen so much endless blue water in her life. It was as if life had never been on any ground at all.

49

When Callie was in grade school, she pictured Florida as a stuffed Christmas stocking. Now she pictured a black speckled pistol pointing west. After all the police and customs documentation was over in Miami, she was finally freed. They collected her evidence from her phone, corroborated her story with Angus, and subjected both of them to several rounds of interrogation. Their history as US Army MPs, their records of drug use and rehab after their service, and their few months in Guatemala had not been easy ones to vet.

Finally, both Angus and Callie were free to go back to Philadelphia on their own recognizance. The police refused to say where all of the others had been taken, but it was clearly to a Customs and Immigration detention center. They would research that as soon as they were home and could locate Ixchel and Sylvia.

For two days, she debated whether to hand over Slinger's papers to the Miami agents. She did not. She wasn't ready to reveal those until she knew everything that was in them and what they meant. With corruption and cartels so difficult to trace, she decided it was her only card and to hold it, unsure what she would do with them until she could read through the details and connect with Ixchel. She had the notion that it was part of the leverage that would bring Ixchel and Sylvia to Philly.

As they entered Miami airport, Callie was paranoid Evers's La Cadena was waiting for them behind every pillar. But all they could see was a self-absorbed girls tennis team buried in their cell phones and Accenture advertisements on the walls. Pre-recorded Homeland Security announcements blasted the air around them.

She spoke with Dillon and Beth once they were at the gate. They would be at the airport when she and Angus landed. Beth had been quiet but obviously relieved.

Beth put Dillon on the phone.

"Dillon, I'm so sorry. I'm coming for you. I love you."

"It's okay, Mommy, Aunt Beth took care of me while you were gone."

Callie didn't know what to say. She turned away from Angus toward the wall, pretending to try to hear Dillon's voice, but really to keep him from seeing the tears welling in her eyes. She said, "I'm coming for you. You be good for Aunt Beth, okay?"

"I will Mommy. I'll be good."

She sat rocking in a homey white rocker with Slinger's leather case in her lap. She recalled the last weeks—*the day she arrived at the ranch, Mrs. Granger's holy Jesus faithful life, sitting with Angus on the street with Gallo beer, Slinger's and Lina's inseparable mouths, Ixchel's continental dreams, the clinic where Sylvia was born.*

Rocking in the chair, she stared out across the crisscross of taxiways and runways. Everything and nothing had changed. Farmers in Bolivia and San Olvidado planted, paste burned, and flights and truckers were still moving like the tides. Evers had to be waiting for her. Angus rocked next to her. He knew the guilt and the duty struggling in her and he let her be. She loved that about Angus—he was very good at letting things be. They just sat quietly watching planes land and take off across the field.

They took their seats on the plane, "You could come live with me if you want," Angus said with an innocent hope.

Callie sorted through many of Slinger's papers on the first few hours of the Miami flight and had fallen asleep with her head on Angus's shoulder. Lake Petén Itzá and its sunken valley were like distant family members who'd overstayed their welcome. The disaster of the ranch killings and the negotiations with Evers hung over her just as intensely as anything she had seen in Iraq. She was now tied for the rest of her life to the Guadeloupe Ranch. *Mrs. Granger's blood all over her hands and arms.*

Callie wanted to say yes. She hunched down in the seat and put her knees up and slid her head against the window. *Slinger's brown leather satchel of Evers papers beneath seat in front of her.* "I don't think I can, Angus."

He reached over and wound her dreads around his fist. "Not that way, just roommates."

She needed a deep sleep to cross into the States. "I know. You can come with me to see Dillon, though."

"I'd like that."

"So what are you going to do with that?" he said, nodding beneath the seat at the satchel.

"I don't know yet."

They didn't need to say more. They both knew now that the papers revealed bank accounts, contacts, cartel leadership, shipping and logistics logs, supply chain networks, customs and government bribes and employees. It was years of evidence compiled. They both knew there were two possible lives in the satchel: one that would turn over the papers anonymously and another that would turn herself and the papers in as evidence against the Evers Corporation and end the Callie Byrne they knew.

50

When they arrived in Philadelphia, Callie sprinted through the concourse. Outside, planes glided slowly out on the tarmac and snub-nosed tractors buzzed on errands. Men with orange batons waved at black women on courtesy carts laughing with each other as old ladies faced backwards, staring at the past and then disappearing into the crowd. Dillon was waiting for them on the other side of the simulated mall of anxious capitalism and beautiful marketing images. The air-controlled PGA Golf, Eddie Bauer Specials, and Bulgari Jewelry were empty of people but full of glass displays. An imitation pushcart of Sunglass Hut eyes were stacked in columns and glared at her.

As they exited security and headed for the street, looking for Beth's Land Rover, she saw so many cars, people, and taxies. She felt like her grandmother from County Cork standing on the deck of the *Mary Elizabeth* in 1927 trying to understand Lower Manhattan.

Then she saw him. A little boy in a Ryan Howard shirt holding hands with a woman in with black hair and a bandage wrapped around her forearm.

She ran to him and was suddenly wrapped in small arms around her neck.

"Mommy, where were you?" That nearly broke her. She'd been the lost one, not him. For days, she had imagined her plan backfiring,

Dillon as an "Amber Alert" kid. Billboards on the Turnpike. Posters in the Wawa convenient stores.

"Honey, I was trying to get back to you," she said quietly into his ear. She felt the tiny rib cage of her son, his arms still gripping her neck.

"I want to go home. Can you come too? We can read the blue balloon book. I remembered it. Aunt Beth and me told it to each other every night."

Blue balloons.

She stared at an airport employee at the taxi stand. He was flagging a row of taxis and yelling. She had done something—one small thing—that counted for Dillon. A yellow line became a blur through her tearing, almost happy eyes. Angus was behind her, and she introduced him to Beth and Dillon. He leaned down and shook Dillon's hand. They headed to pick up Ramona and to transfer Slinger's papers into the pile of clothes in the back seat.

Later, they sat in Beth's family room overlooking the kidney-shaped pool and back yard. It was like being in a movie set where somebody had made an American dream in CGI. Dillon was down on the lawn with Angus trying to catch a football. The suburban worries of soccer, football concussions, and winning at the organic Whole Foods line seemed so foreign. How much money that had built the suburbs was blood money? Was illicit and corrupt, landfills of human garbage beneath neighborhoods? The pool's winter cover was a forest green. Canadian geese were flying south in twilight air with busy calls. There were local police who would come any time you called.

"Callie, why did all this happen?" Beth asked. It was a surprisingly innocent question.

"They told you about the trafficking and the sex ring?"

"Yes. Only the basics though. What did it all have to do with you? With us?" The tone wasn't accusatory. In fact, she was subdued, shaken in a way that Callie could tell had broken the ordered and organized life of the old Beth. There was just a genuine concern and confusion.

Callie tried to think how to answer that. Finally, she said, with no qualm, "It didn't Beth, it didn't have anything to do with us, or me. We just ended up in their way. And they kill whoever they think is in their way. They drowned a friend of mine Rachel in a lake down there because she had seen a list of girls being trafficked. One of them became, well, a friend of mine while I was down there. She was one of the smuggled girls. I couldn't leave her, or ignore what was going to happen to those girls. So we decided to go with them and try to take the smugglers down."

"Jesus, Cal. Are you crazy?"

"Maybe. But Tony Maul, you remember him? The guy who threw sangria on you? He's the center of all this. He's the one who was trying to get to you."

"Where is he now?"

Walking in his black pants across scrubbed soil, lost, maybe reading north by the sun? Buried alive? Shot in the head and left for birds?

"I don't know."

"And you cut a deal with him?"

"And with a guy who was undercover DEA agent who went rogue. And Manual Evers, a cartel kingpin. There was a drug ship-ment worth fifty million. That's all they cared about. Tony was going to have you and Dillon sent out on a fishing boat."

Beth didn't say anything for a minute. "Callie, I know you had that priest come out here. And the security team that's been here out front."

"Father Tim came here?"

"Just once. He said to stay with the security team."

"We're going to bring them down, Beth. I'm going to bring them down."

"Well, whatever you did to help protect us, thank you."

Callie finally said, "You're welcome."

"But aren't they already arrested?"

"Well, some. The ones on the ship were. But not any of the car-tel men."

"But how can that be? There's police, DEA, billions of dollars for the drug war."

All she could think to say was something Slinger might have said. "Beth, there's no explaining the ugly world to beautiful people."

"Don't patronize me," she said.

"I'm not. I just have no way to answer your question. I'd have to write a book. I don't even understand it all. The one thing I can't figure out—how the Coast Guard knew about the ship? I mean there's a hundred different people who knew about a cargo ship going from Belize to Jersey, but not so many who knew a container on that cargo ship was full of girls headed for Atlantic City."

Beth stood up and walked to the windows.

"What's wrong," asked Callie.

"I called it in."

"What?" Callie was in disbelief.

"When you called me from that car I heard Tony say something like that. And then when you called from the Guatemala police station after the ranch killings. You told me you had one more thing to do. I called the FBI."

"You? You called it in?"

"Callie, you basically told me that you were smuggling drugs, something."

"Yeah, so I could nail their asses! Do you realize you let Hector Perez get off? They have no evidence he was the recipient at this end of the shipment. We needed to get to Elizabeth and have him and his people come pick up the girls."

Beth didn't say anything for a minute. "And you really had nothing to do with all this? You weren't selling? Dealing with Tony?"

"No, Beth, I had nothing to do with this! Not that it has anything to do with what we're talking about, but well, I was connected, just not in the way you think. The friend of mine I told you who was in trouble when we were at the pool? Well she *was* in trouble. Rachel asked me to try to help her get out of it. That was it. That was all it was."

Callie got up and went outside to see Dillon.

It was a spur-of-the-moment decision.

"Dillon, let's go for a ride."

Angus asked if she wanted him to come.

"No thanks, I want to be alone with him for a while."

"You are looking at me like a dog you need to put out of its misery," he said.

"Angus, don't be a fucking idiot. I don't know yet what I'm going to do. And don't say everything is going to be fine. That's what people say when things are fucked up."

51

The ride in from Beth's into Philly was a strange panoramic view of the familiar skyline pointed with American office towers. Dillon sat in the front seat. She watched the Schuylkill Expressway and the layers of Manayunk row homes sloping down toward an ordinary, dirt-brown river. She had still heard nothing from Ixchel, nor did she have any notion of where they were being held. She presumed they all were in Florida somewhere.

She wanted a coffee. She pulled into a Starbucks, the corner store of twenty-first century American stimulants. She ordered the Guatemalan blend and tried to avoid the irony. It wasn't funny. But she tried to joke with a young girl in a green apron ringing her up. "Maybe Howard Schultz has a witness protection program benefit for baristas?"

Before she went to Iraq, she had the belief that things would always happen for a reason. As she stood in the Starbucks, she realized there are no reasons, other than the confluence of time and events colliding through your life. And now she had collided with Dillon and wanted to extend their time any way she could. She simply wanted to get in the car with Dillon and head south toward Ixchel and Sylvia.

She pulled Ramona onto the Expressway at Fourth Street and headed for Society Hill.

She and Father Tim had exchanged texts to confirm a meeting at the Grave. There were a few things she needed to do, not the least of which was kiss his cheek. Ramona bounced over the colonial cobblestone streets and came to a stop, she looked at the same Olde City signage, as if nothing in the world had changed since the 1790s. But it was a different Callie Byrne who got out, one who was no longer seeking to make peace with anybody or reclaim anything or become someone she could not become.

She unbuckled Dillon.

A woman walked by, bent over, hair disheveled, leftover 1960s vibe, face determined. For a minute, her mind registered her as Mrs. Granger. *Mrs. Granger standing across the yard with a telescope.* She felt the threads of what happened fraying apart, and she could see Dillon looking around the city street with curiosity. She felt the deadness and shame slide away forever. She had simply done her life as a flawed human, a woman of clay who jumped in the kiln and broke when she came out. She had been on a mission that remained incomplete as long as Ixchel and Sylvia were lost in the system and as long as Slinger's papers sat in the back seat of Ramona.

"I don't want to go," Dillon said.

"I just want you to see where Mommy works, or used to work" she said, nodding at the front door of the Grave. "And Father Tim's inside, I bet."

She pulled Slinger's satchel over her shoulder. *Rachel lying on a stainless steel table in a body bag. Slinger walking across the dirt airstrip toward oblivion. Ixchel falling four stories into the Atlantic.*

She entered the bar towing Dillon gently by his little hand.

She went up behind Father Tim and Sym and placed a hand on each of their shoulders, "Can you slide over, I need some space here." She was greeted with a large hug from both sides that somehow confirmed that she was still alive and back home even more than seeing Beth had. They pulled up a barstool between them for her, and she sat at the Grave's long dark oak bar for the first time. A new bartender—a strawberry blonde, godawful strawberry too—was working in her old place.

"Take off the bag and have a seat!"

She kept the satchel hanging over her neck.

"She pours a Guinness all wrong," Father Tim muttered to her, "and I've tried to teach her three times."

"Well nobody pours an Irish temper like me," Callie said, kissing him on the cheek. "I owe you my life for helping us," she said. "How'd you get Hector to lie for you?"

"A little Catholic guilt. Let's just say the man owes *me* now," and that was all he would tell her about it.

"Dillon, this is Symington the Third, who is going to fund your college education. And say hi to Father Tim."

"Never," Sym huffed. "Full of theorizing liberals. Bah!"

"Has there been any word?" Callie asked.

Father Tim shook his head. "Not from the Guatemalan woman. But I did get a call from Beth while you were on your way down here."

"From Beth? I just left her."

"She asked me to ask you if you would stay at a hotel tonight with Dillon, but then bring him back in the morning?"

"She did?"

"Yeah, she did. Probably not a bad idea."

She felt almost like a grown up, realizing that bringing her son back to her sister was probably the right thing. She said with resignation, "Okay."

"You okay? You got into a lot of mess, eh?"

She felt the weight of the satchel on her shoulder. She heard Slinger's voice. *My life's work.* "I'm not sure I will ever not be in a lot of mess, but it could have been a lot worse." Callie looked at Dillon, searching for something, still trying to make sense of what she needed to do. "You're supposed to have faith in me, Father."

"I do have faith in you," Father Tim said. "I know you love him."

"What good is love that has no place to go?" Callie asked, then turning to look at him. "Don't answer that, please."

Sym didn't bother looking at Callie or Father Tim but said is his deadpan way, "No place to go? I've been wanting to go to Tuscany for months, my dear, and it's about time you came back to me. Because all of my love has been sotting my liver without you. We'll leave tomorrow." He took out an iPad. "Otherwise, Steve Jobs is sucking away my life with this—what do they call it—this *device*."

"Let me borrow that for a minute," she said. She searched Google to see if there were any news items about a ship interdiction or a drug plane bust in Arizona or southern California. It was only a few minutes of searching, as if everything that ever happened were somehow on Google if you knew what to search for.

An anonymous wire service journalist dispatched a brief into the digital ether, and it came across to Callie as an AP wire story in *The Miami Herald* that condensed into one paragraph all she had lived since she had left the Grave:

NARCO TRAFFICKERS AND POLICE
BATTLE ON MISSIONARY RANCH

Guatemala City, Guatemala—An execution-style shooting and gun battle was reported by local police and military authorities in the northern region of Petén today. The killings were apparently part of territorial drug wars, with a long-time Catholic missionary, three ranch employees, and four policemen killed in a gun battle with men thought to be associated with the Manuel Evers drug cartel, one of the most violent and far-reaching cartels operating in Central America, Mexico, and the United States. The Guadeloupe Ranch, located near Lake Petén Itzá, Guatemala's largest lake, was apparently involved in organizing anti-trafficking protests and local Catholic services for the poor.

But there was nothing about any ship interdiction. The Coast Guard must have still been prepping their news release.

She handed the tablet to Sym, "I'll be right back. Can you two watch Dillon for a few minutes?"

"Sure you will, you're always leaving me," Sym said.

Callie left the three men behind her and walked to the waitresses' station, past the blonde into the back bar toward the register. She scanned all of the decorative beer logos, coasters, notes, and stickers on the back bar. She unpinned the photo of her and Dillon at the beach, and then looked at a different woman with a drained, sunburnt face. It was not a face of a happy woman. It was the face of a lost woman. She put the photo in her pocket. She didn't think she would be coming back here.

"We told them to keep right there," Father Tim said, this time kissing *her* on the cheek.

That was the thing that made her lose it.

She refused to break down in the middle of a bar—which was behavior permitted in her mind only for end-of-night drunks in the midst of break ups. She walked through the kitchen to the back alley. She sat down on the stoop. A flood rushed into her mind and heaved through her chest.

52

Still sitting on the alley stoop of the Colonial Home Shop, Callie Byrne was head down, shoulders shaking, her dreads hanging off the side of her head, and her arms wrapped around Slinger's satchel of papers sitting heavy on her lap. A slim band of sundown reached up the alley. *An old woman sitting in an alley weaving. Mrs. Granger sitting next to her now on the street. Next to Mrs. Granger, Ixchel. Next to Ixchel, Callie. All four of them working their own backstrap looms, but each with a remnant of a blanket, taking them apart, one strand at a time, reversing the creations into nothing but piles of string.*

Her cell phone rang.

The interior shaking subsided like the palms in the breezes of the ranch. She cut off her grief, looking at the foreign area code and number.

She answered the phone. "Callie Byrne."

"Callie, this is the Broward County Transitional Center for Immigration and Customs Enforcement. We have a woman here in detention that has asked to speak with you."

An officer put Ixchel on the line.

"Ixchel?"

"Colocha." It was a voice so quiet it was barely alive.

"Ixchel, I'm so sorry."

No response.

"What happened?"

Callie let the long pause of interrogation discomfort do its work, but Ixchel didn't answer. She just said, "They want to send me back."

"Did you tell them about the pictures? Did you take more?"

"Yes, they have them, and they say they are good. They will turn them over to the FBI they said. They arrested Jorge. Just like Evers said."

"I'll help you Ixchel. But I don't know what's going to happen. I can't get into this now, but Slinger gave me a lot of material that is going to help us. Your photos are going to help you. I'm going to ask them to get you up here to Philly. People here will help you."

"I don't care anymore," she said.

Callie tried one more time, "What happened, Ixchel? Why did you jump?"

There was a pause. "I don't know," she said. "It was just all over."

"Did you let Sylvia go?"

"No, I tried to grab her," Ixchel said There was a long pause. "The blanket was too heavy; it slipped off of me. We were supposed to stay together. But that man saved her."

There was another long silence between them.

"Colocha, we probably won't see each other again."

She thought about that. Too many people had been lost in Callie's life for her to believe in old friends. Paths crossed. And uncrossed. And the crossing of Callie and Ixchel had been a blessed catastrophe. Callie said, "Yes, we will. Come to Philadelphia. You're coming here. Father Tim's going to be on your case. Father Tim Lugano. You talk with him. Promise me?"

Ixchel said, "Bye, Colocha."

She hung up. She texted Angus Ixchel's location. She knew he would go there.

She sat on the stoop, the alleyway now in shadow, and another night of diners and drinkers in the Grave to turn over. She headed back into the tavern, and as quickly as she had arrived she said goodbye to both Sym and Father Tim.

She went to the Four Seasons Hotel and booked a room.

That night, she slept with Dillon in a monstrous king size bed of immaculate linens.

53

The next morning, she checked out of the Four Seasons with the credit card number Beth had given her.

She still had no idea what she was going to do, and her mind weighed the options over and over. Drive south with Dillon and hopefully disappear. Or take all of Slinger's work to the FBI at the Federal Courthouse and turn it all over, ask for witness protection—and give Dillon back to Beth.

She put Dillon in the car.

It was only a few minutes' drive to the six hundred block of Arch Street. She drove purposefully but with ease out of the colonial reproduction brick toward the commercial strip of electronic stores and sneaker shops on Market Street. She turned west on Market, toward Center City. She stopped and bought a coffee, watching outside for any SUVs, vans, any car that would swallow her like the lake did Rachel.

She picked up Slinger's case, resting like a potent responsibility. It would be the only justice she would get for the Evers Corporation and the men who put Rachel, Mrs. Granger, and the ranch hands into their graves. Everything Callie had seen since leaving Philadelphia and going to Guatemala was in that satchel. Fragments of Tony, photos of Slinger as a young DEA agent, the linked stories of Rachel and Ixchel. Real people became memory, actions had histories, and imagination became a horrid reality. Threads had woven into a shroud. In a way, nothing happened until she saw it backward, gathering her pieces in the Grave, watching the past become part of the rest of her life.

Love, responsibility, loss.

And around it went.

The ephemera of responsibilities and wanderings.

And it was an unlikely person that jumped into her mind: *Inspector Piñada sitting in the room overlooking the Lake with a laptop full of shoe images.* She did not want to live like he did, trapped in a never-ending state of fear and corruption, doing just what he had to, to survive. It would be only a matter of time before Evers broke down, abandoned, closed, killed, and shut off anybody that had been associated with John Slinger.

She had to do it now.

She looked at Dillon, and turned off the engine.

They walked quickly now past the astronomically humming debt of the US Mint's *money money money money money* and arrived at an institutional block of office buildings and the dark-red-and-black William Green Federal Building. She passed Slinger's case through a metal detector and asked one of the security guards standing nearby, "Can you tell me what floor the DEA is on?"

"Ninth floor. That way," he nodded.

She held Dillon's hand, who was enamored of the expansive lobby and the number of people crisscrossing it.

She tried to focus on the mission and the good: somewhere, there was a collection of men who did not know what was coming for them, who had been tracked for years and would have their sick world blown apart by her covert war, by special forces, by raids, by extradition, by compounds under attack, by another round in an endless war. Including the men who had drowned Rachel and murdered Mrs. Granger and the others.

She headed toward the elevator, watching strangers come and go with court dates and procedural delays and such ordinary lives twirling in an infinite set of unordinary circumstances. Two old black men were talking loudly about their disputes with the IRS. Lawyers in suits crossed in and out of their daily jobs navigating federal regulations and processes wherever people's lives were gummed up into knots like their ties.

So much and so little human effort to live a simple life, she thought, though she had never had one. Trying to compose herself, sensing now she was safe but heartsick inside this building, she paused, not because she was unsure what she would do, but because of how massively unknown the future seemed. Her old life was over. Again. She held Slinger's case on her shoulder, leaning against the wall, letting Dillon hop on and off a bench.

She wished Angus had been there, and yet somehow his presence was. *You're doing the right thing.* She watched the deadened and serious faces of those with court appearances, idiotic mistakes, tax and fraudulent confusions, and indictments of every kind buried in people's worried brows.

She watched them all. She knew the feeling. Hardly any face showed any relief or joy of any kind—it was a parade of troubles, a shuffling around of broken pieces hoping for some unexpected miracle or technicality to save them from the ache.

How long would they need to bury her in witness protection for? Would Dillon have to stay with Beth?

Time was rushing and running out and starting again slowly all at the same moment.

She got up and walked across the lobby, just one of the crowd, but the only one with a young boy in tow. She let him push the *up* button three times.

When the elevator opened, a massive legal bureaucracy and responsibility waited above. She had doubts it could serve much justice, whatever that meant at this point. But, like everybody else in the lobby, it was the only choice. She got on the elevator with a grandfatherly gentleman wearing a government ID carrying a plastic convenience-store bag of bananas who smiled warmly at her, as if he had done the same routine for decades and was in no hurry at all.

She smiled down at Dillon, holding Slinger's records close to her body. She would call Beth from upstairs.

"Here we go for a ride," she said to Dillon.

Christ, an underground life fits me anyway, she thought.

The doors slid shut, and she and Dillon rose in the dingy light.

Acknowledgements

For a first book, it seems the proper moment to thank the writers and editors who helped inspire and sustain a writing life: Peter Balakian for his stance in the world with poetry; the late Frederick Busch for insisting something be at stake and his Living Writers course; Bruce Duffy, for the empty journal and a full backpack; Ken and Betsy Fifer, for their votes of confidence in starting my career; Thomas McAloon, for his wonderful magazine editing; Stephen Myers, for his incisive, generous spirit; and the editors of *Discovery.com*, for my first published pay check.

For this novel in particular, thank you to the two key editors, Lisa Borders and Alexis Orgera, both of whom were wonderful professionals and critical for developing and completing the book. Flaws remain mine. The readers of its various early childhood incarnations were: Amy Bourne, Chip Cheek, Michelle Clark, Kate Flora, Lissa Franz, Laura Gabel-Hartman, and Alan Rinzler. Thank you to Francisco Goldman for his book *The Art of Political Murder*; and to David Grann and the many other journalists for their excellent reporting from Guatemala and Central America.

The following organizations offered vital support: New England Crime Bake; The Distillery Gallery, Boston, MA; Grub Street, Boston, MA, and Genzyme Corporation, Cambridge MA, for which

I made several trips to Latin and Central America as part of my day job in rare disease medicine. I'm grateful for the side effects.

Finally, my family abides my bouts of solitary writing confinement with both patience and relief: Susan Foley, my critic-at-large, and Kirstie and Stephanie Jones, the two farmers I love most on the little planet, who kept up the refrain of "Don't Give Up on Callie" for however long it took.

Made in the USA
Middletown, DE
05 January 2017